The Eye
of the Storm:
A.R.I.E.S. Files #1

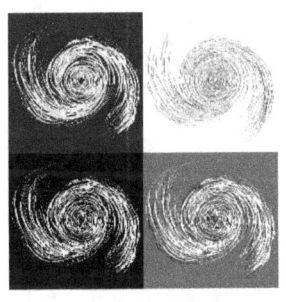

M.T. Falgoust

Printed in the United States of America

First Printing, 2015

ISBN: 0692523901
ISBN-13: 978-0692523902

Wagging Tales Press
P.O. Box 113294
Metairie, LA 70011-3294

www.waggingtalespress.com

DEDICATION

To those who assisted me in weathering the many storms. You helped me
keep the faith.

PROLOGUE

Boston, Massachusetts
March 18, 1990

Mother Nature wasn't Irish.

Not from a meteorological standpoint, anyway. If she was, he reasoned, it wouldn't have rained. Granted, St. Patty's Day had officially ended a little over thirty minutes ago, but there were still some die hard revelers searching through the damp mist for more green beer. He squinted with slightly almond-shaped eyes through the beading moisture on the windshield. He checked the urge to try and wipe his view clear. Hell, if he wasn't on the job he'd probably be one of them – even though he didn't have so much as a shamrock tattooed on his backside.

The faint suggestion of an epicanthic fold lent a sleepy, Far Eastern James Dean character to his rounded face as he peered through the sodium yellow haze of the street lamp. He readjusted the eight-point service cap atop his domed head, however, and grunted with a distinctly American disgust as a teetering pack of teens stumbled from a nearby apartment building. Two of the teenagers broke off from the group. They executed a lopsided, unsteady piggyback toward his car parked on the east side of Palace Road. He certainly didn't need two under-aged drunks making his job any harder.

His partner shifted suddenly in the passenger seat. The standard-issue knee-length nylon rain coat swished with the abrupt movement, reminding Jimmy Dean his reticent partner was in the car. He didn't talk much, but his companion's severe gaze carried on whole conversations. Jimmy Dean glanced over, assessing the nervous tic in the deep-set, dark eyes darting behind square gold-rimmed glasses. Forget searching for worry lines in the craggy, weathered face. It was a road map. But Jimmy Dean could tell. The man was nervous.

Jimmy Dean held up a warning hand. His head shook but a fraction. Glasses eased back into his seat.

Meanwhile, the boy and girl outside swayed uncomfortably close to the small, gray hatchback. Then, a switch flicked. The girl's obnoxious drunken laughter fell soberly flat. The girl slid abruptly from her mount and gestured toward the car.

"Cops." The four-letter word vibrated with the intensity of a guitar string tuned too tight.

With the brain cells that hadn't drowned in green beer, the young man puzzled the incongruity of uniformed cops in a dinged-up hatchback. Even without a viable answer, the blue and yellow Boston police patch on Jimmy Dean's shoulder prompted a nervous step backward. Whatever the police were doing here, the answer wasn't worth getting busted over and jeopardizing his pending high school diploma. The young couple beat a hasty retreat and scampered back to join their friends, away from the watchful eye of authority.

Jimmy Dean and Glasses felt the relief of release as they both let loose the breaths they'd been unconsciously holding. The only motion now on the street came from the shudder of rustling leaves in the oak trees. Jimmy Dean lifted the edge of the blue cuff on his left wrist. The old Seiko read 1AM.

He turned to Glasses. "It's time."

Reggie Abbott fingered a wicked run on the slender neck of his Fender Stratocaster. His signature, wide-brimmed Stetson slid forward on his pale forehead, pushing his unruly mop of curly brown hair into his eyes, but he didn't jump a single fret. That was the beauty of an air guitar. You never screwed up. He sighed.

If only life were an air guitar.

He paused his impromptu jam session and took a requisite look at the bank of video screens behind the security desk of the Isabella Stewart Gardner Museum. Normally, his job as a night watchman at the museum was just a long, quiet rehearsal period between gigs with his band, but tonight had been different and he was on edge.

At 12:30 AM, a fire alarm had sounded in the museum's conservation lab. It had taken several seconds for Reggie's brain to even translate the sound. Normally, the only thing he heard while patrolling the museum's dark corridors and Venetian courtyard was the soft whisper of bats' wings, or the aged squeak of the floorboards in the abbreviated hallway of the Short Gallery. A hasty examination of the lab had revealed nothing but a false alarm.

After a slow, pensive walk back to his post wherein he mentally compared the merits of AC/DC's Bon Scott to Brian Johnson, an alarm sounded again. This time it was the carriage house. A lanky, mad dash again proved nothing was amiss. Now, here he was, a little less than an hour later, when two serious-looking figures stepped into frame on the screen that supported the camera feed from the museum's side door.

As he took note of the police uniforms, Reggie started to squirm. Sure, they could be here because of the wacky alarms. Then he thought of the few times he and his band members might have smoked a bit of the local shrubbery to loosen up after a gig. He might have come into work a little loopy afterwards. Then there *was* that time he'd snuck some friends into the Dutch Room of the museum after hours. It wasn't like they had killed anything, except, well, maybe a few bottles of cheap wine. Mostly they had just stared, drunkenly slack-jawed, at the works of the masters.

An involuntary groan escaped his lips. He was in deep shit.

The cops pressed the white intercom button mounted next to the imposing wooden door. The one with the glasses leaned in to speak. His voice roughed over the speaker like sandpaper. "Boston P.D. We heard there was a disturbance in the courtyard. Let us in."

Reggie thought about all the crazy alarms. He supposed it was possible someone had managed to sneak into the courtyard. But, the museum had a security policy in effect. *Never* let anyone into the museum. Reggie forced a swallow. But they were cops, he reasoned.

Oh, well, he thought. Damned if you do, damned if you don't.

His forefinger gave a half-hearted push on the buzzer.

The wooden door swung open and the two policemen marched toward the watch desk. Fat, wet drops left a dripping trail behind them. The taller of the two policemen hung back. Glasses strode toward the counter.

He jerked his head toward the interior of the museum. "Any other guards here tonight?"

Reggie's head bobbed on his thin neck. "Just Randall, sir. Randall Hurley."

"Get him," Glasses ordered.

Reggie scrambled for his walkie-talkie. Static squawked as he called his partner.

"Hey, Randall? We got, uh, a situation. Could you come to the watch desk?" Reggie's Adam's apple bobbled as he took another nervous swallow. He pushed the button on the radio again. "Please?"

Glasses swiveled his head toward his partner. Jimmy Dean nodded his head over crossed arms. Glasses turned back to Reggie. Suddenly, his eyes narrowed at the young man. His next words turned Reggie green.

"Don't I know you?" Glasses ignored the vehement shaking of Reggie's head. "Yeah. I think we have a default warrant out on you. Get out from behind that desk. I'm going to need to see some I.D."

Reggie took his biggest gulp yet. His legs wobbled uncertainly beneath him as he stood. He cast a wistful glance at the panic button. A nervous titter burst from his lips. Who could he summon if he pressed it anyway? More cops? He was in enough trouble with the ones who were already here.

Reggie stepped from behind the desk. He fumbled in his back pocket for his wallet. He fished out his Berklee student I.D. and Massachusetts' driver's license. Glasses snatched the two thin cards from Reggie's shaking hand.

At that moment, the other security guard jogged into the room. With his scraggly brown beard and the way his uniform hung ridiculously loose on his scarecrow frame, he looked as if he'd be more at home on a random street corner begging for loose change or a square meal than in a palatial museum guarding priceless works of art.

"What's up, Reggie?" Randall Hurley began. He'd just barely gotten the words out of his mouth when Jimmy Dean launched forward and thrust him, spread-eagled, against the unyielding wall.

Randall's voice strained over the definitive click of the handcuffs that were being snapped onto his bony wrists. "What's going on? Why are you arresting me?"

The answer came abruptly. "This is a robbery."

Reggie groaned under Glasses' gorilla grip.

Yup, he thought. Deep shit.

CHAPTER ONE

Willamette, Oregon
Current Day

The sound rumbled low in the early morning darkness, almost certainly audible over the late-night infomercial droning on the television. He could feel it, reverberating up through the ground, faint but unmistakable. He froze, chest flattened against the pine planks of the cabin floor. He only had one chance at this.

The minor tremor passed. It wasn't uncommon for earthquakes to strike the Pacific Northwest. Nearly 17,000 quakes had been documented in Oregon and Washington since 1970, with fifteen to twenty occurring strongly enough to be felt each year. Oregon sat smack in the Cascadia Subduction Zone, its coastline in close proximity to the convergence of the Juan de Fuca and Pacific tectonic plates.

But, he wasn't here for a geology lesson. He had a job to do. He waited until the murmur of the television was again the only sound in the room. Carefully, he resumed his inching commando crawl.

There was just the one guard. If his reconnaissance was good, he shouldn't be a problem. He risked a sideways glance at the clutch of empty beer bottles littering the floor.

Yeah. Definitely not a problem.

A brilliant silvery moonbeam dissolved through the green glass of the abandoned bottles and emerged on the opposite side as an emerald patch of shimmering light. It might have been pretty. Too bad he was almost color-blind.

Focus! He silently admonished himself. The morning sun would be crawling up the horizon soon. The clock was ticking.

A sudden onslaught of smells assaulted his olfactory receptors. His brain calculated and whirred through the identification process.

There was the hint of stale beer lingering in the bottoms of the countless bottles. There was a musky, slightly sour odor hovering just over that. He cocked his head to the left, trying to place the scent.

As his pupils dilated, absorbing as much of the light as the semi-lit room had to offer, they suddenly picked up a large lump haunched in the corner. Damn! Had he missed a guard? Every muscle in his body bunched in readiness, poised to spring. His upper lip curled involuntarily.

The pile of dirty laundry, however, posed no threat. He allowed some of the mounting tension to melt from his body. A stronger, familiar scent wafted on the air, instantly commanding his attention. Something recognizable niggled at the back of his brain. A building sense of anticipation mixed with fear. The blood thrummed in his veins. In his excitement, he knocked into one of the bottles.

A nanosecond hovered as the bottle wobbled on an uncertain edge.

Last chance.

The bottle sloped into a slow, hundred and eighty degree spin before it chinked into one of its compatriots and they dominoed into a chiming cacophony.

The infiltrator lunged.

Almost as instantly, Jake Riesen launched, instinctively, to a kneeling position on the bed, snatched back the slide back on his SIG P-229, chambered a round, and aimed at nothing. He was alone.

"Great." He growled like one of the bears he sometimes saw while on patrol. He sank back on his heels. "Another friggin' nightmare."

The moonlight reflected off his bare, pallid skin, shadows cutting the defined detail on his abdominal expanse. His bloodshot eyes tried to translate the hazy red numbers floating in and out of focus on the alarm clock.

0510. The bear considered crawling back into his down comforter cave and going back into hibernation, but what was the use, really? The same crap would be here when he woke up. Ah, well. Breakfast, then.

The ring on his left hand clinked palpably against the base of the ceramic nightstand lamp as he reached over to turn on the light. He squinted against the unfriendly bulb.

An unsteady hand fumbled for the economy-sized bottle of aspirin. He dumped several tablets into a rough palm and popped them unceremoniously into his mouth. His face barely betrayed a wince as his muscled jaw ground the bitter pills.

A facedown photo frame enjoyed the dubious duty of coaster to another orphaned bottle of beer. A few inches sloshed around as Jake picked it up and chugged back the last swallows. As his brain began to come online, he searched the surface of the end table. He could have sworn he had a slice of deep dish leftover from the night before.

He swung his legs over the edge of the queen-sized bed and initiated the drill of his morning routine. He grabbed his phone.

Hell. Three missed calls. He scrolled through. The first one was from Fogelberg. Jake hit delete without hesitation.

"Dick," Jake mumbled.

The second was from Nell, down at the trading post. Probably calling to let him know that Cody's harness was in. Jake looked around the lonely room. Where in the hell was that damned dog, anyway? He made a mental note to swing by Nell's after lunch.

The last number caught him by surprise.

He hadn't talked to Kat Sørensen since her graduation ceremony in Cambridge. That was what, three years ago? Jake found himself hoping nothing had happened to Oddball.

Theodore Oddmund Sørensen, had been his S.O. during his tenure with the Federal Bureau of Investigation back in Boston. The brawny, surly agent of the property-theft squad was a first generation American who was proud of his Norwegian heritage and pissy about "blue flamers", the dubious moniker bestowed upon neophyte agents by more seasoned veterans. So when Jake came onto the squad so gung-ho and fired up he had that tell-tale blue fire shooting from his backside, a few eyebrows raised when the gruff older man took Jake under his wing. Maybe it was Jake's inclination to speak only when spoken to, or his succinct ability to answer the question asked. Maybe it was the framed print of *The Scream* by famed Norwegian Edvard Munch that Jake had hung reverently behind his desk at the Bureau. Whatever the reason, Sørensen demonstrated a keen interest in grooming the young man to be a spectacular agent, and on some of the most unusual cases the Bureau had to offer.

Sørensen, unlike most F.B.I. agents, liked to work museum cases. His counterparts preferred the big headline grabbing cases. The ones where big-name mobsters received their come-uppance, and South American drug cartel operations were ground to a halt. In other words, cases that made careers.

Sørensen was an oddball, however. Most of his fellow law enforcement types liked to operate in world of black and white. They simply didn't understand the subtleties of art. If it walked like a duck, Sørensen supposed. Sørensen, however, was perfectly willing to believe in a duck that mooed if an artist perceived it that way.

He also enjoyed the chess-like strategy of art crime cases. There was a grace in the ability to think two steps ahead of your opponent. Unfortunately, when he had started at Bureau, art theft was almost not even viewed as a real crime. To Sørensen, to lose a painting, a drawing, a sculpture or a song, was to lose a piece of history, of culture – like when his beloved Norway lost *The Scream* in an almost farcical heist.

So, while he worked the bread-and-butter cases common to the Bureau, Sørensen also worked closely with the Boston police department and chased down pieces of the past. Jake had become his willing apprentice – and the only agent who got away with calling him "Oddball" to his face.

Jake spent hours at the Sørensen home, poring over case files with his boss. That's where he had first met a young Katarina Sørensen. She was certainly smitten with the green-eyed young man who often ate *kjøttkaker* with them. Jake needled her with all the jovial mischief of a big brother. Often, his sophomoric pranks would earn him one of the meat pies in his face.

Jake was there when Oddball lost his wife to cancer at an early age. He was there when Kat had needed a shoulder to cry on.

And they had been there for him.

Jake looked at the clock again. It was too early to call Kat back now.

He'd try her later.

His stomach rumbled. He was positive there had some of that pizza left! He wasn't that drunk. What had happened to it? And where in the hell was Cody?

As he stood, Jake's right foot planted squarely into what was left of his pizza. Only, after being processed through the system of a one hundred and five pound Siberian Husky it was the last thing Jake wanted.

"Cody!" Jake bellowed.

CHAPTER TWO

Miami, Florida

A black diamond.

Exceptionally rare, and thought to be the extraterrestrial by-product of an exploding star, it was a fitting crown jewel for the Aufrecht, Melcher and Großaspach performance shop. Even now, the familiar three-pointed star on the grille of the Mercedes-Benz SLS AMG Black Series chewed up the concrete ribbon of the Palmetto Expressway with the blazing fury of a supernova.

Granted, there was no true trace of carbonado, the main element of black diamonds, anywhere on the sleek sports car, but for the vehicle's rarity in the United States and its sleek black exterior sparkling in the shine of the Miami sun, it might as well have been a jewel from outer space.

The mechanical beast growled forward toward Miami Beach with all 622 horsepower. Melina felt the G-forces pulling her into the supple leather of the passenger seat as Remy Laurent urged the needle on the RPM gauge toward red then abruptly let it plummet to a less consequential number, as he put the vehicle through its paces, bobbing and weaving through the morning traffic.

As the tell-tale green sign overhead signaled the impending arrival of I-95, Melina instinctively gripped the door handle as the car lurched south, then just as quickly commanded her muscles to relax. Melina Flores might be uncomfortable hurtling through space, but Melina *Garcia*, semi-legitimate art dealer and broker, should be used to taking chances.

Melina repeated the unfamiliar name over and over in her head, like a mantra. *Melina Garcia. Melina Garcia. Melina Garcia.*

She always kept her real first name. Keep the lies at a minimum. That was the rule. The more you tell, the more you have to remember.

Melina snuck a glance at the driver from behind her mirrored aviators. Remy Laurent was a cool fish. Even as the mercury climbed toward the average October temperature of 84.6 degrees Fahrenheit, Laurent looked fresh and comfortable in his collared pink polo shirt, casual jeans and leather boat shoes. He could have been ready for an afternoon sailing on a yacht out of Miami Harbor, which, let's face it, was exactly where they were headed, Melina thought. Of course, there was the matter of the six stolen paintings in the trunk.

Wrapped in anonymous brown paper and sealed with cheap, clear cellophane tape, the ordinary packaging belied the extraordinary pedigree suggested by the art hidden within: a $500,000 Dalí; a Picasso *sanguine*, a drawing roughed out in red earth, similar to a charcoal sketch; Mondrian's *The Mill*; two lesser-known Van Goghs; and a long-missing painting by Breughel the Elder. But the artwork by these well-known masters were only the hors d'oeuvres – an *amuse-bouche* before the main course.

This sale represented a calculated strategy. The rumor mill had suggested Laurent, for all his legitimate business holdings, had a penchant for dabbling in the gray area of illicit art trade.

Fancy a Fabergé? Laurent could use his web of international connections to acquire it for you. Dying for a Degas? Laurent could dig one up – for the right price. Melina had set up today's "sale" as an introduction into Laurent's world. It was her shot at proving to Laurent that she was a serious player, one who could successfully broker the illicit sale of one of the greatest collections of stolen art ever – the Isabella Stewart Gardner collection. The infamous Gardner heist had claimed Vermeer's *The Concert*, which alone was estimated to be worth a quarter of a million dollars per square inch, a Flinck, a bronze *ku* from 1200 BCE China, Manet's *Chez Tortoni*, the finial from Napoleon's battle flag, and several other priceless pieces. A tragic loss of history and culture. But, one of the most memorable works that vanished into the fog that night was Rembrandt's only known seascape, *The Storm on the Sea of Galilee*. A striking representation of a familiar New Testament tale - Jesus and his apostles at the apparent mercy of the savage weather - the painting was a brilliant study in chiaroscuro, depicting an intense contrast between light and shadow.

A wry grin tugged at the corners of Melina's full lips. She dealt between the light and the dark on a regular basis. Such was the life of an undercover asset recovery specialist.

Her thoughts turned back to the Gardner collection. Stolen decades ago, it represented the great white whale of the art world, and Melina meant to be Ahab.

Remy swerved erratically in front of a seafood truck to jump off the interstate at the next exit only to hop back on 100-feet later. Forget the main course. At this rate, they were going to get pulled over before they even got to the table.

She slid a hand down Remy's thigh. His quadriceps rippled as he alternated between the clutch and the accelerator. Melina mentally gut-checked herself when she felt a surge of warmth wave through her.

"Take it easy, *querida*," the Cuban beauty cautioned, half to herself, half to Remy. "As much as a girl loves attention, Highway Patrol was not exactly what I had in mind."

Remy's brilliant smile flashed against his tanned skin as he nicked into the marina lot and deftly tucked the sports car into a parking spot.

"This is how one drives, no?" His Parisian accent still lingered, even after nearly twenty years of living in the States. "To avoid the tail?"

Melina stifled a groan. Remy had obviously watched one-too-many Paul Walker films. Oh, well. No sense in downshifting now.

"And just what 'tail' are you trying to avoid, Mr. Laurent?" She smiled coyly. As the gull wing door shushed open, Melina gracefully swung her legs, all forty-four golden inches of them, out of the car and slowly stood. "Certainly not mine, I hope."

Momentarily forgetting about the illicit cargo in his trunk, Remy's eyes devoured Melina as if she were on the menu.

"*Absolutement pas.*"

CHAPTER THREE

Gakona, Alaska

Alan Davenport looked less like a human and more like a matzo ball with feet. The short, round forty-seven year old was naturally a bit doughy around the middle, and the extra layers over his pudgy frame didn't do his physique any favors. As white flurries swirled around the ankles of his severe weather Baffin Shackleton's and the humidity of his own breath froze on the lenses of his bifocals, the space physicist didn't care if he looked like the Frosty the Frigging Snowman. It was an unforgiving thirty-two degrees below zero. Fashion could kiss his frostbitten ass.

He negotiated his way down the icy steps, off the wide porch, and across the snow-covered clearing. The log home nestled snugly in one of the countless timber stands that carpeted much of the forty-ninth state – large, uninhabited tracts of pungent spruce known colloquially as "the bush." He crunched through the thick veil of snow and ice toward his Land Cruiser. He growled like a stuck Kodiak when he discovered he'd have to dig the tires out.

Again.

Ah, the joys of living in the Alaskan wilderness.

It wasn't all snot icicles and snowplows, though, he admitted to himself as the small shovel bit into the white ground. Summer months meant fly fishing for salmon. Or, if you were less patient, there was always kayaking on Prince William Sound. Log jams deposited by high waters and sweepers, the low branches and trunks of trees that had fallen flat against the water, could prove problematic for the unwary, but as long as you back paddled away from the bank, they were easily avoided.

A natural voyeur? There was no shortage of wildlife to be viewed. An observant spectator could watch Beluga whales gambol in the waters of Cook Inlet, or spy kittiwakes or even puffin nesting in the rocky shoals along the coast. Big game more your speed? How about the cinnamon-colored Alaskan brown bear, moose, or caribou? Alan wished he had a caribou right now. It might have gotten him to work faster. He wasn't even supposed to go in today. It was his day off. But, he'd received a frantic call from the office. Something was wrong.

"Probably can't tune in 650 KENI, talk radio," he mocked in his best deejay voice. Of course, that wasn't really what the ionospheric research instrument was used for. He thought about the thirty-three acre array of dipole antennas on the facility's property. The IRI was a high-power radio frequency transmitter – not a receiver – and it could do far more than send the Charlie Daniels Band floating over the airwaves.

The last tire freed from the clutching snow, catching Alan by surprise.

"Yes!" he jabbed the blade of the shovel into the air and wobbled in an awkward little victory dance. The celebration was short-lived as a brisk gust blew up the hem of his coat and threatened to freeze dry his manhood.

Alan quickly chucked the shovel into the backseat, jumped into the driver's seat, and fumbled the key into the ignition with thick, gloved fingers. The lights on the dash dimmed as the Land Rover's engine groaned in protest. Alan groaned in kind. He thunked his exposed forehead against the steering wheel. Was the government pension really worth all this? He gave a last, desperate twist on the key. Thankfully, the engine roared to life and the SUV began the crawl to the paved, two-lane road just beyond the tree line.

As the griseous first light nudged over the summit of one of Alaska's many dormant volcanoes, the bluish gray reflected off the ice covering the highway. Alan found himself drumming his thumbs to the steady, thumping rhythm of the frozen tires. If he concentrated, he could actually make out the driving pulse of the opening measures of Ozzy Osborne's "Crazy Train". The tires had frozen flat to the ground overnight. Alan wasn't worried. They would resume their natural roundness once they warmed up.

The vehicle's heater, however, had just barely managed to defrost a nine-inch hole in the hoary frost covering the windshield. The snow, too, Alan had tracked into the car over the course of the freakishly early winter season, had remained clumped and solid on the floorboards. Occasionally, the sole of his boot would squeak along the frozen surface like a worried mouse.

Alan might have been worried, too, if he'd known what awaited him beyond the main gate.

CHAPTER FOUR

Boston, Massachusetts

Theodore Oddmund Sørensen's brow creased with worry. The cell phone connection warbled persistently in his ear. He let it ring. The voicemail his daughter had left had sounded urgent. Distressed, even. He hadn't listened to the message until this morning.

"Daddy? I need you to call me as soon as you get this. It's important. Something weird is going on at work, and, well, I need your advice. Wait. Somebody's coming. Look, just call me okay? I love you." Katarina's voice had an uncharacteristic tremor in it as the recording clicked off.

He'd missed the phone ringing the night before. He guessed the Knights of Columbus hall had been too loud. It had been Ken Sharpton's retirement party and he'd tied one on.

Ugh! His head pounded. Maybe he'd tied one too many. Back in his S.E.A.L. days, he could pound them back with the best of them. At fifty-nine, not so much. He fumbled in the kitchen cabinet for the pain reliever. Ah, there it was. He shook the bottle.

Damn. Empty. Maybe some coffee would help the throb in his head. He doubted it would help the building acid in his gut, though.

A grizzled cheek clenched the cell phone tightly against his shoulder as both hands fumbled with the espresso machine on the kitchen counter. A Father's Day gift from Kat.

He was so proud of his daughter. And not just because she knew how to make this damn machine work! He let out a frustrated yowl as steaming, semi-caffeinated water spewed from the loose seal between the porta filter and the group head and Rorschached the front of his white oxford.

God, how he missed his Mr. Coffee! Years of military service coupled with a decade of heading up the F.B.I.'s Boston field office had taught him one critical skill - how to brew coffee.

This – he thought as he daubed futilely at the brown stain blossoming on his shirt – this is not coffee.

No, you needed a PhD from MIT to run this confounded contraption. A fatherly smile spread across his face. Maybe that's why Kat deftly pulled two shots of dark energy into two delicate cups whenever she visited. His daughter *had* a PhD from the prestigious Cambridge University. Only three short years ago, she had matriculated from the Department of Earth, Atmospheric and Planetary Sciences with her doctorate in atmospheric science and climate physics. Job offers had flown in from companies all across the globe, both in the governmental and private sectors.

But, in the end, the apple didn't fall far from the tree. Like her father, Kat had opted for a safe, government job. Theodore harrumphed. No such thing. But then, he was a skeptic. Came with the training.

Kat had accepted a position with the U.S. Air Force as a lay scientist with the High-Frequency Active Auroral Research Program facility stationed in the remote Alaskan wilderness. Technically speaking, the

H.A.A.R.P. facility was a joint project funded by the Air Force, the Navy, the University of Alaska and the Defense Advanced Research Projects Agency.

U.S.A.F.? U.S.N.? D.A.R.P.A.? H.A.A.R.P.? Harrumph again. Alphabet soup. Theodore got a little queasy when that many acronyms were involved. The fact that Kat wasn't answering her phone only magnified his gastrointestinal upset. It wasn't like her at all.

He looked at the clock. 0930. That meant it was 0530 in Gakona. Sure, it was early for some folks, but Kat had always been an early riser. Where could she be?

CHAPTER FIVE

Gakona, Alaska

Katarina Sørensen stared up at the heavens. Her arms and legs splayed out, as if ready to create a snow angel.

The eighty-two feet separating her from the ground, however, made it an unlikely endeavor. The crimson-stained rod of the crossed dipole antenna jutting from the center of her chest, didn't help either.

Alan Davenport stood in protracted silence at the base with Shep Hinds, the head of H.A.A.R.P. security.

He never should have answered the damned phone.

His voice was little more than a croak when he finally spoke.

"Call Kirtland."

Shep nodded wordlessly. He would call Kirtland Air Force Base. But, there was another call he had to make first.

CHAPTER SIX

Miami, Florida

Melina stood on the sundeck of the sleek Navetta 33. Her company had rented the luxury yacht for today's dog-and-pony show. She'd nearly broken a crown when she had seen the name lettered on the stern. *La Obra Maestra.* The Masterpiece? A Twitter post would have been more subtle.

Melina made a mental note to kick Larson's ass. The senior investigator had probably chosen this particular yacht just to piss her off. She knew he hadn't been happy with the decision to put her on lead, but to ambush her like this? Laurent seemed harmless enough, sure, but his connections had roots in La Brise de Mer - and European mobsters did not enjoy a reputation of appreciation for being played by undercover agents and snitches. Melina knew all too well that a single slip-up, one off-key comment and a case, or a life, could be lost.

Screw Larson and his boys' club mentality.

The skies echoed her mood. A distant rumble echoed across the water. Melina's honey-colored gaze drifted toward the billowing thunderheads rolling in from the Glades. It was late October. Still well within Atlantic hurricane season. While there had been a peppering of tropical depressions off the Gulf coast, no major storms had yet developed. Melina resisted the temptation to knock on something wood. Like Larson's thick head.

A soft brush of fingers lifted her hair. An even softer brush of lips whispered at the dip where her neck met her shoulders.

"I hope the weather will not ruin our little party." Remy wrapped an arm around Melina's waist as he sidled up behind her. She turned into his embrace with a smile.

"Hmmm. No, indeed. What was it? *Absolutement pas?*"

Remy smiled at the thinly veiled flattery. "Then, how do you say? 'Let's get this show on the road'?"

Melina couldn't have agreed more. Like her cover identity, the rented yacht, and the forged artwork currently cached in one of the staterooms, none of the players – the crew, the South American "drug dealer" Melina was selling to, or his entourage – were real. Everyone aboard the vessel, with the exception of Remy Laurent, was an employee of Robbins International Adjusters. It was all one big show. And it was all for Laurent's benefit.

As she allowed Remy to guide her to the buttercream leather side couch, Melina surveyed the stage.

The role of Antonio Guzman, Columbian drug lord and would-be art collector, was being played by Anthony Larson. A thick, golden rope chain rested on an exposed chest which had not earned its tan anywhere close to south of the equator. South of Northwest 36th Street, maybe, in a midtown tanning salon.

Larson's exercised more of a "shoot first, questions optional" policy, a holdover from his days with the Miami police department. He was coarse and vulgar. As he slapped the rounded backside of the bikini-clad female agent sitting in his lap, his lewd behavior reminded Melina of an early Cezanne - rough, unrefined, a riot of thick brushstrokes and color.

"Beautiful, right?" Larson posited as the female agent scurried off to refill her champagne glass. The stone in the heavy diamond ring on his right hand caught the bright Miami sun as he waved grandly. Remy raised his own manicured hand to shield his eyes from the blinding flash.

"I am not certain the weather would agree with you, *monsieur*," Remy gestured to the growing cloud bank on the horizon.

Larson hardly gave it a second glance. He gave it a dismissive wave. "Pah! The weather in Miami is like a woman. You don't like it, wait around a little while and something better will come along."

Larson cast Melina a suggestive glance. She replied with a withering stare, virulent enough to sterilize future generations. Larson chuckled.

"Speaking of beautiful things," he continued, letting his eyes rove lecherously down the length of Melina's shapely leg. He turned to Remy. "I understand we share an appreciation."

Remy rested a protective hand on Melina's knee. His weight subtly shifted toward the forward edge of the couch.

"Yes," he replied. "I have a great...respect."

Tension chiseled a hard edge on the consonant. He lingered on the word before he continued. "For the aesthetic."

"You gentlemen flatter me, but I must insist we get down to business," Melina interjected before things slid south.

The tension hung thick for a moment, then dissolved with the popping bubbles in Larson's champagne flute as he tilted it back for a healthy swallow. He returned it to the glass-topped coffee table with the resounding thunk of a judge's gavel.

"Yes! Business before pleasure!" he bellowed. The steward leaned forward to clear away the empty flute.

"No," Melina corrected. "Just business."

Her eyes locked momentarily with Larson's. The message could not have been clearer. He shrugged.

"Business it is then." He leaned against the backrest and stretched out his arms. "So, Mr. Laurent. I keep no secrets about what I do. Perhaps you could share what type of business you are in?"

"I have many interests," Remy replied. "My company, Phoenix Research Unlimited, allows me to pursue them."

Larson feigned interest. He tented his fingers thoughtfully. "Such as?"

Remy smiled. "Oh, this and that. Cancer research. Alternative energy resources."

An abrupt boom of distant thunder elicited a high-pitched yelp from one of the bikinied agents. Melina's brow furrowed as she inventoried the agent's scant wardrobe. Where in the hell did she stash her sidearm?

Remy gestured to the darkening sky. "Atmospheric study and evaluation. We hope to one day understand Mother Nature. Perhaps then we can help deflect dangerous storms like Hurricanes Sandy and Katrina. With luck, we could quell them altogether. We gather data every day. Perhaps you have heard of SBX-1, or the H.A.A.R.P. research facility in Alaska?"

Larson scoffed. "Alaska? Too much snow! Not enough skin!" He grabbed one of the women onto his lap. She laughed on cue.

At that moment, the ring of Remy's phone radiated from the pocket of his jeans. He stole a quick glance. He turned to Melina and whispered under his breath.

"I am most sorry, but I'm afraid I must take this call."

Melina nodded as Remy excused himself. When he had stepped out of earshot Melina lunged toward Larson.

"Laying it on a little thick, aren't we?" She snapped.

Larson grinned. "Take it easy. I'm just playing the part."

"Oh, really?" Melinda spat. "Well 'part' of your 'part' is convincing Laurent this whole set-up is real, and you're two steps shy of blowing it."

"Aw, whatsamatter? You afraid your Parisian Thomas Crown is going to slip out of your hands?" Larson needled. "Hell. It wouldn't be the first time you lost a man."

Melina's arm cocked back, but the intended slap never had a chance to connect.

A gasp freed itself from Melina's throat as Remy's grip clutched her arm in mid-swing. Her free hand drifted slowly toward her concealed Glock 22.

"I do not think that would be wise," Remy warned.

A paralyzing chill momentarily froze Melina's heart. Remy dipped his head toward Larson. The tension in her body began to dissolve. Her hand drew silently away from her concealed weapon.

"Besides," Remy continued. "We really should return to shore as quickly as possible."

He turned towards Larson. "Please forgive us, but I'm afraid our transaction will have to wait."

Larson puffed his chest, still fulfilling his role as a bristling cock of the walk. As much as he had been needling Melina, he needed this bust, too. He had no intention of letting Laurent off the hook that easily.

"Why should I wait? Just because you say so?" He verbally chest-poked Laurent.

Remy shook his head.

"No, *mon ami*." He pointed towards the east. "Because a storm is coming."

The wall of clouds that had been lingering over the Everglades now resembled a fierce, roiling freight train, and it was bearing straight for Miami.

CHAPTER SEVEN

Albuquerque, New Mexico

He was going to bring the rain. And no one was going to stop him.

He drove the heels of his corfams along the length of the tiled hallway. The sharp pants crease of his dress blues sliced through the air with surgical precision.

This is what happens when you get civilians involved in a military operation. He seethed silently.

Colonel Lowell Mason was never one of those children who liked to share. It wasn't a trait that stemmed purely from unadulterated selfishness. His mind drifted briefly to the squawking seagulls in that movie about the fish.

"Mine. Mine. Mine."

No. That had never been the driving force that motivated him.

Mason was driven by lack.

Born into a family of farmers, Mason ruminated on the family history. Patrick Mason, the family patriarch, had come to America from Ireland in the latter half of the 1800s when the Great Famine had witnessed record emigrations from the Emerald Isle due to the blight that devastated Irish crops. With disease and hunger running rampant, Patrick, like so many others, set his sights on America. And when a fair share of Irish whiskey landed him on the fair side of a landlord's daughter, the doubled incentive of death finally urged him to pile with the huddled masses aboard a steamer bound for the hopes and dreams of a better life.

At first, it seemed as though he had found it. He found an honest woman and married her. The great land rushes in Oklahoma territory afforded Patrick a plot of land to call his own and he started a modest cattle ranch, then graduated into row crops. Over the years, the Masons grew everything – from tomatoes to almonds, to garlic, to wheat and alfalfa, and even sugar beets and cotton. It was a hard, but honest living.

Crops came and went, and in time, so did Patrick, but the family continued his farming tradition. As the years pushed on, however, new troubles set in. The increasingly high cost of farm equipment and input costs countered the farm's productivity. It wasn't merely the designs of men, though, that would eventually destroy the Masons' livelihood. Just as had happened all those years ago in Ireland, it was the fickleness of a woman – a woman called Mother Nature.

The infamous "black blizzards" of the 1930s left the Dust Bowl region of America a veritable desert. Brought on a period of severe drought, the huge dust storms drove many families from their farms, crops ruined and mortgages foreclosed, forcing them to leave their homes and most of their belongings and find work elsewhere. Once again, the Masons had nothing.

The family never truly rallied. No Mason had amounted to much after that, each generation just barely scraping by, living paycheck to paycheck. That is, until Lowell Mason.

The year was 1968 and the world was in the throes of the Vietnam War. The Viet Cong and North Vietnamese Army had just launched the Tet Offensive, a vicious campaign of surprise attacks throughout South Vietnam. A pimply-faced eighteen-year-old Lowell watched as thousands of young men shipped off to fight in what was quite possibly the most dubious war in U.S. history. While no war could ever be considered easy for those who fought it, the Vietnam conflict was fraught with difficulties that American soldiers had rarely faced: physical challenges imposed by the unfriendly, sub-tropical climate and terrain; few conventional objectives, like territory held, a defined frontline, or even a definitive theatre of war; and a "ghost army" of invisible enemies, ones who hid in Viet Cong-dug tunnels, or blended seamlessly into the civilian population, American eyes untrained to ferret friend from foe.

Over the next years, some burned their draft letters or fled to Canada to avoid participating in the horrors of war, but not Lowell. He had barely gotten his high school diploma in hand before he rushed down the Air Force recruiting office and scrawled his name on the dotted line.

He didn't see much action during the Vietnam War. By the time he'd received his air training, Lyndon B. Johnson had already begun pulling U.S. troops out of the Vietnamese conflict. Fortunately for Mason, humans are hard-wired for war. There would be plenty of other opportunities to defend life, liberty and the pursuit of happiness.

Lowell's dossier stretched back to Operation El Dorado Canyon, Ronald Reagan's 1986 Libyan campaign against Muammar el Qadaffi, where he flew an A-6E in bombing raids on Benghazi barracks. He also flew the C-130 Hercules tactical transports with the 317th Airlift Group over Panama in 1989 for Operation Just Cause.

"I gain by hazard." That was the motto for the 317th AG. The slogan had its roots in World War II when the 317ᵗʰ flew out of Australia and New Guinea, pioneering flights in new and previously uncharted territory.

Mason harrumphed. New and previously uncharted territory. That was H.A.A.R.P. in a nutshell. How else could you describe the brainchild of the 1996 white paper that bore the ambiguous title AF 2025, a three-thousand plus page report compiled by a motley assortment of scientists, armed forces personnel, and even, Mason shuddered, science fiction writers?

The latter point was not as far-fetched as the crisp Air Force Colonel had originally thought when he first became involved with the project. Bringing H.A.A.R.P. to fruition had all the earmarks of a Michael Crichton thriller novel. First, a group of scientists had to cozy up to a US senator. Clandestine deals were cut with an oil company. Lastly, the Pentagon had to be convinced that the project might revolutionize war. That was where AF 2025 came in. It contained just enough science to show the fiction could be fact.

Whenever government and science became bedfellows, however, the conspiracy theorists wormed their way out of the woodwork. For example, Kirtland was within spitting distance of the mecca of all conspiracy theorists – Roswell, New Mexico. So, it shouldn't have come as any great surprise when enough conspiracy theories surfaced regarding the remote Alaskan facility to rival the famed Area 51.

H.A.A.R.P. as an earthquake inducer.

H.A.A.R.P.-induced Extremely Low Frequency (ELF) waves to effect mind control.

H.A.A.R.P.-created super storms.

Mason paused at that last. Sometimes what the public didn't know was in their best interests. But now a member of that damned public had gone and gotten herself killed on his watch. And if there was one thing conspiracy theorists loved more than alien autopsies, it was a government cover-up of a murder.

Yeah, he hated civilians.

CHAPTER EIGHT

Miami, Florida

The living room of the apartment appeared empty. No one sat on the white leather sofa with matching white throw pillows. No one thumbed through the huge, over-sized coffee table books boasting vibrant, colorful reproductions of Picasso, Chagall, and Gaugin. The only evidence that anyone had recently occupied the space was an empty bottle of Jameson's Select Reserve Black Barrel on the kitchen counter top and single hi-ball glass, a thin layer of whisky still lingering near the bottom.

The chrome frame of the Dali-inspired wall clock framed the hour just after 12:00. Anyone looking out of the apartment window might have assumed it was 12:00 midnight for the darkness that had settled in over the city. The black clouds that had rolled in from the Glades had exploded and were now unloading their insistent cargo on the city. Forceful drops knocked at the pane of the sliding glass door, insistent in their syncopated rhythm. The single bulb of the parking lot's security floodlight threw the drops' melting shadows across the expanse of white carpet, persisting the clock's memory theme.

Another shadow crawled slowly across the warp and woof of the Berber. Unlike the liquescing drops of rain, however, this shadow originated from within the apartment. It spread through the apartment with familiarity, leaving the kitchen, pausing at the art books. It wandered to the curio cabinet filled with small, but valuable treasures. It had nearly reached the cabinet, surely intent on relieving it of several of its inhabitants, when the rattle of a key in the door sent it dissolving quickly into the deeper shadows of the room.

The door exploded open in a sudden fury. Melina tumbled in, arms and legs akimbo.

"Damn!" She let the epithet fly as she picked herself up from the ceramic tile of the foyer. "Stupid door! How many times do I have to ask the super to fix it? Argh!"

Melina looked less like the Cuban beauty of several hours ago and more like a drowned rat tossed off the Lusitania – after it sank. Ringlets of dark hair plastered against the high cheekbones streaked with dark lines of running mascara. Her gauzy dress clung suggestively, leaving no curve private. The pointed push of her hardened nipples announced the chill that permeated the room.

An involuntary shiver rippled through her, suggesting an immediate exchange of clothing. She gave the door an exasperated shove closed and started for her bedroom.

The loud squelch of her toes inside her designer heels earned a disgusted roll of the eyes.

What next, she wondered. Although years of working as a South African Foreign Service Officer for the State Department should have proven the inanity of that question. There was always something next.

Always another bad guy waiting around the next bend. Another dictator. Another coup waiting to happen. Another thief.

Sometimes they weren't even around the next bend. Sometimes they were standing right beside you. And sometimes they stole your heart.

Larson's comment aboard the *La Obra Maestra* had hit a little too close to home. She had lost someone – because she had let down her guard. Well, it was a mistake she wouldn't be making again.

She leaned against the white wall, her wet hand leaving a damp palm print, and tugged each shoe off, leaving each one where it fell.

She was just about to continue for the bedroom when she stopped cold. Her pupils dilated wide in her golden irises. She stared at the carpet before her then drifted up to the moist hand print she had left on the wall. Her gaze narrowed and she reached instinctively for her Glock. She looked back at the carpet and the large, wet footprint that lay there.

She chambered a round with a definitive *ca-chick.*

She took a cautious step forward. She kept her finger off the gun's trigger, but poised at the ready, resting along the length of the slide. She pulled her arms in close, gathering her elbows.

"Tuck it in, dummy. Don't give them your gun." She tipped the muzzle downward.

She swiveled her head, scanning the room, looking for hints of unfamiliar color, contrast, or furtive movement. She analyzed every shadow, every shape. Her ears pricked for unusual sounds. The patter of rain continued on the patio door, pulling her gaze. More wet footprints originated at the base of the glass door. She quickly scanned, low to high. The trail led into the kitchen area.

"Damn it," she thought. A waist-high breakfast bar separated her from full view of the small kitchen. Anyone could be hiding, concealed behind the four-foot counter. She took two wary strides, adrenaline pumping.

Suddenly, a ball of white fur launched onto the countertop. Only years of training kept Melina from emptying her clip into Frost, her pedigreed white Persian, as he vaulted onto the bar's surface.

"Jesus, Frost! What the hell?" At that moment, she noticed the near-empty glass on the counter.

"You're outta Jameson's," a gravelly voice rasped from the shadows behind her.

Melina whirled, gun ready.

"And outta practice. I had the drop on ya, darlin'."

Melina dropped her weapon to her side as Connor O'Flaherty stepped from the shadows. A few days of silver stubble glinted on the old thief's jawline as Melina flicked the light switch.

"Well, if I'm out, it's only because you drank it all, and no, you didn't. I knew you were there the whole time."

O'Flaherty flounced onto the sofa and scoffed. "Like hell ya did."

Melina pointed to the coffee table books. "Gaugin's on top."

O'Flaherty's gaze dropped to the art books. "*Shite.*"

"You always were a sucker for hippy island girls," Melina continued. She set her weapon to the side, but kept it nearby. Connor O'Flaherty came off as a friendly old man, but he was still a thief, and a craftily dangerous one at that.

O'Flaherty threw his hands up in mock surrender. "Aye. Guilty as charged. Something about swaying palms and coconuts." His voice dwindled to the dreamy tone of daydreams as he hefted his two hands before him, as if evaluating two pleasantly rounded objects.

Melina reached into a cabinet for a bottle of Dewar's. She walked over to the armchair and plunked two fresh glasses on the coffee table. O'Flaherty curled up his lip in disdain as she broke the seal on the bottle.

"Scotch? Have I taught you nothin'?"

"Fine," Melina began, and reached to clear O'Flaherty's glass. His arm shot out, grabbing her hand in his. Age spots belied his strength. He was still plenty virile.

"Then again," he began, "Scots and Irish have been known to gather for a good game of hurly, so I suppose it'd only be sportin' to raise a toast in their honor."

Melina smiled. For all his grousing, the only thing O'Flaherty was truly picky about was his art.

O'Flaherty had gotten into art theft for the noblest of reasons. At least, that was the company line he paid lip service to. He claimed that most art never got the opportunity to grace the walls of such storied institutions like the Getty, or the Metropolitan Museum of Art where thousands could share in the raw emotion of it.

"Art makes you feel," O'Flaherty insisted. In his opinion, too many canvases and fine sculptures sat, unappreciated, gathering dust in storage or were sold off to finance the acquisition of bigger and better pieces. Harrumph! Better in which bureaucratic arsehole's opinion, he'd grumble. He hadn't qualm number one about relieving said institutions of these works.

"I'm liberatin' it," he'd often joke.

It was in the midst of one such "liberation" that O'Flaherty crossed paths with Melina. As an adjuster, Melina's biggest concern was not the whodunit. That was law enforcement's job.

Recover the art, not capture crooks. That was her focus. So, rather than turn O'Flaherty in, she accepted his assistance in locating a missing

Degas drawing in exchange for not ratting him out to the boys in blue. It began a long and fruitful, if guarded, relationship.

"Why are you here, Connor? We both know it's not for the Scotch."

"Straight to it then. All right." O'Flaherty set his glass on the table. "Scuttlebutt has it a beautiful woman is asking around Miami recently about the Gardner stash. Ordinarily, I wouldn't have even given it a second thought. Every now and again, some jackanapes pokes their head up inquiring about those paintings."

"Of course," Melina offered. "If those paintings were recovered, it would be a coup for the art world."

O'Flaherty raised a knowing eyebrow. "And a big fat recovery fee, no doubt."

Melina huffed and clunked her glass on the table. "It's never about the money, Connor. Not for me. You know that."

"Settle down, darlin'. Settle down. I was only pokin' a bit of fun. Anyway, like I said, I wouldn't have thought nothin' of it, except I heard another name, too. The woman was hanging about with a Frenchman by the name of Laurent. Remy Laurent."

Melina stiffened. O'Flaherty patted her knee. "Tell me you're not shackin' up with Laurent."

Melina pulled her feet up under her. "What if I am?"

O'Flaherty sank back into the sofa, clucking his tongue and shaking his head.

Melina leaned forward, breathless with excitement. "You don't understand, Connor. He has connections. People who can put me in reach of the Gardner paintings."

"And people who can put you in a shallow grave. He's connected to La Brise de Mer, darlin'. I have a temper, but them fellas? Nasty pieces o' work, that group."

"I have to find them, Connor. I have to bring them home. I thought you, of all people, would understand."

"I do, darlin'. I do. But you're like a daughter to me and if you came to harm chasin' the infamous Gardner mirage, it would break this poor Irishman's heart."

"Look," O'Flaherty offered when he saw Melina's infallible resolve. He took a scrap of paper from his pocket and scribbled a name. "If you're hell bent on going after the Gardner heist, you should start with the man who knows the most about it. If anyone can guide you safely to it, it'll be him. He just might need a bit of gentle persuasion. He's a bit of a one-man show since he left the Bureau."

"He's F.B.I.?" Melina asked.

"Former. Aren't you listenin'? Now he's holed up in some backwoods cabin communing with Smokey the Bear, or something. Find him and you'll find the Gardner collection. Just promise me you'll stay clear of Remy Laurent."

Melina nodded as O'Flaherty handed her the scrap of paper. She read the name written in O'Flaherty's loose scrawl.

"Jake Reisen? Who in the hell is Jake Reisen?"

CHAPTER NINE

Portland, Oregon

The seller arrived nearly thirty minutes early. That was all right by Jake. He liked to play it loose.

He couldn't say the same for Dan Fogelberg, the BLM Special Agent trying to look relaxed at the counter. Of course, Jake figured, it had to be hard to relax when you were ordering a medium half-caff, no-foam, non-fat, vanilla soy latte.

Jake liked to keep his coffee to one syllable. Black.

Criminals were notoriously unpredictable. Sometimes they showed up ahead of schedule for a little pre-meet recon. Sometimes they swaggered in well after the appointed hour, if for no other reason than just to establish their command over the situation. Occasionally, they just flat out forgot what in the hell they were doing. More often than not, however, they simply played it loose.

So, Jake sat, rocked back on two legs of his chair, boots kicked up on the table, slowly savoring the Pike's Peak roast steaming up from the 100%

recycled material coffee cup as winter swirled outside.

Jake didn't play well with others. In fact, it was one of the reasons the thirty-five year old had taken the job as a Ranger with the Bureau of Land Management. There were other reasons, but Jake didn't want to think about those right now.

As a Bureau of Land Management Ranger in the Beaver State, he patrolled his parcel of the remote wooded public lands with his ATV or snowmobile, depending on the weather. Sometimes, he even walked the long miles through the tracts of Douglas firs and lodgepole pines, keeping a wary eye for trespassers, wildfires, and pothunters.

The latter was a new group of villains. Not the sexy, curvaceous Lara Croft of Tomb Raider fame, these were common criminals involved the looting of Native American artifacts from public lands. Sometimes it was ancient pieces of pottery. Arrowheads, too, frequently found their way into the pockets of uneducated hikers eager to turn a fast buck. Sadly, the theft could often involve human remains from tribal burial sites. When these "thieves of time" initiated sales of archaeological or paleontological resources – that was when the BLM Special Agents got involved.

It was also when Jake wished his coffee cup held something that could put a little more hair on his chest.

When a Special Agent set up one of these sting operations, quite often Rangers would get brought in to assist. So, when the BLM got a tip that someone was trying to sell "some pots he had dug up", this whole drama was scripted.

Dan Fogelberg, the Special Agent in charge of this operation, was today's buyer. Jake, like most of the "customers" in the café, were BLM employees, there as tactical support.

Two Portland General Electric Company employees sat at a corner table, eating bear claws, eyes on the door. A briefcase-toting redhead stood in line at the counter, jabbering in her cell phone to no one in particular. Even the Rastafarian barista behind the counter was surreptitiously strapped for bear. Jake supposed dreadlocks was there to lend credence to the coffee shop's moniker: "Jamocha Joe's".

Jake closed his eyes and sighed, rubbing his temples. He looked up as the loud clunk of a ceramic cup rattled his table. Fogelberg stared down at Jake with the sour look of the kickball team captain who gets stuck with kid nobody wants.

"Look, Riesen. I don't care what kind of big shot you were with the F.B.I., or how many cases you closed. This is my op, and I've got everything under control."

Jake took a long, slow sip from the lip of his cup. "Yup. I'm sure you do, Fogelberg. No doubt your backstopping's all done up. High and tight. Like your haircut." The sarcastic twitch at the corner of Jake's mouth suggested he knew it wasn't. It was also a pretty open jab at Fogelberg's stereotypical agent razor buzz. The severe cut was losing the battle to camouflage Fogelberg's growing bald spot. Jake's current mop, conversely, trended toward the shaggy side.

"God is in the details, kid." Jake recalled Oddball's favorite aphorism. "And someday those details are gonna save your ass."

Backstopping was tedious, Jake admitted. There was way more to it than just calling yourself Joe Blow and expecting the world – especially the suspicious, seedy characters of the underworld – to believe it. Done right, you had to set up phony email addresses. Fill your wallet with frequent flyer membership cards in your *nomme de guerre*. Store discount cards. Maybe a random receipt or two.

Then there were your bona fides – business cards, phone numbers, and hit or two on your typical search engines. Most of these "credentials" could be put together by an individual agent with some minor elbow grease. The more difficult forms of identification, identification badges from legitimate businesses, the use of a company name – that required a little extra paperwork. But, bottom line, any undercover operative worth his salt, no matter what alphabetical team you played ball for, backstopped.

Fogelberg pulled his neck back like an awkward turtle. "Backstopping? What the hell? This is just some tweaker trying to pawn off some ancient Indian Tupperware so he can buy more meth."

Jake winced. Not just an idiot, but a politically incorrect one.

Fogelberg could have been right about the seller's identity, Jake supposed. There had been a recent surge in the methamphetamine-artifact link. But everybody knew what happened when you assumed.

The uncomfortable thought made Jake's ass twitch.

The temperature in the shop dropped drastically as the front door swung open. Too late now.

Oh, well, he thought. Here goes.

Jake suddenly handed the ceramic sugar packet holder to Fogelberg as if he were just another patron looking for some sweetener. A chuckle twitched the corners of his mouth. They couldn't make enough sweetener for the dill pickle look on Fogelberg's face. "Yeah, buddy. Here you go. And the hair plugs are coming in great."

Jake's smirk disgruntled Fogelberg even further. He grabbed the holder.

"Thanks…pal."

Fogelberg ground his heel into the floor and did an abrupt one-eighty, putting his back to Jake and his eyes squarely on the twitchy young man that had just walked into the coffee shop.

The young man's eyes darted around the room, searching. Dark shadows settled deep under his eyes, as if he hadn't slept in days. Which, Jake thought, if he was tweaking, he probably hadn't. Most users in that stage of meth addiction could go as many as three to fifteen days without sleeping.

"Hey, there. Guthrie?" Fogelberg initiated contact, extending his right hand to shake.

Guthrie kept his hands jammed into the pockets of his lumpy coat, a detail not lost on Jake. Fogelberg noticed, too, but, like the jackass he was, took it more as a personal slight.

Jake, on the other hand, noted it for what it was — a potentially dangerous situation. Not only were tweakers typically sleep-deprived, they also were prone to be extremely irritable and paranoid. A tweaker did not even need provocation to behave or react violently, but confrontation increased the chances of a violent reaction.

Fogelberg was a walking, talking confrontation. Hell, Jake worked with the guy and wanted to punch him half of the time. An uneasy feeling began to roil in Jake's gut. Guthrie gave a barely audible grunt and nodded.

Fogelberg snapped his hand back, visibly annoyed. "Yes, well. I'm Arthur. Arthur Smith."

Jake held back a groan. Fogelberg must have played hooky the day they taught undercover logistics. Always use your own first name. This whole thing was starting to smell like his laundry — sour.

"Let's sit down, shall we?" Fogelberg gestured to an out of the way table in the corner, one out of Jake's sightline. Was Fogelberg trying to louse this up? Jake met the eyes of the redheaded executive who was now sitting at a table near the front door. What was her name? Jake thrashed his semi-caffeinated brain. Heather! The name leaped forward. He made an imperceptible gesture to Heather to stake out the front door. She nodded. Jake slowly stood and brought his coffee to the counter for a refill. The new position gave him eyes and ears on Fogelberg. He cocked his head and listened in.

"So. You have some pots for me?" Fogelberg asked Guthrie. Subtle, Jake thought. No romance. Just slam, bam, and thank you, ma'am. No wonder Fogelberg was a two-time divorcé.

Guthrie nodded, but kept his hands thrust deep in his pockets. "Yeah. I was up on the ridge spur. You know, just hiking."

Fogelberg smirked. If Guthrie noticed the special agent's condescending response, he ignored it. His discolored fingertips drummed an unconscious, but incessant beat into the tabletop. "Uh, huh. Sometimes I have trouble sleeping, you know. So, I go for a walk. Helps clear my head."

Yeah, maybe that and about six weeks of detox, Jake thought. This guy was totally wired.

"Anyway, I was just hiking, like I said, and my boot kicked into something hard. At first I thought it was just a rock or something. But when I bent down, I saw this weird-ass picture on a piece of red clay sticking out of the ground. I dug it out and saw it was some kinda bowl. A buddy of mine told me a bunch of tribes used to live around here and left this stuff behind. He says people would pay good money for this kind of stuff."

"Your buddy's not wrong," Fogelberg replied. "That is, if it's authentic. Do you have the piece here?"

Guthrie hesitated. Not a good sign.

"It's close," he offered tentatively, sitting a little more forward on his chair. "What are you willing to pay?"

Before Fogelberg could throw a number out on the table, a cherub-cheeked grandmother waddled from the ladies' room just behind Guthrie's left shoulder.

Shit! Every muscle in Jake's body tensed. Fogelberg had sworn he'd cleared the place!

Granny had almost passed the two seated men completely when she suddenly stopped and stared at Fogelberg. Her face lit up in a beaming smile.

"Daniel? Danny Fogelberg? Oh, I knew it was you. It's me! Mrs. Duncan!" she exclaimed.

The instincts of every agent in the room suddenly went on the alert.

"I'm sorry, lady. You must have me confused with someone else," Fogelberg floundered.

The old woman slapped him playfully on the arm. "Oh, nonsense! I never forget a student. Especially one who turned out as successful as you! Special Agent with the Bureau of Land Management? A teacher couldn't be more proud!"

At the mention of the BLM, Guthrie shot up, finally freeing his hands from his pockets. It might have been better for everyone if they had stayed there, Jake though as he spied the HK-1037 tactical combat knife in Guthrie's trembling hand. Why did they always bring a knife to a gunfight?

Jake leveled his SIG at Guthrie as Fogelberg tackled the surprised Mrs. Duncan to the ground. Heather had cleared her sidearm from its holster. The power company "employees" also had drawn down on Guthrie.

Guthrie, for his part, may have been on drugs, but he was fast. He took a vicious swing with the serrated Bowie knife in his right hand as Jake deftly ducked and spun around. Guthrie quickly swung the knife in a backward arc and, again, Jake avoided the blade.

He wasn't quite fast enough to avoid Guthrie's left hook, however. The blow rattled Jake's molars, but he was able to maintain enough of his faculties to throw his left forearm up and block the descending point of the knife. The forcible connection of bone on bone knocked the blade out of Guthrie's hand. Unfortunately, it also knocked Jake's gun from his hand. The SIG went skittering across the floor and lodged under the coffee counter.

Jake reached up and gripped Guthrie's right forearm as he lunged for his fallen knife. Guthrie connected another left to Jake's face and immediately cocked it back for a second blow, but Jake ducked backward, throwing a quick right. He followed it up with a solid jab to Guthrie's solar plexus.

As Guthrie doubled over, Jake delivered a driving elbow to the addict's right kidney. The force of the blow spun Guthrie to face Jake who obliged with a quick right-left combination to his face. As Guthrie reeled, Jake jammed a powerful uppercut below his jawline.

Guthrie stumbled backward, eyes rolling into the back of his head. Jake planted a final, solid roundhouse kick in Guthrie's chest and the young man crumpled to the ground. The two male agents rushed forward to take Guthrie into custody and Heather ran forward to assist Fogelberg in righting the disoriented Mrs. Duncan.

Jake retrieved his gun from beneath the counter. He grabbed a handful of napkins and dabbed at the blood trickling from the corner of his mouth. He nodded to Fogelberg as he passed.

"Nice working with you, Dan," he muttered.

"Wait," Fogelberg began. "This isn't over. We're not done."

"Oh, you're done."

With that, Jake pushed open the door and stepped out into the brisk air of the Oregon morning.

CHAPTER TEN

Miami, Florida

In a correspondence to his brother Theo, Vincent Van Gogh penned that: "Great things are not done by impulse, but by a series of small things brought together. And great things are not something accidental, but are willed."

It was no accident that nature was bending to his designs. He had willed it to do so – with a little help from science, of course.

He swirled the 2002 Abreu Cabernet Madrona Ranch in a deep cherry red eddy in the glass. As the jewel-toned liquid spiraled inside the contours of his glass, his eyes raised to the steel gray sky brooding over the Atlantic. He had received word that another vortex had begun swirling over the southern Caribbean. A satisfied grin creased faint laugh lines at the edges of his mouth.

All the small things were coming together.

He leaned his nose into the bowl of his wine glass, absorbing the heady bouquet of berries and spring flowers with just a hint of charcoal.

The bottle had a pricey receipt, nearly eight hundred dollars a bottle, but there was certainly cause for celebration. He took a slow, savoring sip.

Worth every penny.

He fancied himself an artist, a great master like Van Gogh. Anyone could steal a painting. He thought on the catalogue of art theft that had burgeoned since the late 80s.

Bold thieves relieved the Louvre of a Corot.

A DaVinci was absconded from a Scottish castle by brash bandits posing as tourists.

Then there was the young man who walked into the Rodin Museum near closing time and snapped a ten-inch high bronze from its marble podium and walked right back out.

In the world of art theft he mused, however, there were technicians and there were artists. The technicians could get the job done, he supposed. They possessed the expertise, or blind, stupid luck as was more often the case, to pull off the heist, and sometimes impressive ones at that. But the true artists offered something more than just the broad brushstrokes of removing seminal works of art from their current proprietors.

Artists thought beyond the theft. After all, the art in art crime wasn't in the theft. It was in the sale. A thief who stole a piece of art and expected to fetch anything near open-market value was a fool. He'd be lucky to command even ten percent. And of course, the more famous the work, the more difficult the task became.

But the artist – he chuckled – the artist knew looted art and antiquities could be used as collateral, a sort of cultured currency, to finance arms deals, drug transactions, and perhaps the occasional terrorist plot.

At the thought of this last, his smile grew wider. He tilted the last of his wine into his mouth. He set the empty glass on the bare bar, reached down for his carry-on bag, and left the empty condominium leaving nothing behind but echoing footsteps.

CHAPTER ELEVEN

Willamette, Oregon

Jake felt like he'd been gut-checked. The receiver hung limply in his hand, Oddball's filtered voice echoing from miles away. His mind reeled.

It just wasn't possible. Kat was dead?

She had just called him last night! He slowly brought the receiver back to his ear.

"What happened, Oddball? What happened to our girl?" His voice came out as a choked whisper.

Oddball responded slowly, his voice thick with grief. "I don't know, Jake. They're telling me it was some kind of animal attack. A rogue grizzly. They won't release my baby's body."

Jake shook his head. Wouldn't release the body?

"Hold on, hold on, Oddball. Who's 'they'? And why won't they release the body? If it was just an animal attack," Jake began. Oddball cut him off.

"That's just it, Jakey. I don't think it was."

The short hairs on the back of Jake's neck bristled as Oddball continued.

"I got a call. From Kat. Sometime last night."

"Me, too, but she never left a message," Jake interrupted.

"Well, she left one for me. She was scared, Jake. Something had my baby girl terrified. Something to do with her job at that flaky government think tank."

"I thought they just studied the Aurora Borealis. You know. Nature's awesome light show?"

"I thought so, too. But, something had her spooked and I don't know what." Oddball paused, choking back a sob. When he regained his composure, he continued. "Listen. Do you still have that friend of yours, your buddy, the conspiracy nut?"

"Digger? Yeah. He was supposed to come around tonight to watch the game," Jake replied.

"Ask him what he knows about that H.A.A.R.P. facility. I wouldn't get you involved, Jake, but you're the only one I trust. I hate to ask," Oddball began.

"That's the beauty of it, Oddball. You never have to."

Jake suddenly froze. His ear picked up a faint white noise in the background. Staticky. He wasn't sure if it was coming from the phone or from the growing blizzard outside.

No, it was definitely coming from the phone.

"Hey, Oddball, did you just drive into the TWT?" The Ted Williams tunnel, one of the underground arteries that resulted from Boston's Big Dig project sometimes interfered with cellular reception.

"No," Oddball replied. "I'm holed up at home. Why? What's up?"

That was the answer Jake feared. He heard the scratching again.

"Oddball, I think we've got ourselves a party line."

The tension hung thick as both men fell instantly silent. A loud click suddenly popped over the line. Well, hell, Jake thought. That was a capacitive discharge if ever he heard one.

"Jesus. What in the hell is going on, Jake? What did my baby get herself mixed up in?"

"Oddball, hang up. I'll contact you later." Oddball didn't need further prodding.

As the disconnect sounded in Jake's ear, his mind raced. He was fairly certain the mystery guest had signed off, but somebody was awful curious about his conversation. He would grab a burner phone down at Nell's later, after the snowstorm ebbed. Meanwhile, he'd do a little digging. If they were studying more than the Northern Lights at that facility, he was going to figure out what it was. Oddball and Kat were family.

Family. Jake cast a longing glance toward the face-down picture frame on his end table. He'd already lost too much. And now, Kat. Such a sweet kid. Who could possibly want her dead? And why?

The biting question urged him to place his palm flat against the case of his cell. No extraordinary tell-tale heat radiated from the case. It was unlikely the suspected tap was on his line. It had to be Oddball's. Still, no use risking it.

The blizzard had blown in suddenly, catching the region by surprise. The meteorologists on KPTV had no reasonable explanation for the uncharacteristic onslaught of winter fury. Snow and ice weren't unusual. This much, at all once, was.

A sudden low pressure system had sprung from nowhere, spawned in the frigid Gulf of Alaska, and inexplicably deepened with tightening pressure gradients. As warm winds blew up from the jet stream, the resulting front was dumping winter on Portland's doorstep.

Jake figured that was weather-geek speak for "Keep your ass inside 'cause it's friggin' cold out there!"

The freak storm wasn't the only anomaly being discussed on the news. Apparently, the morning's quake was grabbing its share of headlines, too. Mostly because it hadn't been the only one. Apparently four micro-quakes hit the Portland area during the night and early morning hours, all between 1.4 and 2.2 on the Richter scale. People had started clamoring. Was this a prelude to "The Big One" that geologists were predicting?

Jake had other things to worry about right now, like why Cody was suddenly barking fiercely at the swirling snow outside. The Husky had both of his massive front paws braced against the sill of the window, alternating low, fierce growls and spats of frenzied barks. Huskies were fairly non-committal when it came to barking, so it gave Jake pause for concern. Jake quickly grabbed the dog by the scruff and tried pulling him back, but Cody was frenziedly adamant to address something outside.

"Cody! What are you barking at, you ridiculous dog?" Jake squinted out into the white blindness as a deep growl rumbled in Cody's chest. Jake caught a momentarily flash of shadow against the bleached backdrop. Jake started. Did he just see someone large leaning against the flurrying gale? He looked again, but the image dissolved just as quickly as it had appeared.

The room plunged into sudden, unexpected darkness. Cody backpedaled, pulling free of Jake's grip. His nails skittered on the wooden floor as he scrambled under the bed. Jake stared after him.

"A little snow and you're Rin Tin Tin, but kill the lights and you're friggin' Droopy? Stupid mutt."

But when the goose bumps raised on his arms and the hairs stood up again on the back of his neck, Jake considered maybe Cody was onto something. The power *could* have gone out because of the storm.

Jake scrambled for his sidearm. Gun in hand, he pressed himself flat against the wall next to the window. He snatched a quick look out the window. It was there again. The dark figure. Only this time, he knew it wasn't a figment of his imagination. It was there and it was close.

He watched as the figure slowed, then collapsed in a heap only thirty feet from his front door.

Jake weighed his options. The mysterious visitor could have something to with what happened to Kat — someone who silenced her and had now been sent to silence the last people she had tried to contact before her death. If that were the case, he felt completely justified in leaving the stranger out in the elements.

Conversely, unwary hikers had been known to lose their way out here. The storm had blown up so suddenly and fiercely, it wasn't such a stretch to believe that some poor schmuck had stumbled out of the woods and happened upon his cabin. If that was what was going on here?

Jake refused to add any more red to his ledger.

He pulled on his North Face parka, yanked the fur-trimmed hood over his head, tugged on his gloves and opened the door. A dervish of snow whirled in the resulting convection current as the frigid air outside met the comfortable warmth inside. Jake pressed against the gusting storm, crunching through the snow toward the fallen hiker. He still couldn't make out much detail, squinting as he needed to against the wind. Tears trickled from the corners of his eyes, impairing his vision even further.

As he approached the hiker, he was surprised at how slight he was. In that initial flash, Jake swore he had seemed larger. Jake kept his gun trained, and toed the hiker over.

"Holy cow!" Jake exclaimed. He nearly dropped his gun into a drift when he saw the bronzed skin of the Latin beauty lying in the snow. Granted, she was favoring a more bluish tinge at the moment.

Jake shook himself from his initial shock and swept the woman into his arms. He needed to get her inside before hypothermia or frostbite set in, if it hadn't already. She didn't look well.

He turned and headed back for his cabin. Cody was back at the window, yapping through the pane.

"Oh, yeah, Genius?" Jake yelled above the howling wind. "Why don't you get out here and help me! You're bred to pull a friggin' six hundred pound sled across the Alaskan wilderness for crying out loud!" Cody just cocked his furry head sideways and let his tongue loll out the side of his mouth.

Sweat rolled down Jake's forehead. The effort of trudging through the snow was grueling. Even though the unconscious woman probably only weighed a buck twenty-five soaking wet, slogging her deadweight coupled with his own body mass was a workout.

He was so intent on reaching the cabin door, he didn't notice the intent gaze of a second dark figure watching from a nearby copse of trees.

CHAPTER TWELVE

When Melina opened her eyes, it was still dark. The softness of the down comforter pillowed around her like a cloud. She thought for one minute about floating back into the peaceful oblivion of sleep when a wet tongue slobbered generously across her face.

Consciousness slammed back to her like a pile driver on a pylon.

Backpedaling away from a deluge of sloppy canine kisses, Melina scrambled to a standing position. She searched the room, struggling to get her bearings and piece together the last few hours.

She forced her brain to recall the chain of events that had gotten her here. Wherever "here" was. After her meeting with O'Flaherty, she had packed an overnight bag and caught the next flight out to Portland. She had rented a car. Economy 2-Door. Ford Fiesta. Yeah. That was right. The first snow had started to hit just as she had pulled into Nell's Trading Post.

When she asked around on where to find Jake Riesen, gregarious Nell was only too happy to offer directions. Apparently, Mr. Riesen didn't get too many visits from exotic-looking women. Or any women for that matter, Nell hinted. She suggested Melina wait until the weather cleared before she continued her journey. There were plenty of warm rooms at the Lodge where she could wait it out. The trail up to Jake's place was difficult enough to navigate under clear skies let alone in the blinding white of a snowstorm. Melina was adamant, however. She had to go tonight. Against her better judgment, Nell provided Melina with snowshoes, a more appropriate winter parka and a water bottle.

Now, as a distinct draft drifted across her taut belly, Melina was slowly realizing she had neither snowshoes nor parka on. She didn't even have so much as the water bottle to cover her totally naked body.

"Whoa!" Jake exclaimed as he walked in from the next room. He nearly capsized the tray carrying steaming tomato soup and a hot, grilled cheese sandwich.

Melina flushed nearly as red as the tomato soup as she instinctively fumbled for the comforter. Cody translated her frenzied pulling as an invitation to play tug-o-war. He plopped his furry mass squarely in the middle of the down square.

As Melina wrestled the belligerent dog for the blanket, Jake executed a discreet about-face. A jumbled apology tumbled from his lips.

"I am clothes. No. Not sorry. What I meant was, I am wet."

"What?" Melina spluttered.

"No! Damn! Sorry! Not me. Your clothes. Wet. Hypothermia. Fire." Jake gave up and slapped an open palm against his forehead.

"Food." The last word came out more as a Neanderthal grunt as pointed to the tray and walked back out the way he came.

"Your owner's not too bright, is he?" Melina asked the Husky. She gave one last tug with all her might, just as Cody bounded from the bed releasing Melina and the comforter in an unceremonious tumble. A beat passed.

"And, apparently, it's contagious." Her muffled voice muttered from under the folds of linen. She dug her way to the surface and peered out.

She swore the Husky was grinning behind the grilled cheese gripped in his teeth.

Jake busied himself with stoking the fire. Melina's clothes hung over the fireplace screen. The power was still out so the dancing flames were the only illumination in the room. He was glad. Maybe the shadows would conceal the complete embarrassment on his face.

It wasn't her nakedness that embarrassed him. He'd certainly seen his share of feminine flesh over the years. He snorted. Okay, maybe a little more than his share. The human body was nothing to be ashamed of. It was a beautiful thing – one of Nature's works of art. No, what embarrassed him was his Freudian slip in admitting how her body affected him. It had been far too long since a woman had been able to scramble his brain like that and make the words come out so very wrong. What was worse was he didn't even know who in hell she was yet or what she was doing up here in the backwoods in the middle of a freak blizzard!

"Great first impression, Jake," he muttered to himself.

"I was impressed. Most guys I know can only burn water." Melina's voice startled Jake. He dropped the poker. It clattered to the ground. Melina stifled a chuckle.

"It looked impressive, anyway. The dog seemed like he was enjoying it." She thumbed her way in Cody's direction.

Jake regained his composure at the mention of the dog. "Cody? Oh, come on. You're kidding me! Shoulda named that chow hound Oliver."

"Please, sir. May I have some more?" Melina giggled.

Jake grinned. "Good one. So, uh, do I call you Oliver, or do you actually have a name?"

Melina stepped forward, hand outstretched. "Of course. I'm an idiot. I'm Melina. Melina Flores."

Jake shook her hand. "Jake Riesen."

Melina started at the name. Jake continued before she could find her tongue.

"Well, Miss Flores, you want to tell me what you were doing way up here in the middle of a blizzard?"

Melina shifted her weight in embarrassment. Nell had warned her about the storm, but she had ignored her. The Gardner collection was just too important.

"I suppose it was pretty stupid," she offered.

"Stupid? No. Stupid is choosing the high school quarterback over the president of the chess club. Just ask the girl before Melinda Gates. But hiking in the mountains during a snowstorm? That's suicidal. You must have been after something really important."

"I was," Melina floundered. "I am."

She flopped into the easy chair and sighed.

"I need you."

"Me?" A puzzled crease furrowed between his eyebrows.

Melina drew in a deep breath and prepared to launch into her well-rehearsed sales pitch.

"Mr. Riesen, I am an adjuster with – ," she began before Jake abruptly cut her off.

"You want to talk about the Gardner case."

"Actually, yes. An acquaintance told me you were the expert when you worked with the FBI."

"Worked. Past tense. I'm not an agent anymore. I don't work those kinds of cases. Especially not the Gardner case. End of story." Jake went back to stoking the fire, angrily, until a brilliant flame erupted from the glowing embers.

Melina slid to the very edge of her seat. The burning in her eyes rivaled the glow emanating from the now roaring fireplace. "Don't you realize how important this case is? What it would mean to have these pieces back?"

Jake whirled on the defensive. "Sometimes things are lost. And no matter how much you want them back, they're going to stay lost."

A crackling pop punctuated the end of his sentence, an audible exclamation point. Melina would not be dissuaded.

"Is that why you wear that St. Anthony medal around your neck?" she pointed out. Her quick eyes had noticed the religious icon resting on a silver chain near the hollow in Jake's throat.

"St. Anthony of Padua," she continued. "Patron saint of lost things. I couldn't help but notice. Does it help?"

Jake's hand went instinctively to his throat. He clasped his thumb and forefinger around the small medal.

"Not that I can tell," he mumbled in reply.

"I always understood that things like that only work when you have faith," Melina suggested.

Jake was just about to whip back with a sharp retort when a sharp retort of another kind shattered through the windows of the cabin.

Jake tackled Melina to the ground as a spray of bullets strafed the wooden walls. A line of bullets peppered the wall at what would have been chest level had the pair still been standing. Melina's eyes flew wide. Jake found himself lost fleetingly in their golden topaz. Another quick staccato of bullets shook him from his reverie. He braced himself up on his muscled forearms.

"You packing?" Jake asked Melina briskly.

Melina looked down at her twisted comforter wrap and grimaced. "Does it look like it?"

Jake rolled his eyes and scrambled low for his spare Ruger. He reached his hand up into his bedside table drawer, fumbling blindly. No sense in giving the anonymous gunman or gunmen a clear target.

A low whine issued from under the bed. Cody cowered beneath the box spring, hiding behind the dust bunnies. Jake checked the magazine. Good. Full clip. He turned to the dog.

"Bark at a pretty girl, sure. Bark to let me know there's a guy with a semi-automatic weapon? No. You make like a Roomba. I really think we need to reassess this relationship."

Cody threw an embarrassed paw over his nose as Jake scrambled back to Melina's post behind the sofa. He handed her the gun.

"You know how to use this?" he asked.

"Gee, I don't know. How does it turn on? Yes! I know how to use it!" She quipped tersely. "I just wish I knew what or who I was shooting at."

Jake thought back to the early morning debacle with Fogelberg. He supposed that Guthrie the Tweaker could have friends, but didn't think they would have the wherewithal to know who he was let alone where his place was located. He was damned surprised Melina had found it, snowstorm notwithstanding.

In between volleys of wood-splintering bullets, Melina pulled off a few shots through the shattered window. She ducked back down for cover.

"Don't you have a phone up here? To call 9-1-1? The forest rangers? Somebody?"

The phone. Melina's suggestion fueled Jake's second concern. If someone had the chutzpah to tap a few phones they could figure out who he was. He was also fairly certain they would have the skills to track him down. If they suspected Kat had shared information, information they didn't want anyone to know...oh, well. Shoot first. Figure out the answer to the questions later.

He squeezed off several rounds and nose-dived as they were returned even more enthusiastically. Glass shards showered Jake and Melina as the side lamp exploded into shrapnel.

Melina instinctively covered her head. "Jesus! Connor must have been right!"

"Who's Connor? And what was he right about?" Jake voice strained over the crashing gunfire.

"Connor O'Flaherty. The one who sent me to you. He said if I kept poking into the Gardner thing, La Brise de Mer might, well, let's just say they might get a little upset."

"A little upset? La Brise de Mer? As in the European mob?"

Melina nodded and went back to firing.

Jake fingered the St. Anthony medal around his neck, then looked over at the strange, half-dressed woman shooting beside him. As she leaned her rounded breasts into the cushion of the sofa and used the backrest to steady her aim, the comforter slipped dangerously low, settling just above the "V" of her buttocks.

Jake sighed heavily. Seems like the only thing Saint Anthony had helped him find was trouble.

CHAPTER THIRTEEN

Virginia Key, Florida

Residents of tropical climates planned their year around it. Natives of the southern U.S., in cities like New Orleans and Mobile, threw parties for it. Stores stocked shelves with batteries, bottled water, and emergency generators for the duration of it. And when massive, revolving storms boasting winds that broke most speed limits, swept across sultry waters and lumbered clumsily, but destructively onto coastal lands – that was when Mother Nature announced the fifth season of the year – hurricane season. In the Atlantic and eastern Pacific, they were called hurricanes. Typhoons swirled in the western Pacific. The Indian Ocean birthed cyclones. By any name they were monsters – sometimes killing thousands and causing billions of dollars in property damage. And nothing, absolutely nothing, stood in their way.

Or did it?

As he gazed at the monitor screen, he wondered. The science that hinted at environmental modification was sound. You just had to plug the proper variables into the equation. He thought about the birth of the fearsome atmospheric phenomenon.

Hurricanes developed innocently – clusters of thunderstorms over tropical waters. Seas in lower latitude areas traditionally harbored the warmer waters that fed moisture and heat to the atmosphere, climes where humid air could stick your clothes to your body. Heat rises. And when it did, condensation occurred and clouds ballooned in the skies. The process released heat. That heat evaporated even more moisture into the atmosphere until it reinforced itself in a perpetual feedback. In time, Mother Nature blinked, and the eye of a hurricane formed.

At least, that was how things unfolded when Nature was left to her own designs. Sometimes, she needed a little extra nudge in the right direction.

It was in the direction of the Nicaraguan coast that his attention was currently trained. A fairly loose, disorganized system burbled in the Caribbean. Nothing to warrant any great cause for concern. Yet.

If all went as planned, however, the calm, centrifugal heart of their little experiment would be the only haven for hundreds of miles.

He had developed a thick skin when his contemporaries had scoffed at the idea of clobbering an enemy with a blizzard, or starving him with an artificial drought. It was the stuff of science fiction, they cried. But, then again, so was the talk of atom bombs before 1946.

The damage caused by tropical storms was indeed horrendous, the energy they contained rivaling any bomb Oppenheimer had ever conceived. One storm equated the energy of a 10,000 one-megaton bomb. That was one-sixteenth of Hiroshima's infamous "Little Boy". Like a vengeful god, the Allied Powers smote an entire population. But, splitting the atom was not the only time man dared trod the slopes of Olympus.

Indeed, it would be Hercules, as the C-130 transport planes of the Vietnam War era were aptly dubbed, that would carry members of the 54th Weather Reconnaissance Squadron into the heavens – first over the Laotian panhandle, then north over the 20th Parallel and into the south over A Shau Valley. The 1967 cloud-seeding mission flew over Vietnam to "make mud not war." Silver and lead iodide were released into the existing clouds. The combined latent heat that released as billions of water particles turned to ice morphed the clouds into towering cumulus to scrape the ceilings of Olympus itself. Then the burgeoning nimbus tore open, dumping their heavy, watery load onto the Ho Chi Minh trail in an effort to wash out river crossings, turn roadways into sucking muck, and cripple enemy mobility.

A wry grin contorted his bearded face. Vietnam was a mere finger-flick from the gods.

A mosquito droned passed his ear. His heavy brow furrowed as he waved an angry fist at the buzzing insect. There had not been many mosquitoes in his boyhood home in Tashkent. Here, in the sub-tropical Keys, however, they may as well have been the state bird. A beefy hand reached for his cell. He dialed a long series of numbers and waited.

He tapped the glowing, radar heart of the developing meteorological skirmish blipping on the screen. The thick, ridged nail on a fat finger chapped by years of Russian winters chinked an uneven rhythm on the monitor. "Grow my *malenkyi odna*. Grow and we will show you the way."

The irritating buzz hummed past his head again as the mosquito alighted on a heavily-matted hand. Before the insect could puncture his rough skin with its needling proboscis, he crushed it into a blackened, bloody smear, his other hand meting out justice from above.

Like a god.

CHAPTER FOURTEEN

Willamette, Oregon

He peered through the sight of the F-2000 from his hidden vantage point in the trees. Even in the low light he could make out the two low slung humps in the shadows of the cabin. He ducked behind the pine as one of the shadows fired several shots in his general vicinity, then he quickly returned fire.

He wasn't overly concerned about giving away his position. The F-2000 came equipped with a flash suppressor that cooled and dispersed the hot gases escaping from the gun's muzzle. Though the initial concept of that particular design was intended to prevent shooter blindness in low light conditions, it had the secondary benefit of partially camouflaging the shooter in the dark. Nature played her part, too. The surrounding woods bounced the echo of each volley of shots. It was nearly impossible to discern their origin.

The F-2000 was a military weapon, a Special Forces bullpup assault rifle capable of firing eight hundred-fifty rounds per minute. Over the years, however, a few of the guns had migrated surreptitiously from their official channels, the Libyan Army, Pakistani SSW, and other organized armies and onto the arms black market. It was not his first weapon of choice for wet work like this. There was no finesse, no class. Just the abrupt brutality of shredding whatever you pointed at. It also required a degree of intimacy with which the shooter was not entirely comfortable. Up close and personal. Not his standard operating procedure.

But the freakish weather had called for a drastic policy change. No chance of effectively employing a standard sniper rifle in this gale. Had he had his druthers, he would have employed the longer, sleeker British L115A3. With a range of nearly fourteen hundred meters, it let him dole out judgment from a discreetly anonymous, almost godlike, distance. And his judgment could be bought by anyone – for the right price.

His current client had certainly tithed the right price – a cool million to neutralize the target. He didn't know why his intended quarry had been marked for disposal. He also didn't care. He had no need to see the big picture. He only needed to focus between the frenzied flakes of blowing snow, through the telescoped view of the magnifying reticle, and squeeze.

Inside the cabin, Jake's mind raced to find a solution for their predicament. In the battle between fight or flight instincts, flight currently had the winning edge. If an assailant had a rifle immediately at your back, muzzle nosed up against your shoulders, you stood an outside chance of disarming him. Wheel into the barrel with your shoulder, and take the weapon. A risky move, but plausible.

At this distance, though, there was only one option, but it was absolutely crazy.

The burning halogen eyes of the Abominable Snowman bore down on the would-be assassin accompanied by a fearsome roar. The churning snow masked the vicious swipe from an unyielding appendage that knocked the F-2000 from his hands. He looked on helplessly as a nearby snowdrift swallowed the gun. The temporary halo of light faded and cover of darkness returned. A foreign epithet escaped his lips, almost Italianate in inflection, but it was drowned out by the returning roar of the beast. Twin shafts of light flooded the clearing once again. As an unmistakable *braap* cut through the wintry gale, he realized quickly it was not snowman, but snowmobile. A Polaris Edge XC 600, to be exact. A sardonic grin wormed its way onto his scarred face. Mythical beasts might have given him pause, but a mere man on a snow-fitted motorcycle was simply a matter of a well-placed bullet. He just needed to find his gun.

He scrabbled through the snow, searching for his weapon. A satisfied smile spread as his hands closed on the hammered steel barrel. But, before he could raise it any higher than his waist, he was clotheslined by the driver of the snowmobile rocketing back through the clearing. The lower half of his body swung forward in an awkward, pendulous arc, while his head flew backward and connected hard with a section of packed snow and the unyielding rock beneath it. He fell still, a crimson stain leaching into the surrounding white.

The driver of the snowmobile powered down his vehicle and raised the snow goggles from his face. The wary, beady eyes of Grover Kelley looked down at the fallen hit man.

"Guess you didn't see the 'No Trespassing' signs," he muttered.

"Digger!" Jake's voice filtered through the winter howl. Digger jumped off his snowmobile and trudged through the snow toward Jake. Even at a distance, Jake was visibly taller than the bundled rider. When he got close enough, he grabbed the shorter man in a hearty embrace, patting him solidly on the back.

"Digger, my man, you are a God-send."

"Yeah, I'm not so sure where I stand on that whole religion thing. I talk to him and I'm praying, but he talks to me and the docs call me schizo."

Jake smiled. Grover "Digger" Kelley was not a huge fan of the psychiatric community.

"Witch doctors in Hugo Boss," he would often grouse.

A decorated veteran of both the Iraqi and Afghanistan wars, the Master-at-Arms Second Class SEAL bore the Navy Cross and the Silver Star. Unfortunately, he also bore the weight of an acute case of post-traumatic stress disorder. While in Afghanistan, his convoy had come under heavy enemy fire. He had instinctively leapt from his hummer and began returning fire, while also pulling a wounded Afghan soldier to safety. Once he had secured the man behind the engine block, he endured showers of Chechen gunfire to rescue a Marine trapped behind the wheel of another vehicle. Ammo shredded through Kelley's fatigues as he alternated tending the wounded men and returning volleys of defensive fire. Amidst the melee, Kelley monitored the medical evacuation of the injured, then led a ragtag Afghan force to quell the ambushing Chechens. He followed up on the conditions of the men he had rescued, but was devastated to learn the young Marine had not made it. He couldn't come to grips. The young man's injuries had been serious, but not immediately life threatening. Kelley was never quite the same after that. He began to see conspiracies everywhere he looked.

After finishing his last tour, he began another one – this time in various VA hospitals. After a well-tailored psychiatrist flipped open his

Physician's Desk Reference and declared aloofly "let's see what meds you haven't been on yet", Kelley excused himself from the doctor's office, disappeared down the hallway and into the woods of the Pacific Northwest. He only ventured out for the regular meetings of the Saturday Night Eaters Group that met at the local Denny's. Somewhere between Moons Over My Hammy and the more traditional Grand Slam, the eclectic assortment of scientists, writers, and armchair UFO investigators dug into every new conspiracy concept to roll out of Area 51 and beyond.

"You know, pal, you really should consider building a reinforced perimeter around this place. Especially if you want to keep the riff raff out."

As Jake smiled, his teeth chattered against the cold. "Then how would you get in, buddy?" He jovially slapped the odd little man on the back. Concerned, he looked toward the inert body of the gunman, then back at Digger.

"You still got that shortwave back at your place?"

Digger nodded. "Yeah. Of course. Why?"

"Gonna need to call streets and sanitation about this guy." He thumbed towards the dead man. "And I've got a little infestation problem."

Digger threw a thick glove down into the snow and stamped a foot. "You see! It's PRISM, man! The NSA's all over domestic surveillance now. That's exactly why I won't touch a phone. And don't even get me started on the internet."

Jake tried to reel his friend in. "All right, Jerry Fletcher."

The reference to the 1997 Brian Hegelund film gave Digger pause as the two men started the slog back to Jake's cabin. "You really think I look like Mel Gibson? I always thought he had a better butt."

Jake smiled and shook his head. Behind them the snow continued to fall, blanketing the body of the fallen assassin. Nature marched on.

CHAPTER FIFTEEN

Grand Goave, Haiti

In a long line of feminists, Mather Nature was a leader. The female praying mantis practiced the art of sexual cannibalism – one woman who made sure she got hers. In Africa, it was the lionesses who brought home the bacon – er, warthog. And, in the field of meteorology, females hadn't just broken the glass ceiling – they had shattered it.

The meteorological stretch for equality hadn't exactly occurred between a computerized low pressure system and a scattering of thunderstorms dancing across a green screen. No. Nature operated with even less subtlety than Gloria Steinem.

In the decades between the race for the M.R.S. degree and the precedent-setting *Roe vs. Wade* decision, a single violent and inarguable fact developed. Of the ninety-plus hurricanes that had made landfall, scientists discovered that storms with feminine monikers proved nearly three times as deadly as their male counterparts. Mother Nature was woman, and she roared.

Jacqueline Arcueil didn't much care if bad weather was male or female. She certainly did not know a barometer from an anemometer. What she did know was that the staccato drumming on the corrugated tin roof meant she had better step lively if she intended on getting her family's meager crop to market before she resembled one of the drowned rats you sometimes saw in the Port-au-Prince harbor. She had half a mind to crawl back under her threadbare sheet, but when you subsisted on less than two dollars a day, sleep was an ill-afforded luxury.

She swung her dark legs over the edge of her thin mattress. She was accustomed to her rough, calloused feet hitting a dirt floor. She jerked them back in surprise when they hit water instead.

"*Qu'est-ce que c'est?*" she thought out loud. She supposed the morning's rain was actually a holdover from throughout the night. The steady water had now seeped in, finding its way across the threshold. It wasn't much of a surprise when she thought about it. Much of Haiti's forests had been denuded, leaving little root structure to hold the land in place. And the Arcueil house was a simple one, put together by neighbors and other family members after her husband had passed away. It was truly no great engineering feat. She shouldn't be surprised that it leaked.

Vous pouvez tromper le soleil, mais pas la pluie. You can fool the sun, but not the rain indeed, she thought. Ah, well. The market waited.

She clucked her tongue and plunged her feet into the cold, inch-deep water. The moisture had turned the floor into a slick, slimy surface. The walls were fashioned of a similar materials – crude bricks mixed from sand, clay and water, with bits of stick and straw muddled in as well. It was no wonder Jacqueline's mahogany forehead creased with worry when the ground began to rumble. Rippling concentric rings radiated from around her ankles across the water's shaky surface. A survivor of the 2010 quake that had devastated much of Haiti and, in fact, had claimed her husband's life, Jacqueline feared the increasingly violent vibration radiating up through her feet would rattle the walls of her family's hardscrabble home to the ground, trapping them inside.

Jacqueline's head swiveled at the sound of a small slosh coming from the direction of the second room. Her five-year old daughter shuffled through the water with a sleepy look of confusion. The ragged teddy bear in her left hand drooped dangerously low to the increasingly dirty water. The little girl rubbed the errant crumbs of sleep from her eyes.

"*Maman? Thierry mouillée leur lit à nouveau,*" her soft, high voice mumbled.

As the rumbling grew with the insistence of a barreling locomotive, Jacqueline sincerely doubted her six-year old son's questionable bladder was responsible for the rising muddy water. Still, she wondered. After a moment's hesitation, she swooped her daughter into her arms and was about to rush into the other room to wake her son and other family members when a loud crash reverberated throughout the entire house. Something solid connected with the north wall. It was quickly followed by a rapid banging at the front door and the frantic cries of her neighbor's voice.

Jacqueline set her daughter down and barked a quick order in French. "*Rapide! Rapide! Aller réveiller votre grandmère et les autres! Nous devons quitter! Maintenant!*"

The small girl quickly slopped into the other room to rouse the other family members per her mother's frantic instructions. Jacqueline flew to the door, muddy water peppering a dark splash pattern across the hemline of her skirt. As she reached the threshold, she tore open the door. She completely missed the wide-eyed look of terror on her friend's broad, dark face. Jacqueline's attention was riveted on the undulating motion behind her.

A river of wet earth crashed toward her home.

CHAPTER SIXTEEN

Willamette, Oregon

The sensation was closely akin to being born, Melina imagined.

At first, the blackness enveloped her. Then, suddenly, her eyes fluttered against a brilliant, white light as the blindfold was removed. She held up a shielding palm against the Maglite beam Digger played through the forest shadows.

"I don't get it. Why all the secrecy?" she asked as Digger moved to detach Jake's blindfold as well.

"No offense, lady, but I don't know you, and even if I did, *never* let anyone know where your bunker is." Digger steered the flashlight toward the bunker entrance, a fairly non-descript metal utility door marked with the words "High Voltage".

Melina cast a sideways glance toward Jake. Digger caught the wary stare in his peripheral vision.

"Don't worry. That's just there to discourage the lookie-loos." He had no sooner uttered the assurance when he grabbed the handle and his body began to jerk violently in an awkward 120Hz shuffle.

Melina leapt into action. Her quick gaze darted through the thick underbrush for a fallen branch large and sturdy enough to dislodge Digger from the deadly current surging through his body. She had just picked up a viable candidate, a three-inch round pine about four foot long, and was about to drive it into Digger's torso when she stopped cold in her tracks.

Digger was still convulsing, but not because cardiac-halting amperage coursed through his squat body. Cycles of braying laughter bounced off the nearby spruce and pine as he bent over, hands braced on his knees. Jake tried, unsuccessfully, to stifle his own chuckles as Melina volleyed her shocked stare between the two men. Shock gave way to stormy fury as her golden irises deepened into a fathomless brown.

"Sonovabitch." The *sotto voce* epithet dripped with the promise of retaliation.

"Seriously," Digger managed between gasps for air. "Where do you find these girls, Jake?"

Jake wiped a tear from his eye. "They find me, man. They find me. But, right now I'm more worried about who *else* might find me, so can we put a little hustle into it?"

"Yeah, yeah. Sure. Be warned, though. I wasn't expecting house guests. Didn't exactly have a chance to tidy up."

"Not here because you're Martha Stewart, bud," Jake quipped as they followed Digger into the black void of the compound.

Jake winced as he took Melina's well-placed elbow to the ribcage. "Your friend is funny. No, really. He could play Vegas."

"Oh, come on," Jake defended. "Digger's just a little, well...off."

"Off is not exactly what we need right now. Somebody shot at us. We need the authorities."

All traces of joviality drained from Jake's voice. "We *need* to find out who shot at us and why. We *need* information. And when it comes to information," he jabbed a thumb in Digger's direction, "Digger's the best there is. Not to mention, if there's going to be any more trouble, you want him on your side."

Melina took the admonishment silently. After all, Jake and Digger had saved her life. She decided to hold her tongue for the moment, and give Digger the benefit of the doubt.

A few steps into the antechamber, her pupils dilated to flat, black saucers. Little moonlight seeped its way past the portal to the outside night. A resonating clang echoed through the antechamber and they were plunged into sudden blackness.

"Nine thousand dollar bullet resistant steel door," Digger boasted from somewhere in the darkness. "Yup. This puppy is FEMA-rated to withstand an F5 tornado with debris up to a hundred miles per hour. That is, if you can believe anything those bozos say. How they have time to rate anything when they're so busy building mass internment facilities for when they declare freakin' martial law, I don't know. Now, where's the damned light switch? Oh, here we go. Ta da! Home sweet home."

A narrow, antiseptic white staircase dropped a hundred feet into the earth. As Melina followed Jake and Digger down the steps, she quickly realized the stairway might well have been the cleanest place in the whole bunker.

They entered what appeared to be a living room. Melina surveyed the motley assortment of odds and ends: a collection of crumpled, discarded cans of energy drink; cork boards rife with blurred 8x10s of what were presumably UFOs in various shapes and sizes; a map of Silver Falls State Park, pin-pricked with pushpins – sightings, she supposed – next to a thermal photograph of a tall, bestial form; a dog-eared, note-scrawled copy of a government white paper, *Weather as a Force Multiplier: Owning the Weather in 2025*. She wasn't certain, but she thought she even spied a tinfoil hat peeking out from under a tented copy of Coleman's *Cryptozoology A to Z*.

Digger followed her gaze and quickly snatched the aluminum, crumpling it into a tight ball and lobbing into a nearby trashcan.

"Takeout," he grinned half-heartedly.

Melina started. Digger had peeled away the layers of winter outerwear, leaving a new, but equally odd person standing amid the clutter. She took in the fresh details. His razored light-brown hair did little to hide the spider-webbing of scars over his scalp. Melina thought back to Jake's comment about wanting Digger at his side in a fight. She surveyed the thick-barrel chest straining against the white tank top and the solid biceps under the lumberjack flannel and was inclined to agree. The evidence of repeated head trauma might explain a few things, though, she thought, too. His eyes were dark, close-set and twinkled with a mixture somewhere between quirk and crazy. Heaven only knew what the endless pockets of his cargo pants contained. Digger was an enigma, and an enigma he would have to remain. At least for now, Melina thought. She had other puzzles to figure out at the moment. Not the least of which was figuring out who had fired on them at the cabin.

Digger reached into the refrigerator and pulled out a beer. He tossed an amber bottle to Jake who snagged it in an expert catch – obviously, a practiced game between the two men. Digger thumped into an office chair near the desk. "So, what's the sit rep, Lieutenant? Bugs? Bullets? Who'd you piss off this time?"

"That's part of the problem. I don't have the first clue."

"That's not entirely true," Melina offered. She reached into her pocket. "I dug this out of one of your porch posts. Left a little bit of a hole. Sorry." Melina shrugged. "A 5.56 mm NATO round."

The interjection left the men momentarily flummoxed. Digger found his voice first.

"Great! That narrows it down to a list of only around fifty weapons, or so." The sarcasm wasn't lost on Melina. "We're gonna need a little more than that to go on."

Jake leaned in and took the bullet from Melina. "Yeah. Like telling me why an insurance adjuster knows so much about ballistics. As I recall, Picasso didn't use a Walther PPK to sketch out *Boy in Blue*."

"Foreign Service. South Africa. We had a lot of trouble with the Boko Haram and the splinter faction Ansaru. Some terrorist attacks and some kidnapping for ransom. I helped get some of those people back. Now? Now I just get artwork back." She shifted uncomfortably in her seat. "Paintings don't bleed."

"Yeah? Well, I do. Back at the cabin, you said something about La Brise de Mer having something to do with the Gardner paintings, the ones you're trying to recover."

"The Corsican mob guys? That's just great!" Digger burst. Jake silenced him with an arresting palm, but never took his eyes off Melina.

"La Brise de Mer. Tell me about them."

Melina studied Jake's face, sizing him up as a potential ally. She sucked in a huge breath and began to speak.

"I met a guy. An expat French businessman in Miami. Rumor has it that if you want something particular in the art world, this guy can get it for you. Especially, if you aren't too particular on provenance. I set up a deal to get my foot in the door with his people, La Brise de Mer, but, I don't know. Something spooked him and he called the deal off. I think he might have been headed back to his business in Paris. Phoenix Research Unlimited. The business is squeaky clean. Lot of government contracts."

"Phoenix Research?" At the mention of Laurent's business, Digger launched into a flurry of activity. He fingered through stacks of papers and reports, hunting, searching for something. Jake and Melina watched as a dervish of papers convected into a rag content funnel cloud. Suddenly, the funnel collapsed in on itself to reveal Digger clutching a newspaper. He smacked the front of the paper for emphasis.

"Phoenix Research Unlimited! Bingo! I knew I'd heard it before!" he announced.

"What?" Jake asked.

"P.R.U.! I've been watching the H.A.A.R.P. facility in Gakona."

"H.A.A.R.P.?" Jake started at the familiar name. "What about H.A.A.R.P.?"

"So, I've been watching, right. And it's had all these white vans moving in and out of the gates. All of them are marked on the side with this big, red bird and the letters P.R.U.".

"Phoenix Research Unlimited," Jake and Melina chimed in together.

Digger nodded. "Probably has something to do with the transition between government monitoring and civilian control. There this whole big article in the paper about it. They're supposed to be hosting a big event at the Getty Museum as a formal kind of announcement. Everyone who's anybody that's been involved with H.A.A.R.P.'s gonna be there."

"Sounds like I need to pay a visit to this H.A.A.R.P.," Jake mused.

Digger shook his head vehemently. "Nuh, uh. No way. No how, buddy. "If the government is doing something hinky in there, I don't want to be anywhere near it. A buddy of mine swears – all those antennas? Mind control." Melina caught Digger's gaze drifting toward the trash can and his discarded tin foil. She suppressed the smile curving the edges of her mouth. Digger continued his rant.

"Besides, what do you think they're going to do? Let you walk right in through the front door?"

Jake grinned. "That's *exactly* what I think they're going to do."

"We'll have to go see Oddball, of course," Jack scratched the persistent stubble on his chin. He turned to Digger. "You have a tux?"

Melina's left eyebrow arched. "Oddball?"

Jake blew off her curiosity and spoke directly to Digger. "He can use his FBI connections to rustle up a good, solid cover."

Melina tried shouldering her way into the men's conversation. "Who's Oddball? And why does he need a tux? I thought we were going to the H.A.A.R.P. facility."

Digger began to chew on his non-existent thumbnail. He turned to Jake. "Um, he still in Boston?"

Jake nodded. "We'll have to meet him somewhere loud. Someplace where it would be impossible to listen in."

"Who's listening?" Melina tried again.

Digger's eyes squeezed shut, his hands clasped together in fervent prayer. "Please tell me you mean what I think you mean. Please, please, please."

The small grin tugging at the corner of Jake's mouth dropped to a shocked "O" as two manicured hands caught him square in the chest. He stumbled back, landing in Digger's lap. The two startled men looked at the seething Latin beauty, her hands now cemented on her shapely hips.

"What in the hell are you two cooking up?" she trumpeted.

"You like hotdogs?" Jake grinned sheepishly.

"Hotdogs? I guess they're okay," she responded warily. "If they have yellow mustard with relish and onions on them."

"Yes!" Digger jumped up, dumping Jake unceremoniously on his ass. The short man bounced up and down like a Big Papi bobble head. Melina blinked confusedly between the two men.

Jake slowly stood, rubbing his backside. "Then you're gonna love Fenway."

Digger leapt into the air, punching a fist upward in victory. He began an awkward little jig that took him deeper into one of the honeycombed rooms. They could still hear him singing "Take Me Out to the Ballgame" wildly off-key well after he disappeared from view.

Melina jabbed a thumb in his general direction. "What is he so excited about?"

"Game seven of the Series. The Sox are tied with the Yankees."

CHAPTER SEVENTEEN

Santiago de Cuba, Cuba

Hester Farnsworth was giddy with excitement. Well, at least she had been when she originally booked this solo trip to Cuba. After the long, rough flight in – the pilot had had to reroute to avoid some burbling inclement weather in the Caribbean, but still encountered sick-bag turbulence – she wasn't so sure anymore.

Originally, she had been looking forward leaving her stuffy office cubicle behind in Scranton and dipping her toes in the azure waters of the Caribbean. She had even prided herself on choosing Cuba. Anyone could have a pre-packaged, all-inclusive generic Sandals resort vacation. But, Cuba? Cuba had history! Sugar and coffee plantations. Pirate attacks. The final resting place of charismatic revolutionary Che Guevara. She had looked forward to soaking up the vitality of the old colonial quarter which rang night and day with the driving rhythm of drums and the bright, peppered notes of brass horns.

Right now, though, the only thing that she was soaking in was her own sweat. The helpful man at the airport had insisted the hotel was an easy walk. Now, as she dabbed the beads of perspiration at her hairline, she questioned the five dollar tip she'd passed him. The October mercury in Cuba hovered near a sultry eighty-four degrees. And Santiago, spreading outward from the bay and cradled in the crook of the indomitable Sierra Maestra Mountains, had little breeze to relieve the humidity that could oftentimes oppress the unwary traveler.

Unwary traveler? Hester gave an abbreviated chuckle. Guilty as charged, she thought.

A sudden, strong wind whipped through the quarter, rustling through the nearby palms.

Oh, thank god! She leaned into the current of air, grateful for any relief. Her respite was short-lived, however. As she tried to navigate her way through the higgledy-piggledy streets and narrow alleys to get to her hotel, a group of hawking *jineteros* suddenly descended upon her. Cuban streets were home to the outwardly-friendly, quick-talking swindlers, eager to relieve unwary tourists of their "excess" baggage and money.

"*Hólà*, my friend! *América? Francia?*" one dark-skinned man queried as he jogged up on her right.

"*Buenos tardes.* You need some new shoes?" Another man threw his arm around her left shoulder. He pointed to her less-than practical heeled sandals. "I know a guy."

"Um, n-no thank you," Hester replied shakily. She tried to shimmy out from under the unwanted embrace. Why, oh, why hadn't she just taken a cruise?

She hefted her carry-on a little higher on her shoulder and quickened her pace. The men were not so easily dissuaded. One man in particular swooped directly in front of her, halting her dead in tracks.

"Let me help you with your bags, *senorita*. You should not have to carry such a heavy burden." His dark eyes flashed with a shadow of ferocity that warned Hester she probably should not refuse his services. Her own head swiveled around the square, searching anywhere for help, or an escape route. She took two wary steps backward, ready to run.

A sudden flurry of activity to her right caught not only her attention, but it caught the attention of the man in front of her. A thin, barefooted man raced out of a nearby bar where a television was showing disturbing pictures of mudslides washing away whole homes and massive waves crashing over shorelines. The new arrival frantically tugged at his friend's sleeve.

"*Carlos! Carlos! Dicen que viene un huracán. Es una mala. Van a cerrar los hotels turísticos. ¡Rápido! Paz a esta chica y vámonos de aqui.*"

The man who had frightened Hester took off, looking a little frightened now himself.

Hester tried remembering her high school Spanish. *Rápido!* That meant quick. *Es una mala?* She racked her brain. It's a bad one? What's a bad one? She walked up to the bar, looking at the captions. One word stood out. *Huracan.*"

The color drained from Hester's face. It didn't matter if she'd learned the word in Mrs. Ancona's Spanish class or not. The word was nearly the same in English.

Hurricane.

CHAPTER EIGHTEEN

Gakona, Alaska

The wind howled like a mad monkey. At least, Mason imagined it did. As he watched the convection currents whip the flakes into a white frenzy outside the Humvee's window, it was rather like watching a colorless, silent movie. He half-expected a title card caption to pop up on the dark tint at any moment.

Save us, Sheriff! Please, save us!

He was, of course, cast in the role of white-hatted sheriff in this little drama, riding in now on 190 horses to save the day. The part of the poor, pitiful townsfolk fell, obviously, to the civilian scientists who need the long arm of the law, or at least a disciplined military man, to put things to rights.

The Humvee slowed in the darkness, headlights catching the rigorous iron gate safeguarding H.A.A.R.P. from prying eyes. A bold warning sign cautioned. "Controlled area. It is unlawful to enter the area without permission of the Installation Commander. Sec. 21 Internal Security Act of 1950 USC 797. While on this installation all personnel and the property under their control are subject to search."

"Humph," Mason vocalized. Well, that should make his job just that much easier. He *was* here to search. Search for answers. And he had every intention of finding them.

The horses under the hood cantered impatiently in the cold as the driver awaited verification of security clearance. Too little, too late? Mason wondered. Once cleared, the black gate slowly slid open and the Mason's vehicle crunched through snow and gravel beyond a line of white-frosted spruce. Beyond the trees was a box-like building that far more resembled a grain elevator or an industrial warehouse that a state-of-the-art research facility.

The SUV parked, the beams of its headlights cutting toward the generic white building in matching columns. Their parallel symmetry was broken by an approaching figure outfitted in layers of cold-weather gear.

Mason was not going to wait for Shep Hinds to get completely to the vehicle. He broke the seal of warmth afforded by the door and stoically met the unforgiving cold of the outside night.

"Mr. Hinds?" he called over the insistent wind. His steady voice did not betray even the slightest shiver.

"Colonel Mason," Hinds replied, hand outstretched.

Mason accepted the proffered shake, gripping Hinds' hand firmly. "I will cede on the evening part, but there isn't anything good about it."

He dropped Hinds' hand and strode purposefully toward the command center. Hinds was hard pressed to keep up with the taller man's loping gait. He vigorously rubbed feeling back into his hand and he eventually fell in step with Mason.

"So, where's this firework show I understand you're supposed to have up here?" Mason threw a vague gesture toward the clouded sky.

"What?" Hinds began. "The Borealis? Oh, you wouldn't be able to see it on a night like this. The skies need to be clear and dark. You should have been here last night. Before this storm moved in, the whole sky was lit up. Blood red."

Mason stiffened visibly at the security chief's choice of adjectives. Hinds immediately regretted opening his mouth. He withered under Mason glowering stare.

The two men reached the building's entrance. In a quick, but surreptitious move, Hinds entered the security code on the keypad.

"How many people have that code?" Mason probed.

"Everyone who has access to this building has their own personal identification code." Hinds anticipated Mason's next question. "The only code entered last night was Kat Sørensen's."

The door clicked open. Hinds gestured toward the interior. "This way, sir."

Mason turned his head sharply and stepped inside. After an imagined eternity, Hinds exhaled and stepped in after the brusque man. The security lock obligingly snicked closed, keeping H.A.A.R.P., and its secrets, safe from the outside world.

Alan Davenport didn't grasp what he was looking at initially. He sat at Kat's desk, trying to organize what may well have been her last thoughts on earth. Kat's research dealt primarily with the aurora borealis. She studied the beautiful, atmospheric phenomenon in an effort to understand the physics of aurora and its related solar storms. In doing so she, and other scientists, hoped to be able to predict when our technologies in space, like satellites, might be affected.

So, why then did Kat have all this research on her drive relative to weather anomalies and natural disasters the world over?

Davenport sifted through data and pictures of the 1985 Puerto Rican floods, the 2011 Japanese quake and resultant tsunami, and even the recent California drought. He couldn't see the connection between the polar lights and these devastating events. Then again, it might have nothing to do with it at all. Even government think tanks experienced snow days. Especially in the Alaskan wilderness.

When a blizzard kept you trapped inside for days, you had better find a mental hobby, or you were likely to succumb to a vicious case of cabin fever. To that end, many of the H.A.A.R.P. scientists had taken up crossword puzzles. Some dabbled in watercolors. Davenport himself had daubed a fair faux-Monet. In fact, it currently hung on the wall behind him, there in Kat's office. Kat had had a love of the Masters and she had always been encouraging to him with his hobby – even if sometimes his Picasso came out more like a Pollock.

Some of the researchers, like Kat, took on little micro-projects to occupy their time. Sometimes, they were even able to cull a publishable paper out of it. What was the old adage? Davenport thought. Oh, yes. Publish, or perish. He shrugged. Maybe all this interest in weird weather had just been Kat's snow day project. She had been an atmospheric scientist, after all.

He gathered up the loose papers on her desk, tapping them straight. He was about to do the same to the wandering thoughts in his head when a yellow flutter caught in his peripheral vision. He followed the motion and saw a sticky note land on the drab tile floor. Davenport was about to reach for it when Shep Hinds and Colonel Mason stepped into Kat's office. Mason's stern countenance halted any motion to retrieve the paper that Davenport may have been about to execute. He had never served in the

Armed Forces. Hell, he had never even been a Boy Scout. The concept of any type of strenuous activity made him break out in an all-over body rash. But, Mason's stern gaze brought Davenport to his feet immediately in a quick, if awkward, attention.

The Air Force Colonel's quick gaze darted to the twenty-two inch monitor over Davenport's right shoulder. In a measured march, he passed the doughy scientist and snapped off the power to the computer's screen. The HD images of mudslides and flooding faded to black nearly immediately.

"Name?" Mason demanded.

"Davenport. Alan Davenport."

Mason circled Davenport in a way that recalled lions on the savannah. "You were phoned when the decedent's body was found?"

"Yes-s-s," Davenport stammered. "Miss Sørensen worked directly under me. I was also the one who instructed Mr. Hinds to alert Kirtland. We're still operating per installation protocol. Haven't made the transition to civilian control one hundred percent yet."

"Yes, and now that I'm here, can you tell me what Miss Sørensen might have been doing near that antenna array?"

Davenport looked momentarily confused. "Actually, no. Her work was mostly data analysis. There was no justifiable reason for her to be out near the pad."

"Then what in the hell was she doing out, or rather, up there?"

"I'm certain I have no idea. I was just going through her things, to see if there were any personal effects that could be passed to her family."

"No!" Mason barked almost instantly. "*Nothing* leaves this office. Is that clear?"

"Yes, sir!" The mirrored military reaction kicked in again.

Davenport's whole body trembled. He was excessively eager to get out of the office and the mounting tension. The discovery of Kat's body had been unsettling enough. Admitting there was no way in hell it was accidental just made matters worse.

"You can go, but I want radio silence on this whole fiasco. I mean muzzles on everyone," Mason ordered. He turned to Hinds. "Everyone."

"Yes, sir," Hinds responded.

"And I want everyone searched before they set foot off this installation. I don't want a shred of information leaking out. Understood?"

Davenport nodded nervously. "Not a shred."

With that, Davenport spun anxiously on the ball of his Shackleton's and hoofed it down the narrow hallway, unaware of the small, yellow hitchhiker that had affixed itself to the bottom of his boot.

CHAPTER NINETEEN

Boston, Massachusetts

The monster rose. Thirty-seven feet and two inches of green towering over the left field at Fenway Park. As they made their way down the concourse, Melina was hard pressed to keep wonderment from dropping her jaw.

"It's incredible," she said.

"Yup," Jake replied. "Do you know the Sox won the very first game they ever played here, April 20, 1912? Didn't even get a mention in the papers."

Melina looked at him, puzzled. "Why not?"

Digger bumped past, making a beeline for their seats. "There was this little boat mishap in the North Atlantic around that time. The *Titanic*. You might have heard of it? Wasn't an accident. It was part of an Illuminati plot to establish the Federal Reserve."

Jake brushed off his friend's brusque behavior. "Yeah. Don't mind him. He's cranky. Digger's not big on crowds."

"Then why in the hell did he come to a baseball game?" Melina gestured to the seats burgeoning with baseball-capped, beer-toting whoopers and hollerers.

Jake shrugged. "He's a Red Sox fan."

If Melina understood, her poker expression didn't show it. For anyone who had ever been a Sox fan, however, it was tacit truth. A game at Fenway was like going to church, a veritable religious experience – and faith was unswerving.

N°· 4 Yawkey Way was a gateway into another time. It didn't boast an aquarium behind home plate, or a chic nightclub dazzling left field. It didn't exude boardwalk celebrity with a novelty ferris wheel or a carousel populated by thirty hand-painted tigers. No fly ball would ever splash down in an outfield swimming pool.

Granted, the beer may have been overpriced, but not because it was handcrafted by some guy with a PhD in brewing from the University of Brussels in Belgium. And there was no trendy infield boutique shopping with the stars, no matter how "charming" they were.

Things remained simple at Fenway. From the hand-changed scoreboard to the familiar tri-mark logo that held a place of honor over the left field fence, Fenway refused to be dominated by progress, by overbearing marquees heralding the names of colossal insurance companies or telecommunications behemoths. If you concentrated, you could still hear Sox fans' hearts breaking as pint-sized Bucky Dent sent a towering Yankee hit sailing over the wall. Feel the swell of pride surge through the bleacher seats as Ted Williams clinched his last Sox at bat with a 440-foot homerun bomb. Experience the stadium shake with the 2004 roar that reverberated through the stands when the Sox rallied back from a 0-3 deficit to beat the Yankees in the American League Championship Series and reversed the infamous Bambino's Curse.

Fenway simply offered what it had for the past one hundred years – an unadulterated dose of Americana served up with a side of beef and pork wrapped in a white bread bun.

Jake held two of the famous hot dogs in his hands and inhaled deeply. He closed his eyes, almost reverently.

"Smell that?" he asked Melina. "That's what baseball smells like."

He handed one of the relish and mustard-laden franks to Melina as they bumped up their pace to catch Digger. Melina held up her dog.

"You sure you don't want one?" Melina asked Digger.

Digger's nose wrinkled in disgust. "Are you kidding me? Do you even know how they prepare those things?"

Jake scoffed. "Aw, come on, Dig. What's a little dirty water dog between friends?"

"Dirty water dog?" Melina asked. One perfectly arched eyebrow raised in quizzical puzzlement.

Digger was only too happy to explain. "Yeah, they fix 'em just like they do in those sketchy little pushcarts you see in Jersey and New York. You know. The one's with the blue and yellow umbrellas on them? Anyway, the mystery morsels sit in the same murky water all day long – this kind of churning, gray foam – until the vendor fishes one out, slaps one in a bun, and some poor unsuspecting schmuck snaps through the 'natural casing' with their teeth."

Melina was almost afraid to ask. "Natural casing?"

Digger paused. "Pig intestine."

Before Melina could turn green, Jake swept to the rescue. "Consider it a spa day for tube steak, Dig. A hot tub for hot dogs. And millions of Americans massage it with a little mustard and snarf these bad boys down without a second thought." He slapped his pal on the shoulder.

Digger actually froze in his breakneck tracks. "And so it continues. The downfall of this once great nation."

"It's not the demise of civilization, Digger." Jake admonished. "It's a hotdog,"

Digger shook his head sadly then recommenced his former pace.

Jake turned to Melina. "Oddball should be here any minute now."

A sarcastic snort escaped as she jabbed a thumb in Digger's general direction. "You sure he's not already here?"

The narrow look on Jake's face made her clear her throat with some discomfort. She tried again, with less cheap humor. "Who's this 'Oddball' again?"

Jake mumbled through a mouthful of masticated beef and pork. "He's my old S.O. from the Bureau. If your buddy O'Flaherty was right and Laurent is in bed with La Brise de Mer, Oddball will be able to help me with a solid cover to infiltrate their organization."

Melina grabbed Jake's arm abruptly, nearly causing him to lose his grip on his dog. "You? Wait. You mean us, right? This is just as much my investigation as it is yours, pal."

"Not exactly, sweetheart. You had your run at Laurent in Miami. You blew it. It's my op, now."

Melina huffed loudly. Jake wiped a spot of mustard from the corner of his mouth before he continued.

"I could give a rat's ass about the Gardner paintings. Besides, my main priority here is finding out what happened to Oddball's daughter. Art may be irreplaceable, but so are people."

Some of the fire died from Melina's gaze.

"Oddball's done a lot for me over the years. The least I can do is give him some closure." Jake tossed his trash in a nearby receptacle just as Theodore "Oddball" Sørensen walked up. A roomy Red Sox jersey covered his burly girth, the bright red letters of Boston's team name cutting a swath through the crowd. Jake could see the older man clenched a thick manila envelope in his left hand. The dark shadows beneath his eyes weren't cast by the cap he wore low on his forehead.

"What's up, Jakey? This the little lady you were telling me about?" Oddball dipped his head in Melina's general direction.

"Melina Flores, Mr. Sørensen. Robbins International Adjusters. I am so sorry for your loss." Melina extended a firm, but gentle hand which Oddball shook gratefully.

"Beautiful and polite. You'd better hold on to this one, Jakey." Melina drew back her hand awkwardly as Jake toed the ground sheepishly.

"Okay, okay. Lighten up, you two. You don't have to pick out a China pattern just yet. I do appreciate your sympathy, Miss Flores. Good people around you, like Jakey here, help you sort through it. You start to think maybe there's hope on the other side." A moment of silence hung between them.

"Or at least a clear shot at the bastards responsible," Jake interjected. "We ready to get this show on the road? Digger's got the seats."

They headed for the bleacher seats. As he grabbed the stair rail, Oddball looked up and noted the sign. Section 42. Oddball glanced sideways at Jake.

"The red seat?"

"The red seat."

The trio found Digger ensconced in his chair back seat in the lower bleachers of right field. In an odd way it tickled Jake that Digger, usually so determined to blend seamlessly into the anonymous background, went out of his way to choose the one red seat in a sea of dark green ones. The seat marked the spot of Ted Williams' monster home run. Red Sox fans, Jake thought again. Nothing like them.

The newcomers took their seats next to Digger who waved frantically, trying to spur them on. "Come on, come one, come on! Capuano's pitching! They brought him in to replace Dempster and I want to see if he can get some heat on the ball."

Oddball ignored the little man. As he sat, he pulled a crisp copy of the Parisian newspaper, *Le Monde*, from the envelope.

"La Brise de Mer. One of the most powerful criminal organizations in France. Didn't start out so bright, though. Rumor has it that when these guys started back in the seventies, they had to cancel a few gigs because they forgot their weapons. I dunno. Too much red wine, I guess. They started off pulling some pretty basic smash-and-grabs. But now, these Corsican-based goombahs now have their mitts in everything from racketeering, night clubs, casinos, and money laundering which, I believe, is where your interest comes in, Miss Flores."

"The Gardner collection," Melina replied.

"The Gardner collection." Oddball nodded. "The art market is ridiculously opaque. Can't think of another business better suited to transfer assets and hide illicit profits than through a business which allows both the seller and buyer to be listed as 'private'. Even the art itself makes it easy to move between countries. Roll up a Renoir, stuff it in your luggage, and you've got yourself a priceless souvenir."

"My mom got me a 'Somebody in Branson Loves Me' t-shirt once. Oh. Hey, Oddball," Digger blurted briefly, and immediately went back to watching the game.

Oddball waved a bear paw in response. "Shoot, if you list the value of a piece as less than two hundred dollars no customs forms or declarations are needed. No tax even has to be paid on it when it comes into America. All you have to do is say a fifty million dollar painting is only worth fifty. A bit of a stretch, but I'm sure you see where I'm going with this." Melina nodded.

Jake picked up where Oddball left off. "Art crime is a six billion dollar a year business. But, I'm guessing you know that."

"And given what Connor said, you think La Brise de Mer now has a piece of that pie?" Melina asked.

"With your friend Laurent's help. And since he may have had something to do with what happened to Kat, we want a piece of him. We can't be sure your cover's not blown, and I, for one, am not willing to let you dangle you as bait to find out," Jake stated.

"I agree," Oddball responded. "That's why we're sending Jakey in as a rep from the Getty."

A sudden, solid crack of leather on wood shot through the air. Jake instinctively ducked, still a little gun shy after the previous day's encounter. Digger, on the other hand, was up on his feet, showering the row with peanut shells.

"Kill it, Big Papi!" He growled hoarsely.

Melina was on her feet as well, but not because she felt any allegiance to Number 34.

"The Getty?" she cried. "As in the J. Paul Getty Museum? In California? And I thought he was crazy!"

She leveled an accusatory finger at Digger, then tempered the gesture with a cautious apology. "No offense."

Digger shrugged as he sat back down. He popped a peanut into his mouth. "None taken."

Jake coaxed the agitated Melina back into her seat. "Easy there, chief. Trying not to draw attention here."

"But, why the Getty?" Melina moaned.

"Two very good reasons. One, the name Getty screams money. Old Man Getty was notorious for dropping millions on art work year after year, sometimes upward of two-hundred and fifty million. And I can guarantee you, we dangle the Getty wallet in that sea of sharks, we won't have to wait long to get a bite. Two. While the Getty is famous for its rampant acquisitions over the years, it's almost as famous for some of its more not-so-legitimate dealings. Gross expenditures by senior staff. Clandestine contracts with overseas dealers to procure looted antiquities."

"Now, the Gardner doesn't have enough dough to tempt the crooks into the open. They've already offered a five million dollar bounty for the return of the collection. All they've succeeded in getting is holes in their shoes from running down every crazy tip that's come off the wire," Oddball offered.

Jake leaned in. "But as a Getty representative, I could offer to negotiate *sotto voce* on behalf of the Gardner."

"And Laurent will be negotiating on behalf of La Brise de Mer," Melina finished.

"Everybody gets what they want." Jake leaned back in his seat. Another cheer rolled through the crowd.

"So, what's our next step," Melina asked.

Oddball handed the manila envelope to Jake.

"Jake Reisen disappears. Jake Roberts will take his place." Oddball pointed to the envelope. "There's a credit card in there with Roberts' name on it and a California driver's license. There's also a Getty Museum employee ID with your mug, official business cards, and even some personalized museum letterhead. If they check any deeper, I had my guy at the Getty doctor the payroll records back a few years. You're listed as a roving scout working immediately and exclusively for the Director. That way, if somebody gets really itchy, it will make sense if no one further down on the Getty ladder knows exactly who you are. Godspeed, Jakey. Keep an old man in the loop, huh? I'd love to see you get those paintings back." He hesitated at that last.

"Some things," he paused. "Some things are just priceless."

With that, Oddball excused himself and scooted sideways through the bleacher seats. Jake watched his old mentor shuffle away, shoulders stooped.

A few respectful moments of silence passed, at least as silent as they could be with fifty thousand fans, including Digger, roaring in the stands. Then Melina dug in her heels.

"And what am I supposed to do?" Melina fumed. "Just sit on the sidelines and wait? Like a good little cheerleader while the quarterback runs the play?"

Jake was hard pressed to suppress the smirk niggling at the corner of his mouth. He had to admit, she was cute when she was feisty. He immediately dropped the dopey grin when he caught Digger smiling at him.

"Ahem," Jake embarrassedly cleared his throat. "No. We don't just want you to sit around. You were Foreign Service. Use your contacts. Poke around. If La Brise de Mer is using the Gardner paintings as collateral for something big, we need to find out what it is. It could very well have been what got Kat killed. We want to avoid anyone else suffering the same fate. But, we need to know exactly what the end game is. We don't need another nine-eleven on our hands."

The gravity of the thought quelled Melina's agitation. No civil human being wanted another disaster like the one that had hit New York on that clear, early Tuesday. The impact of the Boeing 767 and its 20,000 gallons of burning jet fuel left a gaping hole in much more than just the side of the North Tower. She instinctively reached for her chest, clutching her heart.

She was supposed to have been in that building that day. If only --- the thought floated.

"And what are you going to do?" Melina asked when her thoughts came back to her.

"Me? I'm gonna go kick over an anthill. See what comes crawling --".

"OUT!" A sudden, thundering roar filled the stands. Everyone around them was immediately on their feet. Red Sox fans were hugging each other. Tears were streaming down faces. Even Digger found himself enveloped in the 350-pound embrace of a hairy, sweat-stained, tank-topped gentleman.

"What the hell just happened?" Jake asked his purple-tinged friend. Digger tried to extricate himself from the celebratory choke-hold.

He managed a strangled reply. "Capuano just pitched a no-hitter."

A no-hitter. Jake's brow furrowed with concern. He thought about Oddball and Kat and what they both meant to him. Everybody who might know something about what happened to Kat would be at the museum's gala event. Including this Remy Laurent. When you had your fingers in as many pies as Laurent supposedly did, you were bound to pull out a plum sometime.

The crowd noise continued to surge. Jake sighed. He didn't need a no-hitter. What he needed was a home run.

CHAPTER TWENTY

Los Angeles, California

When driving along the 405 from San Diego toward the City of Angels, if you weren't too dazzled by the stars and diverted your gaze toward the one-hundred ten acre expanse of hillside sprawling across Brentwood, you might notice a curious sight. Sprouting from the verge was a burst of bright, Italian travertine sliced in angular clefts and married with curvilinear design elements.

The architectural "flora" was the brainchild of architect Richard Meier. A museum that stepped out of the conventional one-box-fits-all mold and looked more like a strip mall genetically spliced with Disney's California Adventure. Carefully mapped walkways stretched between attractions, dotted with a balanced mix of coffee bars, strolling musicians, and quaint stilted puppets. If you fancied a light lunch, there was a menu of cafés offering gourmet salads and healthy, sprouted fare.

Sometimes, however, it was not the palate that needed to be sated. Sometimes the order of the day called for something more substantial – a full and rich degustation of world art and culture – food for the soul. No place catered to hungry minds better than The Getty.

Jake leaned on the rounded cherry-wood reception desk. The tailored seams of his tuxedo protested as the fourth tray of *foie gras* passed Jake. Cody, on the other hand? That hound of a Husky would not have been dissuaded by a mild case of bloat.

Goose liver, caviar on petite toasts, exotic-flavored quiches – Jake was pretty sure there had been a Thai curry one. He cringed a little. Not a fan. He could definitely use a drink, though.

As if on cue, a waiter glided by. Jake swooped a champagne flute from the surface of his tray and sipped. An older woman wearing Barbara Bush pearls also helped herself to the contents of the waiter's tray. She slipped Jake a serious come-hither stare over the stemware. Jake offered up a winning set of his own pearly whites. His were all the original model, however.

The dowager tittered like a school girl. Jake took a moment to drink in the museum's entrance hall over the woman's shoulder.

Aside from assaulting the ocular senses with paradoxical themes – organic, circular patterns, yet sterile and bleached of life – it was a bit like being caught in a Tim Burton movie. White, diaphanous dirigibles – near bus-sized netted balloons – floated in the empty air under the crisscrossed window opening recessed in the high ceiling. A two hundred-fifty foot scroll, speckled with seemingly random dots and dashes, sat poised under the floating, white leviathans. Jake read the title card near the installation.

Tim Hawkinson, not the quirky Burton, was the artist who bore responsibility for the artistic beast. His *Überorgan*, which apparently changed with every installation, interpreted the strange assortment of dots and dashes as traditional hymns, jazzy, improvisational tunes, and bouncy pop music as the scroll passed in front of light-sensitive switches in its player.

One expensive iPod, Jake thought.

His keen gaze passed through the rest of the room. It wasn't lost on Jake that there were a number of stiff-suited guard types stationed around the room. Their coms were subtle, not the pig's tail earwigs Hollywood insisted Secret Service agents always wore, but if you knew what you were looking for, you could still spot them. Jake supposed their presence had something to do with the complex and heady mix of movie stars, arts patrons, military brass, and both current and former government dignitaries burgeoning in the modernist rotunda. He was even fairly certain he noticed one tall, muscled gentleman with a jaw that could probably break rocks, who fit simultaneously into several of those categories. Well, there was that…and the priceless artwork in the museum.

Suddenly, Jake spied what he was truly looking for. He took a swallow of the bubbly libation and set the glass back on the waiter's tray. He turned to the old woman.

"I'll be back."

Jake followed his target past the forty-thousand pound wedge of Indian black granite that began inside the lobby and thrust its way to the exterior courtyard. Jake momentarily wondered how you kept something that heavy from crashing through the floor, then continued his surreptitious tail. The last vestiges of the California sun played off the travertine for a few final moments before it dipped below the horizon.

Jake's ears caught a dancing splash. His eyes darted right for just a moment to see a jutting formation of rocks and boulders with water cascading down their irregular surfaces. He might have stopped to appreciate the juxtaposition of the hard rock against the yielding water, but he had a job to do right now. His head swiveled to train his gaze back where it needed to be, but it was too late. He'd lost the target.

"Damn!"

"Can't disagree with you there, lad. Hard to believe after everything they've been through, isn't it now?"

Jake swung around at the sound of the unexpected reply. He eyebrows raised in surprise.

Resplendent in his tailored tux and neatly clipped goatee, Connor O'Flaherty looked every bit the part of generous patron, one who bought art instead of "liberating" it. A far cry from the rumpled, shabby old man that had recently visited Melina's Miami apartment.

"Connor O'Flaherty." The left side of Jake's mouth turned up in a sardonic grin. "Who let you escape?"

O'Flaherty let out a hearty chuckle. The art thief swirled his aged whisky in a golden vortex in his glass before he took a healthy swallow. "Oh, they'd have to catch me first, boyo. They'd have to catch me first."

"You going to tell me what's so hard to believe? Or, do I have to guess?" Jake bit at the older man's bait.

O'Flaherty waved his nearly empty glass in a wide arc. "This. The museum. Such a beautifully massive collection of riches just beggin' to be liberated. And, of course, John Paul Getty. The art world's big spender." O'Flaherty emptied the rest of his glass.

"Couldn't be bothered to spend a dime when his grandson was kidnapped at sixteen, mind you. Poor lad. Held captive, chained to a stake in a damned cave for three unholy months."

"I think your history's a little muddled. That ransom was paid. That's how they got him back," Jake countered.

"Hah!" O'Flaherty brayed, the whisky raising a florid fire in his cheeks.

"Only after the old man bargained the price down to 2.7 million, like a Kasbah hawker! And even then, the bastard charged his own son four percent interest! Didn't save his grandson's left ear, though. Kidnappers sliced it clean off."

"Sounds brutal," Jake agreed, looking around nervously as O'Flaherty became more animated.

"Mmm. And the bad luck didn't stop there. The old man's son George, by his first marriage? Want to venture a guess how *he* died?"

"I have a feeling you're going to tell me."

O'Flaherty nodded. "Fell on a barbecue fork. Twice."

Jake looked at O'Flaherty dubiously. It didn't seem to faze the old man one bit. The Getty family is cursed, I tell ya."

"Taking a little artistic license there, aren't you?" Jake scoffed.

O'Flaherty poked a gnarled finger into Jake's chest. "Now, you listen to me, you *scanger*, I may not have gotten past primary school, but if there's one thing I've learned in this godforsaken life o' mine, it's art and everything that's related to it. That includes curses. Like the one on the Gardner collection you're chasin'!"

At the mention of the Gardner collection, Jake lunged. He gripped O'Flaherty's arm firmly and steered the older man to a quiet alcove.

"Will you keep it down!?" Jake hissed between his teeth.

O'Flaherty tugged his arm from Jake's firm grip. There was a strength in the Irish bulldog, yet.

"No, boyo. No, I won't, because you need to hear me, and hear me well." There was more steel than whisky now in O'Flaherty's flinty blue eyes. "When I heard sweet Melina was chasing down the Gardner collection, I sent her to you."

"A favor for which I am eternally grateful," Jake replied sarcastically.

The unexpected, yet virile punch to Jake's midsection knocked the wind out of him and nearly doubled him over, but O'Flaherty kept him fairly vertical. O'Flaherty no more wanted to draw attention to his presence than Jake did.

"That girl's the closest thing to a daughter I have, Riesen. Hell, she's headstrong enough to be my own flesh and blood. Now, you an' me? I wouldn't know ya if I slept with your mother and slapped your arse on the day you were born. Opposite sides of the coin, we are. But, there's one thing I know we have in common. We don't let innocent folk get hurt."

O'Flaherty's bold statement was a worse gut check than the fist. O'Flaherty didn't seem to notice. The old thief continued. "I sent her to you hopin' you'd have the good sense to keep the girl outta trouble, but now I see you've got no more brains in ya than a plowin' mule."

At that last, Jake straightened tall. "Now, hold on. I didn't *ask* you to send her to me. I didn't *want* you to send her to me. And I *damn* well didn't want a thing to do with the Gardner case. But, you can bet your pot of gold, you Irish sonovabitch, that I wouldn't do anything to get her hurt."

O'Flaherty backed up, his bushy eyebrows raised so high they nearly disappeared into the snowy white of his wavy hairline. "Oh? You don't say! Well, then, you stupid bastard, maybe you can tell me what in the hell she's doing here with him?"

Jake followed the direction of O'Flaherty's point toward the small platform raised at the far end of the courtyard. Near the podium stood Remy Laurent, looking crisp and powerful in his designer suit. It wasn't the Armani that truly caught Jake's attention, however. It was the long, lithe beauty in hip-hugging red whispering in Laurent's ear. Whatever Laurent's reply, it made her throw her head back, golden brown hair cascading down her bare shoulders, as she let loose a clear peal of laughter, like a bell.

It was Melina.

CHAPTER TWENTY-ONE

The sky and its secrets had always held a certain fascination for him. But, if ever there was a moment in time he could go back to and change, it would have been the moment he'd gone to career day in high school and spoken with the representative from NASA at Langley. He'd let himself be dazzled by the lure of discovering about "what's up there". Even at this very moment, he used his Mont Blanc pen to demarcate the points of a random constellation on a cocktail napkin at the bar. His bleary blue eyes roved over the crowd. If he noticed the swarthy, thick-necked man near the end of the bar, his alcohol-soaked brain didn't register it.

Yep. He should have just stuck with pursuing a career in environmental engineering. He'd had plenty of experience with the inside of toilet bowls, courtesy of Chet Winthrop, high school quarterback. It would have been a natural segue.

Plus, he never would have wound up freezing his ass off in the Alaskan wilderness. And he would have no idea what the color red meant in the Aurora Borealis. And he damn well wouldn't be in the predicament he was in now.

"No, seriously." A voice behind Davenport insisted, shaking him from his reverie. In his hazy fog, he saw a short man with a military-style buzz cut gesticulating wildly. The frenzied motion of the man's hands tugged the already too-short cuffs on his sleeve even further over his muscled forearms. The tuxedo looked like it hadn't been dragged out of the mothballs for about twenty years or so. An aromatic waft of camphor and dichlorobenzene seconded the impression.

"I mean it," the man continued to the pretty blonde standing next to him. Davenport supposed he might have been trying to flirt with her. Then he heard the rest of the man's conversation. "Google is freakin' Skynet! Think about it. All the tools and properties people use every single day on their computers. Google controls over half of them, man!"

The blonde stole a furtive glance over her shoulder, her eye trained on the ladies' room. Looking for an escape route, no doubt.

"And what about Boston Dynamics? Google bought them up, and they create all these robots for the government. AI. If the government doesn't get you, the robots will."

Davenport pondered, just for a fleeting moment, if maybe this guy had more problems than himself. A hazy concept began to coagulate in Davenport's head. Maybe it would take somebody like this – someone not afraid to get the information out there, no matter how crazy it sounded – someone completely not like him.

Tiny droplets of moisture splattered from underneath Alan Davenport's Madras as he plunked the heavy-bottomed cocktail glass on the bar, missing the napkin completely.

"Bartender? Hey, bartender?" His words slurred as he waved the server over. "I'll have another."

He thought about for a moment, then amended his request. "Scratch that. I think I'll have two 'nothers."

It was going to take a little more liquid courage for what he had just decided to do.

A few of the wild drops from Davenport's glass caught the cuff of the man standing next to Davenport at the bar.

"Hey, buddy!" the man grumbled. "Maybe you'd better screw the lid back on the flask, huh?"

Davenport blinked behind his fishbowl lenses at Digger who now tried to balance his hors d'oeuvres plate while furiously trying to blot the moisture as if he was afraid the water might shrink the already too-short cuffs further. The blonde used the distraction to make good her escape.

"I'm so sorry. Let me help with that." Davenport pawed at Digger clumsily with his napkin, tipping Digger's barbecue shrimp and dark orange sauce in a cascading rivulet down the placket of Digger's shirt.

Digger stood, empty plate in hand, and just stared at Davenport. Davenport, for his part, turned a sudden, and very unappealing green. He grasped a fistful of Digger's jacket sleeve with one hand, while the other came clamping down across his mouth. Two seconds too late.

"Aw, come on, man!" Digger cried out in exasperation.

"I gotta go," Davenport mumbled through his fingers and took off like a shot in the direction of the men's lavatory, nearly upsetting the vacant seat where the swarthy man had been sitting.

The bartender handed a clean napkin to Digger over the bar. Digger accepted the linen gratefully. He started daubing at the disaster that had been his tuxedo.

"Figures," he said to the bartender. "I wear this thing twice in my life. Senior prom and today. Got puked on both times."

The gray-haired couple behind Digger huffed in disgust and walked away.

Digger shrugged and turned back to the bartender. "Got any beer nuts?"

Out in the courtyard, Jake pried himself from O'Flaherty's grip.

"I don't know what she's doing here. It certainly wasn't my idea. If you two are as close as you say, you know she's got a mind of her own. Regardless of what she's doing here, I have a fair idea of what you're actually doing here. So, unless you want to try to use up all your lucky charms on explaining it to museum security, I suggest you let me do what you sent her to me for in the first place."

O'Flaherty took a moment. Then nodded reasonably.

"No sense in causing a scene," he replied. "Just take care of my girl. As a favor to an old man." O'Flaherty walked away and melted into the crowd.

O'Flaherty's request twinged Jake's conscience.

Take care of my girl.

O'Flaherty might not have been so willing to put his faith in Jake if he knew the truth. He hadn't been able to help Kat either.

But, that was exactly why he couldn't fail now. He turned quickly on his heel and started to cross the wide expanse of the courtyard when he was suddenly blinded by the blue-white beam of a spotlight. He held up a shielding hand as thunderous applause rolled through the courtyard. With the gentle authority of a beloved ruler, the rich, silken voice of Remy Laurent quelled the wave of adulation.

"*Merci. Merci.* I thank you," Laurent humbly replied. Jake side-stepped from the spotlight's prying beam and merged with the crowd. He never took his eyes from Laurent, however, nor Melina. He could see her smiling, nearly as dazzling as the diamonds at her throat. But, he could see her eyes searching, scanning the crowd for someone. Jake surmised it was probably him.

Yeah, Jake thought. And when she found him?

Loooo-cy! You got some 'slpaining to do! The familiar line from another Cuban passed through his head.

Laurent continued his speech. "First of all, I would like to extend a most sincere thanks to the Getty Museum for this magnificent reception." More applause. Laurent smiled and raised his hand.

"And now to the reason for our little soirée. It costs a great deal of money to reach for the stars, and though it seems here in Southern California that they live amongst us, we're aiming a little higher. No offense, Governor." The crowd laughed as Laurent gave a cursory nod to the strapping gentleman Jake had noticed earlier. The man flashed a Kennedy-worthy smile.

"Indeed," Laurent continued, "we could think of no better place to formally announce the passing of the torch than here, among the stars. My company, Phoenix Research Unlimited with all its resources will be assuming control of the H.A.A.R.P. facility in Alaska and its celestial studies. May the knowledge we gain truly be unlimited. Like the stars."

The crowd erupted into wild applause as Laurent stepped away from the microphone. He grabbed Melina around the waist and kissed her. As Jake watched, he felt an odd tug in his gut. He felt another tug – this one at his sleeve. It was Digger.

"Where in the hell have you been?" Jake asked. He took one look at Digger's shirt and then his nose crinkled at the peculiar mix of sour and Worcestershire wafting from it. "And what in the hell happened?"

"I was attacked. By drunk crustaceans," came Digger's reply.

"What? Oh, forget it," Jake quipped. "I can dress you up, but I can't take you anywhere."

"I'm perfectly okay with that," Digger responded agreeably. "I hate this monkey suit, anyway."

"Too late now, Clyde. Come on. Melina's here, and she's with Laurent."

"What? I thought she was supposed to stay at the cabin!"

"How about that, huh? So did I. Apparently, she didn't get the memo. So, let's go take care of business. Now, remember, I'm –."

"Jake Roberts." Laurent's French accent finished Jake's statement. Jake whirled to find the Frenchman and Melina standing immediately behind him. Jake's eyes locked immediately with Melina's as she hung on Laurent's left, her hands entwined over his forearm.

Follow my lead. Jake read the silent order in her honeyed gaze. Jake growled on the inside. This was not how he did things.

Yeah, he also thought to himself. And things have always gone so great for you in the past.

Maybe it was time to shake things up a little.

Jake extended a cordial hand to Laurent. "Yes, Mr. Laurent. I am Jake Roberts. Very pleased to make your acquaintance."

"But, of course. And whom, may I ask, is your friend?" Laurent gestured to the disheveled Digger. A tense nanosecond passed before Jake leapt to an introduction.

"No one," he stated authoritatively. "No one who expects to keep his job if he intends to continue walking around in a suit like that."

Jake jabbed a finger at Digger. "Now, go back into the staging area immediately and get cleaned up. I won't have any member of my wait staff looking like a cheap food truck employee."

It took three blinks from Digger and a nearly imperceptible nod from Jake before Digger launched into motion. "Uh, yes sir, Mr. Roberts. So sorry. Won't happen again."

Digger took off toward the interior of the museum leaving Jake standing alone with Melina and Laurent. He bumped into a solid shoulder as he reached the doorway.

"Oof! Sorry, buddy. Excuse me." Digger kept walking. He didn't seem to notice the beady, black eyes of the swarthy gentleman look from Laurent to him, then fall in stride directly behind him.

As Digger took his leave, Melina smiled brilliantly. "Remy, this is the gentleman I was telling you about. Mr. Roberts here works for the Getty."

"Indeed? Well, again, Mr. Roberts, *merci beaucoup* for your organization's assistance in mounting such a beautiful event."

"I appreciate that but I had very little to do with it. I'm more of a roving scout. I work immediately for the director. I'm rarely here in California. Mostly I jet set all over the world, sometimes to far-off, exotic places, searching out suitable acquisitions for the museum. Like New Jersey."

A laugh burbled from Melina. Jake continued. "I once negotiated in a parking lot of the New Jersey turnpike for a looted seventeen hundred year old South American back flap that had belonged to a Moche king."

Remy's eyebrow raised at that last. "Really, now? You make it sound a bit like Indiana Jones."

"It can be. I find that you get to meet all types in the art world."

"*En effet*," Remy replied. "The New Jersey turnpike? It sounds as if some of them are quite unscrupulous. And you willingly pay them money for items which clearly do not belong to them. *N'est-ce pas?*" Melina's eyes warned Jake to tread carefully.

Jake didn't miss a beat. This was his old turf. He wore the Jake Roberts persona like a second skin. "Yes, Mr. Laurent, it's true. My business sometimes requires me to rub elbows with folks of questionable backgrounds, and yes, I have 'rewarded' some of these characters great sums in exchange for the return of valuable works. But, truly great art, however, has a certain, how shall I put this, scarcity value. So, when I can pay for the infinite with the finite? I'd say I'm getting a damned bargain. Any reasonable man's got to believe that."

A weighty silence hung in the air before Laurent finally spoke. "Art is a faith, not a profession, eh, Mr. Roberts?"

"Yes," Jake replied with a smile. The delicate dance of "I'll show you mine if you show me yours" was over. Laurent had taken the bait.

"I think I may have some information for you," Laurent began.

"I sure as hell hope so," a brusque voice interrupted their conversation. It was Mason, and he looked pissed.

CHAPTER TWENTY-TWO

Bal Harbour, Florida

Any normal human being would have been tickled pink to be in a spectacular, eighteen-story glass castle, redolent with rich European cabinetry, stoic granite work, and breathtaking views of the beautiful Atlantic Ocean and Intracoastal water way. They might even be tempted to dip a toe in one of the sumptuous, stand-alone egg-shaped tubs in one of the one hundred twenty-four suites. And sure, most people would probably melt under the deft manipulation of their muscles by one of the highly-skilled masseurs at the 10,000 square foot waterfront spa. But, Kyle Wiley's particular brand of relaxation involved mile long drift paddle outs, spitting tubes, and infinite lines marching in from the horizon. A surfer's paradise come true.

What it did not involve was an over-privileged thirteen year old, a troupe of Solid Gold dancers, and the throbbing, pulse-pounding rhythm of Christina Aguilera's "Spotlight" in the Grand Ballroom of the Ritz-Carlton Bal Harbour. But, unless he intended to take a page from The Ex-

Presidents and start robbing banks to fund his chase for the endless summer, he needed to do something to pay the bills. So, here he was, pointing his camera at the twenty-foot tall blinking letters of little Adam Horowitz's name while the scantily-clad dancers did their best to give Adam's *bubbe* a heart attack and he, Kyle Wiley, imagined himself someplace else.

He was so busy daydreaming of the perfect section cornering off in front of him that the sudden radiating buzz of his cellphone nearly caused him to drop his video cam. The caller ID read "Slater". Normally, he wouldn't take a call in the middle of a gig, but if Slater was calling, it had to mean something was going down – something big. He had to take the call.

Wiley took a quick glance to make sure the stationary camera was running, then switched off his shoulder cam and set it on a nearby table. He could always edit later. He brushed his unruly mop of curls from his eyes and jogged over to the slightly-less obnoxiously loud rear of the room. He slid the bar to accept the call.

"Slater. What's up man? I'm in the middle of a job," he said. He could hear the siren call of the pounding surf crashing against the break in the background of the call.

"Dude! You have got to get out to the Pump House!" Slater hollered into the phone. Wiley could barely hear him.

"Man, you're gonna have to speak up. I can barely hear you."

"What?" Slater responded hoarsely.

"I can't hear you!" Wiley repeated.

"Just come to the Pump House, man. Six to eight foot rights and lefts! Breaking as far as you can see, dude! It's Paradise, man!"

Slater signed off. Paradise? Wiley looked at his watch. If he floored it up I-95, he might be able to make it in fifty minutes.

Wiley looked back at the stage. Adam Horowitz was now on stage, shaking his white-tux tailed *toches* for all he was worth.

Screw the gig. He could survive on ramen noodles for the next month. He gave a jaunty, two-fingered salute toward the stage. "*Mazeltov*, kid."

He liked his buddy, but there was no way Slater was waiting for Wiley. When he hung up the phone, Slater looked out at the pounding surf in awe. The ocean had come alive. Solid, eight foot faces screamed down the beach, holding up draining barrels. It was like Mundaka in South Florida, he thought. As he watched the heaving lip sections crack into the flats, he couldn't help but recall the famed swells that rolled in from the Bay of Biscay in northern Spain and slammed into the rocky coastline.

This storm that had everyone talking in nervous tones at NOAA and the Hurricane Center – comparing it to killer systems like Hurricane Katrina and Hurricane Sandy – it was music to the ears of every wave jockey within paddling distance. The storm surge was granting South Florida some of the biggest swells it had ever seen. And they were only getting bigger.

A huge grin spread across Slater's face. He grabbed his gun and hit the water. He paddled out for the first wave of the set. The surfer in front of him towed in, riding the wave. Slater followed suit, ready to feel that surfer high, but found himself in a bad position, trapped on the inside. The surge was only bringing in bigger and bigger waves, but Slater scaled waves for the same reason rock climbers scaled impossible, sheer faces of mountains – because they were there.

So, when the ocean served up a sudden fifteen-foot leviathan, Slater tried again. This time, he paddled to the outside. He had made just about two-thirds up the face of the wave when the wave suddenly broke. Slater was hurled, his board snapping in two. As the sheer weight of the water bore down on him, Slater was helpless to stop his torso from impaling on the broken fiberglass of his board.

The waves continued to roll, fleeting crimson, then receded again a stormy gray.

CHAPTER TWENTY-THREE

Los Angeles, California

The cold water shocked some sobriety back into him, although he wasn't sure sober was what he wanted to be. Then again, he wasn't quite certain of anything at the present moment.

As the drips fell from his cherubic face onto the marbled vanity below, his vision came a little more into focus. He found himself wishing a few other things would come into focus right about now. Like how he was going to get out of this mess.

He felt a little better having vomited, but the acid still lurking in his GI system foretold there was probably more to come. When he'd first found the sticky note on the bottom of his shoe, he had panicked. Colonel Mason had been adamant that nothing, absolutely nothing was to leave Kat's office. When he'd seen the familiar scrawl and scratch of Kat's handwriting, Davenport had immediately recognized it as the paper he'd seen floating to the ground just before Shep Hinds and the Colonel had walked into the office. He must have stepped on it, its gummed edge keeping it in place on his sole. After he deciphered her cryptic code, Davenport couldn't believe what Kat had discovered. It was no wonder she had gotten herself killed.

He had no intention of being next on the list. He had to get the hell out of Dodge.

He had some money saved. It wasn't an enormous sum, but it was enough to help him disappear to South America. He had read in Bloomberg's *Business Week*, that Julian Assange had found safe asylum in Ecuador. If it was good enough for the founder of WikiLeaks, it was good enough for him.

He gave a drunken chuckle. He felt a little like Assange himself after he'd slipped the napkin into the pocket of the man with the ill-fitting tuxedo. His own little WikiLeaks campaign. Granted, he had a few pounds on Assange and far less hair, white or no, but he had gotten the information out there, regardless of Mason's gag order. Originally, he'd come here tonight to give the information directly to Mason. But, when he'd seen who Mason was talking to, he second-guessed himself. He couldn't be certain who to trust.

Instead, he'd made a beeline for the bar where somewhere between his third and fourth drinks, he contrived his brilliant Assange-esque plan and strategy to escape. Now, all that was left was to go home, pack some clothes, grab his passport and say *huk ratukama*.

He dried his face, replaced his glasses, and wobbled from the bathroom. He swayed like the nearby palms in the evening breeze while he waited for the valet to bring up his rental car. The young man hesitated as he held the keys out toward Davenport.

"Sir, are you *sure* you don't want me to call you a cab?"

Davenport waved him off. "No, no, no. I'm fine. It's just a rental.

Besides, in two hours, I'll be in the passenger seat 27,000 miles up. S'all good."

The valet still looked doubtful, but watched Davenport squeeze his round frame into the tiny car.

Davenport wasn't the only one leaving the party early. "Staging area" had been Jake's code for "get to the car and back to the hotel." Digger was only too happy to oblige, eager to peel the constricting tuxedo off and exchange it for a tagless tee, broken-in jeans, and an episode of *Ancient Aliens*. As he walked to the top of the drive and waited for the valet to retrieve his car, he heard a distinctly haughty sniff coming from the His-and-Hers Rolex couple standing next to him. Digger just rolled his eyes. Okay, yes. He was a mess. He could hardly disavow that fact. But, he had just about reached his quota of intrapersonal interactions today. He snorted. Who was he kidding? Try the whole damned year! If he saw Jake, Nell, and his buddies in the Eaters' group, that was more than enough for the anti-social conspiracy nut.

Speaking of nuts, Digger watched as the valet helped the kook who had coughed up his cocktail. Man, if anybody should be calling it a night, it was him. The big man was trying to squeeze into a tiny Fiat 500 Abarth. The red two-door compact looked terribly out of place amidst all the luxury cars, resembling a giant red pimple about to pop its overly large driver right on out of it.

Eventually he succeeded in cramming his bulk into the car. Digger overheard the valet ask the bleary-eyed man if he wanted a cab. Probably not a bad idea, Digger thought. But, the man refused and ground through the gears of the five-speed manual transmission with a determination that made Digger's jaw clench.

Clenched teeth were one thing, but Digger became much more

bothered by the sudden feel of the hairs rising up on the back of his neck. Nightmare visions of Afghanistan came flooding back, and every muscle in him bunched. The former SEAL pivoted his head, eyes searching for any incongruity that would warrant the sudden heightened alert his internal warning system had given him.

That's when he saw it. The black SUV, headlights dark, pull from the shadows at the side of the drive and follow discreetly behind the bucking red pimple.

CHAPTER TWENTY-FOUR

Mason roughly grabbed Laurent by the arm and steered him out of earshot.

"Just what in the hell do you think you're doing?" he growled menacingly at Laurent. "It was decided to hold off on the public announcement of Phoenix's takeover until we got the *problem* resolved. Now you might as well have shined a spotlight on the whole damned operation! I oughta have your ass thrown in Leavenworth for obstructing a military investigation."

"Colonel." Laurent's voice betrayed not a hint of distress at Mason's rabid tirade. He calmly removed his sleeve from Mason's vise-like grip before he continued. "It is a well-known fact that the world is changing, and changing rapidly. We are no longer the Neanderthal caveman grunting unintelligibly, powerless to control the world around us. With advances in cloning, we can duplicate the miracle of life. We can genetically engineer our food sources to be bigger, better, more disease-resistant. And we no longer are tethered to this little blue marble we call Earth. We can now walk among the stars, like gods!"

Laurent leaned in close, his gaze narrowing to tiny slits. His voice took on a gravelly, foreboding tone.

"But, even on Olympus, the gods fought. They waged *war* to be certain they were the one in control, and sometimes mortals suffered the cost." Laurent stood straight, his countenance returning to its genteel smile. His voice took on a much more civil tone. "You are a soldier, Colonel. Surely, you understand the casualties of war."

"What are you getting at, Laurent?" Mason insisted. "Are you suggesting you are at war with the United States government?"

Laurent blew a disparaging burst of air from his lips. "Why, ever, would someone admit to such a vain folly? However, I *am* at war, Colonel. George Bernard Shaw said it best. 'Progress is war is against society'. So, yes. I am at war. At war with society. So, it was strategy on my part to announce my company's interest in H.A.A.R.P. After all, any student of war knows that in battle, you keep your friends close…but, keep your enemies closer. Enjoy the rest of your evening, Colonel. The stars are quite lovely. Here among the mortals," Laurent gestured to the beautiful people at the party, then to the sky. "And among the gods."

"What's going on?" Melina discreetly gestured to Laurent and Mason.

"I don't know, "Jake replied. "I was about to ask you the same exact question. You were supposed to stay at the hotel and use your contacts with the Foreign Service to figure out what La Brise is up to."

"I did," Melina responded. The strains of the string quartet suddenly filled the courtyard.

"Quick! Dance with me. Laurent is looking suspicious." She pulled Jake into the wide area that had been cleared for guests to tango.

"Why's it always got to be a tango?" Jake groaned. He nearly succumbed to a minor case of whiplash as Melina pulled him into the basic frame of the dance. Jake awkwardly placed his right hand on her left shoulder, suddenly conscious of the roughness of his palm against her silken skin. He gingerly reached for her right hand with his left. A shiver traveled through his body as Melina rested her left hand midway down Jake's right forearm. Her laugh pealed like a clear bell as she surveyed Jake's stiff body and the conscious distance he was leaving between their bodies.

Jake's eyes flew open in surprise. "What?"

"You do know the word *tango* means 'touch', right?" Melina chuckled.

Jake squared his shoulders and stood a little straighter. "Yeah. Sure. Of course, I do." He cleared his throat and pulled her in, chest to chest, close enough to feel her body warmth. Melina gave him a warm smile. The opening swell of the dance sounded.

"You know what you're doing?" Melina asked. It was Jake's turn to smile.

"Try to keep up," Jake replied, suddenly stepping forward on his left foot, nearly causing Melina to tumble.

Melina swiftly regained her balance, mirroring Jake's movement by stepping back on her right foot.

"Bring it," she challenged. It became a courtship, Jake the courtier and Melina the willing courtesan. Jake stepped forward with his right foot, with Melina following gracefully with a mirrored left. Jake took a quick step forward, collected his right foot then placed it in preparation for the sultry, near-drag of the left so characteristic of the dance. Jake led Melina through a fevered series of tango steps: the promenade; the open fan; and the flashy apache throw-out. The passionate music began to climax, and in the heat of the moment, Jake executed a *corte*, the step backward that put both dancers into a bit of a lunge. Melina and Jake held the position for only two beats. As their chests heaved with the efforts of the dance, it seemed like an eternity.

"Not bad, Mr. Roberts. Not bad at all." Melina gasped between breaths.

Jake smiled, his broad chest heaving with his own efforts. "I had a good partner."

As the music resolved to its closing cadence, Melina and Jake drew their bent legs back and completed the last steps.

The couple suddenly became aware of the rousing chorus of applause surrounding them. Laurent approached them slowly, manicured hands clapping politely.

"Bravo! Bravo. *Très bien.* That was quite a performance," Laurent commended. Jake released Melina. She stood straight, smoothing her dress, then moved to Laurent's side.

"Mr. Roberts was just keeping me entertained while you had your little meeting. Is everything alright?"

"*Mais oui.* But, of course. The Colonel and I were simply having a difference of opinion. He had an opinion. It made no difference," Remy chuckled.

"The Colonel's Air Force, right?" Jake began. "Isn't Phoenix Research taking over H.A.A.R.P from the Air Force?"

"*Oui.* We are. But the military is bound to rules of the government which regulates them. And government can be so, well," Remy paused. "Stifling."

"And you? You're the breath of fresh air?" Jake asked.

"Let's say a good storm every now and again is good for the soul. Nature's way of clearing away the trash." His crooked smile suggested there was more to that, but Laurent gave Jake and Melina no time to ponder. "Speaking of storms, Mr. Roberts, how well do you know your biblical history, hm?"

"I know some," he replied cautiously as Melina's eyes grew wide behind Laurent. This was it. This was what they had been waiting for. "Why?"

"Do you recall Mark 4:37?"

"The Storm at Galilee," Jake replied.

"Rembrandt," Melina nearly whispered. Surprised at the sudden sound of her voice, Laurent turned.

"Exactly, *mon cherie*. When you look upon it, it is quite incredible how the Master's canvas captures the fear of Jesus' disciples in the face of nature's fury."

"Look upon it?" Jake interrupted. "You mean to tell me you know where The Storm at Galilee is?"

Laurent grinned broadly, and leaned in, conspiratorially.

"I know where they *all* are."

CHAPTER TWENTY-FIVE

Digger couldn't shake the uneasy feeling that had crept into his gut back at the museum. As soon as the valet had pulled up with his rented sedan, he practically jumped in and tore off down the drive, searching for the dark SUV that had been following the round, little drunk. Sure, the guy had puked up his prawns, but if something hinky was going down? Digger didn't let bad things happen to good people. He'd never been wired that way. It was why he'd saved that Afghan soldier. And it was why he was now tooling down North Sepulveda Boulevard, playing the part of the unlikely hero.

His dark eyes darted from one vehicle to the other, hunting for the SUV. His gaze bounced between Jaguars, top-of-the-line Mercedes, a few scattered Lamborghinis – he shouldn't have been surprised. The car pointed toward Beverly Hills – parking lot for the rich and famous. His alert gaze combed the passing traffic, but no over-stuffed Fiat and no shady SUV.

As the exit for Wilshire Boulevard drew closer, however, what Digger could see was the sudden, blinding glow of red brake lights. "What the hell?"

He spent the next half-hour inching the rental forward. He craned his neck out the window investigating the hold-up. The only detail he could make out was the steady whirl of red and blue.

"Damn it!" Digger smacked the top of the steering wheel with a solid fist. If the SUV had come in this direction, it was long gone by now. Well, there was nothing he could do now. When traffic came to a complete standstill, Digger obligingly put the car in park, and settled in for what was shaping up to be a long wait.

Besides having lost any chance at finding the SUV, being at a standstill brought with it another problem. There was no longer a moving California breeze aerating the car through the open windows. As he sat waiting for the long line of vehicles to move, the rancid odor of vomit wafted up from his shirt. Digger's nose crinkled in disgust.

"Oh, man! That's rank!" He looked down at the shirt and noticed a chunk of partially digested shrimp lodged near the third button down.

"Ugh!" he groaned. He frantically searched the car, pawing through the dash and digging through the glove compartment, looking for a stray tissue or napkin to wipe away the offending bit of seafood.

Nothing. Digger shook his head. He didn't understand it. Jake was no Martha Stewart at home. Why, then, did he keep his rental cleaner than Kim Kardashian's hoo-haw?

He dug around in his pockets. He brightened when his right hand brushed something promising. Digger dug out a cocktail napkin. He must have shoved it into his pocket at the museum. He didn't recall, but, who cared? It fit the bill.

He was just about to wipe at the stain when a snatch of strange scrawl caught his eye. At first, Digger couldn't make heads nor tails of it. Just a list of numbers – maybe latitudes and longitudes – and names of colors. Stranger still was a diagram of dots and connecting lines. It looked like something out a mad scientist's journal. Before he could look at it too closely, the caravan of cars began to move. Digger shoved the napkin back into his pocket, sat up straight, and dropped the car into gear.

It was definitely police lights. California Highway Patrol shuttled oncoming traffic into a single lane just past the warning sign for Wilshire exit's sharp turn. The yellow and black sign cautioned motorists to slow to a reasonable twenty miles per hour. When Digger saw the crumbled, mangled pile of rubble that used to be the roadway barrier, it wasn't a leap to ascertain that someone had failed to heed the suggestion. Looking at the size of the hole, it looked like they damned well ignored it altogether.

Digger leaned his head out of his window and tried to get the attention of the CHP directing traffic. "Excuse me, Officer. What in the hell happened?"

"Some drunk missed the turn. Plowed through the barrier. Guess God can give you brains, but common sense is a crap shoot," the cop replied.

"Brains?" Digger asked.

"Yeah. One of those high IQ types partying up at the Getty. Some big shindig with a bunch of Einstein-types and the military."

Einstein-types? He recalled the awkward stumble of the funny little man who spilled water on him and how he fumbled with his napkin to wipe it away just before he tossed his cookies.

Digger's eyes grew wide. The napkin!

Digger dug into his pocket and pulled out the napkin with its enigmatic scrawl. Digger was beginning to have a fair idea who might be in the wrecked car below. He was fairly certain that person had also slipped this napkin into his pocket on purpose. And he was ready to bet his VA disability pension that whatever this chicken scratch on the napkin was, it had gotten the dumpy little man killed.

CHAPTER TWENTY-SIX

The blood thrummed in Jake's veins. He wasn't sure if it was because he was getting closer to finding out what had happened to Kat, or if the impassioned tango with the smoky-eyed Melina was to blame. Either way, he didn't bank on getting much sleep tonight. He was wired.

Laurent had admitted to knowledge of the Gardner collection's location. The admission had thrilled Melina. But, it was something else Laurent had said that had caught Jake's attention. Something about a storm – and not Rembrandt's missing masterpiece. He tried to recall Laurent's exact words.

Nature's way of clearing away the trash. Question was, to what "trash" had Laurent's off-the-cuff remark been referring? Had Kat been considered disposable?

Jake had done his homework on Laurent. More specifically, he had dug into the Frenchman's company, Phoenix Research Unlimited. The Global 500 Company had holdings all over the world – Norway, Japan, Peru, Brazil, New York, and, now, Alaska. And the company had made significant contributions to society, decreasing the mortality rate in childhood cancer patients with its strides in cancer research, among other things. On paper, Laurent looked like a saint. But, Oddball's words floated back to Jake.

The devil's in the details, kid.

Particularly, it was the strides in weather research that made Jake doubt Laurent's altruistic intent. P.R.U. had recently acquired Industrum, a Russian enmod company. Enmod, Jake thought. Sounded like an iconic 60s television squad. Industrum was a small company offering environmental modification services to both the public and private sectors. Its client list was far from extensive – by any stretch of the imagination. Its biggest customer was the Malaysian government, who had hired the firm to help clear the impossible smog that plagued the Asian country. Years of burning the rainforests had created a miasma that choked the capital.

Industrum had been only too happy to oblige. The company had filled the government's tall order for clear skies. But, it wasn't like dropping a batch of frozen potatoes in the fryer for a value meal. No, the company had created a typhoon. The ensuing torrential rains and wind effectively dissipated the pall of acrid smoke. If effect, nature had "cleared away the trash." Except, this time, Jake thought, the "nature" was inordinately unnatural. It was entirely man-made.

The concept made his skin crawl.

It was not long after Industrum's foray into playing God that Phoenix Research had purchased the company and the rights to all its environmental modification technologies, and not long after that that Laurent became involved with H.A.A.R.P. and Kat Sørensen. He could almost see the whole picture. Still, Jake felt like he was missing something, something that should be blatantly obvious. The heels of his polished dress shoes clicked against the marbled floor of the Four Seasons' lobby. He wished something else would click, like the last piece of the puzzle.

He headed for the bank of guest elevators when he was suddenly body-checked into a nearby alcove. He instantly felt his muscles tense, poised to fight. He cocked back his right fist just before he realized it was Digger. Jake dropped his clenched hand and smoothed out his tux.

"Dig! What the hell, man?" he groused. "Are you nuts?"

Digger shook his head for a second and gave his friend a dubious stare. "I thought we already established that. Anyway, that doesn't matter. Kat's not the only one."

Jake shook his head. "I don't understand. Kat's not the only one what?"

Digger sighed in frustration. He fished into his pocket and pulled out the scribbled napkin. "This, man!"

He waved it in front of Jake's face. Jake grabbed the napkin from his wild-eyed buddy. He tried to make sense of the scribbles. "What is this?"

"The guy, the drunk who tossed his cookies all over me? He shoved this in my pocket. He was one of those brainiacs from H.A.A.R.P., and I'm willing to bet he knew Kat."

"Wait," Jake paused. "Was? What do you mean 'was'?"

"He's dead, Jake. Road kill at the bottom of the Wilshire exit. They're claiming it was a drunk driving accident."

Jake stared at the scrawl on the napkin in his hand, trying to puzzle out its possible significance. He looked up at Digger. "When?"

"Last hour or so. What are the odds, man? Two scientists from that facility? Dead within days of each other? No offense, but that retirement plan stinks."

"Yeah. It does," Jake agreed.

"And, I'll tell you what else stinks, Jakey. I saw a black SUV pull out from the Getty and follow this guy. I trailed them, but lost them on the freeway. By the time I caught up, roly–poly was flat as a *latke* and that SUV was a ghost! I'm telling you, my gut's churning on this one. No way was it an accident. And no way Kat was attacked by any grizzly bear either. Her and the fat man? They both knew something. And I'll lay you dollars to doughnuts it's got something to do with what's on this napkin. Whatever *that* means," Digger pointed forcefully at the napkin in Jake's hand, "I'll bet that's what got them killed."

Jake's eyes locked with his pal's. "And now we have it."

CHAPTER TWENTY-SEVEN

Van Nuys, California

The Van Nuys Airport sat discreetly in the San Fernando Valley, just within the city limits of Los Angeles. No major airlines took off or landed on its asphalt surface. The two parallel runways usually serviced the private aircraft – upwards of seventeen hundred a day – of politicians, Hollywood celebrities, and business executives looking for a convenient, but anonymous point of arrival or departure.

So, it was no great surprise when the limousine pulled up next to the Gulfstream G150 with stealth, like a sleek black jungle cat. The pilot stood, patiently waiting, at the foot of the stairs that led up into the open door of the aircraft. There was no rush. He was paid handsomely to wait – if that was what his passenger required. His eyes flicked over to the idling limo. There was no immediate movement. So, waiting it was.

A dark-colored SUV pulled in a few minutes later. The pilot couldn't be sure in the vague shadows of the night, but there was a dip, a divot in the polished black quarter panel that suggested the vehicle had recently made contact with something unyielding. Before he could determine if it was just a trick of the uncertain light, a thick-necked gentleman in a dark suit exited the SUV and slipped into the now open passenger door of the limousine.

Inside the limo, Remy Laurent leaned back so comfortably into the seat, it was almost as if he were a part of the Milanese leather. The swarthy-skinned man who had just ducked into the car handed him a thick, generic envelope. Laurent took it with a neatly manicured hand and began to lift the flap.

"Well?" Laurent asked his guest.

"It's him," the man replied, his voice rumbling like so much gravel. "He's the one Sørensen called."

Laurent slid the black-and-white surveillance shots from the envelope. Jake's face stared back at him from the glossy surface. The photo showed the vague outline of a cabin through the swirling snow in the background. Laurent turned to the second photograph. The circular tuft of fur on his hood framed Digger's round face as he stood next to Jake, dwarfed by the taller man.

"The short one killed Victor," the swarthy man continued.

"Hm," Laurent replied. "And the girl?"

The olive-toned man took the photos from Laurent and quickly flipped to the last one. He handed the photos back to Laurent. "She's with them."

Laurent looked at the photo and clucked his tongue. "What a pity."

"Shall I take care of it?" Olive-Skin asked.

Laurent shook his head. "No. I'll handle the girl."

He handed the packet of photographs back to his companion. "Our friends in Paris can handle the other two. Tsk, tsk. It's truly a shame when beautiful things have to be destroyed."

Olive-Skin looked down at the photograph resting on the top of the stack. Taken at Fenway, it clearly showed Jake, Oddball, and Digger conferring with each other. Clearly, Laurent had had the men under surveillance for quite some time.

The photo also showed one other face. It was hard not to be taken aback by the high cheekbones and defined jaw of the Cuban beauty depicted in the photo. It was Melina.

A crooked smile crept into the corners of Olive-Skin's mouth. Too bad she wouldn't be beautiful for long.

CHAPTER TWENTY-EIGHT

Beverly Hills, California

It dripped down her body, warm and wet. She tilted her head forward, letting the cascade of water run over the tight muscles in her neck, down her naked body, and swirl the soapy suds down her long legs into the waiting drain. When she'd gotten back to the hotel after the meeting with Laurent, she had hopped into the suite's marble shower in the hopes that the hot water would help ease the tension in her lithe body. She wasn't certain exactly where the tension had originated. It could have been from Laurent's flagrant pronouncement that he knew exactly where the Gardner collection was. The odd thought entered her head, however, that the proximity of Jake Reisen's well-muscled body could have just as much to do with it as well.

She thought back on their initial meeting at the cabin. He hadn't been at all what she had expected. When O' Flaherty had first set her on Jake's trail, she wasn't sure what she had actually expected the Gardner expert to look like exactly. Maybe older, stodgier – less, well, stacked. But, it wasn't necessarily his god-like physique that had drawn her in. It was his eyes. Melina firmly believed in the old adage – the eyes were the window to the soul. Inside Jake's intense blue irises, she saw a storm raging. Jake Riesen was a man of passions. The eyes gave it away. And it had stirred something in Melina that was thoroughly unexpected.

She hadn't looked at another man that way in a long time. Not since Paul. Paul Stevens had been her partner – in more ways than one. Their paths had initially crossed when his CIA investigation intertwined with her Foreign Service terrorist investigation. They were both working on the investigation of Al-Qaeda. Paul worked out of the CIA Boston Field Office, his eyes on a group of men from Hamburg, Germany that had made their way into Afghanistan, known jihadists. Melina had been investigating the terrorist group since the 1998 African Embassy bombings, where Bin Laden had gotten his start in terror tactics.

Paul and Melina hadn't been able to get out of each other's way since – both professionally and on a more personal level. Paul had even proposed. They were going to meet in Boston and fly out to Los Angeles to get married, honeymooning in California wine country. The day they were due to fly out, however, Paul got a call. There had been chatter, talk that something big was going down in New York. Paul's contact wanted to meet, a source in the World Trade Center. Paul called Melina to urge her to make their scheduled flight, United Airlines Flight 175, out of Logan. He promised to take a later flight out of JFK and meet her in Los Angeles. At the last moment, Melina decided to surprise Paul and traded her ticket for one to New York. Paul was in the North Tower when the flight Melina should have been on crashed into it and brought her world crashing down. She left the Foreign Service not long afterwards.

She splashed a handful of warm water on her face. This wasn't working, she thought. Her thoughts trailed to the hotel room's mini bar. Maybe there was something in there that could help ease the tension threatening to twist her into pretzeled knots. She would have to look as soon as she finished up in here. She gathered up the soap in her long fingers and lathered up a pile of suds before scrubbing the evening's makeup from her face.

The minibar was well-stocked. At least it appeared so to the stealthy figure maneuvering past the open butler pantry equipped with its refrigerated private bar. It was the second door he'd found open as he'd made his way up to the twelfth floor premiere suite. He gripped the weapon in his right hand a little tighter, the leather glove creaking slightly with the effort. He reached the other hand forward and gently pushed the pantry door closed. It obliged with a simple, modest click, but the figure froze as if a cannon shot had just reverberated through the suite. His eyes darted through the room, combing the surrounding square footage for any furtive motion. After a few tense moments it had appeared the sound had not permeated the marbled walls of the lavatory. No sound of concerned furor seemed to come from that direction. Just the steady flow of running water. The intruder picked up his right foot and restarted his path through the suite.

He paused at the glass-topped coffee table. The perfume of a dozen, long-stemmed roses drifted under his nose. He plucked the card from the holder.

"*Belles fleurs pour une belle femme*," it read. Returning the card, he reached down and picked up the airline ticket lying wedged under the crystal vase. The boarding pass indicated a morning flight out of LAX to Charles de Gaulle. He made a mental note, then quietly returned the ticket to the table surface. He gracefully side-stepped the silver stiletto heels and red satin cocktail dress balled into a pile on the floor and started to make his way toward the bathroom, the muzzle of his firearm leading the way.

As he rounded the corner, white clouds of steam rolled from the bathroom door. The roiling water vapor obscured his vision. He did not see the flat, metal expanse of the vanity tray until it connected with the bridge of his nose. Blood gushed in crimson bursts as his gun clattered to the marble tiles. He fell to his knees, hands instinctively grabbing for his bleeding nose. A swift kick to his posterior sent him flat against the floor.

He wasn't giving up without a fight, however. He gave his bloodied muzzle a vicious wipe to smear away some of the blood and scrambled for his gun. His attacker wasn't too keen on him reaching it, though, and made it abundantly clear with a well-placed kick between his legs. He saw stars and his insides felt a sudden and urgent urge to vomit, but he fought through it. He scissored his legs between those of his opponent and leveraged their own weight against them. Melina came crashing to the floor in a slippery, soapy pile.

She tried to scramble to her feet, but the slide of the soap on the tile made it impossible for her to find purchase. The intruder grabbed hold of her left leg and dragged her back just inches from the bathroom doorway. She twisted around, intent on connecting a well-placed fist with something breakable, but the intruder threw his entire body weight on top of her, pinning her and her arms to the cold, bare floor.

Melina writhed and twisted. "Let me go!"

"So you can bust me in the schnoz again? No, thank you. You know, you were much friendlier on the dance floor."

Melina immediately stopped her struggling at the sound of the familiar, if now slightly nasal, voice.

"Not to mention, you had on a few more clothes," Jake continued.

Melina became suddenly acutely aware of her complete nakedness. Her breasts pushed up against Jake's hard chest. The curve of her slim hip fit neatly against the bone of his pelvis. Both of them were heaving with the physical exertion of `their recent bout.

"I – I – I thought you were an intruder," she began, her voice breathy and flustered. "Why the hell were you sneaking in here? And with a gun?"

"I thought you might be in danger. Although clearly the only danger here is you. Anyway, there's been another murder and when I found the door open, I thought – I thought maybe they had gotten to you."

"The door was open?" Melina questioned.

Jake nodded. He was having a difficult time catching his breath, but he was no longer certain if it was due to the recent physical exertion, or the fact that Melina was so close to him. "Did you let anybody in?"

Melina knew Jake was talking about the hotel suite, but, as she looked into the stormy gray blue of his eyes, another thought crossed her mind. Impulsively, she leaned her face up towards him and pressed her full lips against his. Jake's eyes widened in surprise and he immediately pulled back.

"I'm sorry," Melina apologized. "I – I shouldn't have done that."

Embarrassed, she tried to wiggle her way out from under Jake's body. Instead of letting her go, however, Jake softly caressed her cheek, tilting her lips back toward his, and drew her into a long, deep kiss. He pulled her full lower lip in between his, then gently explored the edges of her mouth with the tip of his tongue. Melina hardly noticed the chill of the suite's air against her nakedness as a surging warmth coursed through her.

Jake stood, scooping Melina up into his arms. He carried her from the bathroom into the adjoining bedroom and rested her on the soft down comforter. His eyes surveyed every inch on her tanned body as he stripped the tuxedo jacket, then shirt from his chest. As he lay down on top of her, she brought her hand up toward his face.

"But, what about your nose? You should get some ice," she offered.

"Some things you feel more than pain," he replied, and kissed her hard.

CHAPTER TWENTY-NINE

The morning sun winked happily through the curtains. Melina rolled her eyes miserably. It wasn't that she didn't share the sun's enthusiasm, necessarily. By rights, she was totally a morning person. The morning sun just meant the dream was over. And it had been a blissful dream.

In her dream, she and Jake had spent the long hours of the night, searching, exploring every inch of each other's bodies. They had forgotten all about Remy Laurent and lost art and simply lost themselves in the comfort of each other's arms. But, now, in the harsh light of morning, she was no longer lost. She knew exactly what path she, and she alone, needed to take.

Gingerly, she slid herself from under Jake's warm embrace. He looked so peaceful lying there, his sheepdog hair tousled every which way on the king-sized pillow. Melina smiled and ran a hair through her own wavy mop. It had been damp from the shower when they had lain down. She wouldn't be surprised if she looked like a crazed Gorgon right now because of it. Oh, well. She wasn't trying to win any beauty competitions. She was just trying to slip out in secret. But, she wasn't going to be able to do it stark naked. Her clothes were in the other room. Jake was so entwined in the bed sheets, there was no way she'd be able to steal one without waking him. Her eyes scanned the room. She spied Jake's shirt crumpled in the corner. Perfect, she thought. She slipped into the white, pleated shirt, its tails resting just a few inches above her knees. Her painted toes tipped their way across the plush carpet. She reached for the door handle and winced as it clicked open. She heard Jake stir in the bed behind her. She quickly whirled, but relaxed as his breathing slowly returned to a steady, even rhythm.

Without waiting another second, she slipped through the narrow opening she had allowed herself, fearful that the hinges would squeal an alert if she opened the door any further. As soon as she had closed the double door, a sudden voice sounded behind her causing Melina to nearly jump from her own skin.

"You know, it's customary to put a sock or a tie on the door when you have company," Digger mumbled through the chunk of flaky croissant he had just shoved into his mouth. "By the way, nice shirt."

Melina wanted to crawl under the nearby potted plant. "Hey, it's not what it looks like."

Digger chuckled. "Lady, I may be crazy, but I went to college. You," he waggled an accusatory finger at her, "got lucky."

Melina threw her hands up in surrender. So much for sneaking out.

"Alright, alright. You don't need to make a capital case out of it. We're all grown-ups here."

Flakes of the delicate pastry tumbled from Digger's mouth and came to rest on the dark blue NAVY t-shirt he was wearing. Melina cocked her head doubtfully to one side.

"I think," she amended.

Digger grinned with a mouthful of masticated food. Melina grimaced.

"So, what have you been doing all night," she asked. When she saw the devious look come across Digger's features, she raised a warning hand to dissuade him from making the obvious off-color remark.

"Don't even," she warned.

Digger threw his hands up in mock surrender. "Wasn't gonna."

"Yeah, right," She pointed to the strange markings on Davenport's cocktail napkin. "What's that?"

"I wish I knew," Digger replied. He cleared his mouth with a swallow of dark roast. "Coffee?"

"Yeah, sure," Melina replied. Digger poured a cup of the dark, rich brew into a clean cup and handed it to Melina. She reached across the table, rotating the napkin one-hundred and eight degrees, then back again. "It almost looks like a constellation. I used to love going to the planetarium as a kid. My dad used to take me. We'd sit and look at the stars for hours."

Digger quickly grabbed the napkin back from her and gave it a hard look. "Gimme that. A constellation, huh?"

"What? You get bored and start doodling last night?" Melina asked, sipping the hot coffee from her cup.

"Huh? Me? No. Nuh uh. I'm more of a Van Morrison than a Van Gogh guy. But, the guy who puked on me? Turns out he might not have been as loopy as we thought. He was a scientist at the H.A.A.R.P. facility. He slipped this into my pocket before somebody decided to waste him."

Melina's coffee cup clattered against her saucer. "Waste him? What the hell?"

"Exactly what we've been trying to figure out," Digger replied. Something on the television behind Melina's shoulder caught his attention. While he squinted at the screen trying to read the ticker running along the bottom edge, Melina took another look at the drawing and the scrabble of numbers and colors jotted below. She appeared to come to a decision, but casually went back to sipping her coffee. When Digger stood up and walked toward the television to get a better view, Melina quietly slipped into the other bedroom and slipped into her own clothes. Digger was still standing in front of the screen, remote control in hand, when Melina silently slipped out the hotel room door and out into the hall. Just as she pulled the door closed behind her, she could hear the voice of the news anchor.

"In a surprising turn of events, Hurricane Hera is taking an unpredicted turn against projected hurricane models and is headed for Bahamian archipelago. Meteorologists are baffled by the storm's path, saying that it's as if the storm has a mind of its own and is steering itself exactly where it wants to go."

She pulled the door completely closed, checking her bag for her ticket to Paris. She took a deep breath, steeled herself, and walked briskly down the hall before anyone could appear to change her mind.

CHAPTER THIRTY

The Bahamas

God took a Polaroid. The electric flash of lightning popped through the eerie blue-green filter that had siphoned the remaining spectrum from the atmosphere over the Atlantis resort. For a moment, the stuccoed salmon towers and the signature Bridge Suite arcing between them stood in high-definition contrast against the backdrop of dark storm clouds. Paradise Beach lay uncannily quiet. Even the ocean waves seemed to roll into the sandy shore on mute. Then, suddenly, sound startled Nature.

Twin red flags whipped near the water, snapping at full attention, warning would-be bathers of the dangers lurking under the roiling surf. Abandoned lounge chairs clanged, metal striking metal, as they upturned and bounced down the beach. Upended umbrellas rocked to and fro, creaking, dancing upside-down Technicolor mushrooms. A lone gull soared, trying to climb over the buffeting gusts. He wheeled into a sudden, plummeting dive, caught helplessly in a vortex of wind. He recovered just short of the jutting rocks at the surface of the nearby reef. He surged upward, gliding past the wide windows of the Bridge Suite, and headed for refuge.

Inside the exclusive suite no one relaxed against the gold-fringed damask pillows scattered on the sofas. No one basked in the brilliance of the 22-carat gold chandelier. No one sank into the luxury of the king-sized bed with its four, ebony-spiraled bedposts. A half-filled emerald bottle of imported water sat abandoned on the black and white marble coffee table, its owner discernibly absent. The ten dining chairs around the beveled glass table sat vacant, breakfast plates cast aside, one with a fork still stuck in a fat pork sausage. The entire montage stirred a post-apocalyptic feel.

There was no fall-out, though. There had been no bomb. The Atlantis had gone into lock-down in preparation for the coming storm. The first, fat splatting drops began to smack flat against the window pane. Then heaven pommeled the glass, insisting upon an invitation.

Most guests had fled the island before the authorities had officially shut down the Nassau airport. Management had retained only a handful of employees, enough to keep the restaurants and bars running. Those stayed open to service the few remaining guests and keep the party going. The piña coladas kept flowing and no one seemed to have a worry about the weather commentary of the meteorologist on the bar's widescreen.

"Hurricane Hera is now 185 miles east-southeast of Freeport on Grand Bahamas. She is spinning between Cat Island and Eleuthera, moving north-northwest at 12 miles per hour. Though the storm has weakened to a Category 1 hurricane, meteorologists are concerned about a potential merge with the abnormal winter storm raging down from Canada into the northeast United States. Forecasters are recalling the devastating effects of Hurricane Sandy when similar conditions resulted in the super storm that caused over fifty billion dollars in damages across the Caribbean and eastern seaboard."

Andrew Burke wasn't looking at a fifty billion dollar bill, but as he tried to corral the three family dogs, two cats, and one goat into the relative safety of the garage, he certainly saw dollar bills ripping from his house roof as the punishing winds tore off shingle after shingle. After his unexpected heart attack at 48, he cashed in his 401K and moved the whole family from New York to live a different kind of "island life". It was supposed to be less stressful.   No traffic.   No crazy cabbies.   Long, slow-brewed conversations over coffee in ceramic mugs. Bed sheets blown dry by the trade winds from the south. People who went out of their way to wish you a good day instead of going out of their way to avoid you altogether.

He was beginning to second guess the decision to move – and the one to ride out the storm on the island.

One of the cats cringed beneath the hedge.   As Andrew reached blindly through the snagging branches to rescue the growling feline, it lashed out a slicing claw in feral fear. Andrew instinctively drew back his hand. He dabbed a shirt corner at the welling blood and managed a dry chuckle at the irony. He'd left Wall Street to get away from the senseless blood-letting. A streak of feline fur rocketed past his feet and under the garage door.

"Pussy," he grumbled. The squeak of hinges drew his attention.

"The power lines must be down, Hun. We lost the lights and the television!" His wife shouted over the gale.

"The hand-crank weather radio is on the counter!" He hollered back. His wife nodded then disappeared back into the house. An ear-splitting crack resounded over the winds. Andrew narrowly missed being flattened by the falling guayacan tree as it rent in two. He clutched his chest, the bands of tightness hinting a second heart attack was near. He suddenly found himself wishing for a generic cardboard Starbucks and a rude cab ride to the industrial-dried Egyptian cotton sheets of The Roosevelt.

Mateo Agreeb just wished the world would stay upright. As the gutted sailboat listed hard to port, the crowd of Haitian refugees packed into the hold crushed into one another. Mateo himself wound up flattened against the bulwark, life-sustaining oxygen squeezing quickly from his lungs. Relief flooded back briefly as the boat suddenly lurched starboard and the refugees lost purchase in the opposite direction.

Making the trip from Haiti, hoping to seek asylum in the United States, was an arduous journey even under the best of circumstances. It was expensive, for one, costing nearly two thousand dollars a head for a cramped position aboard an often leaky boat with any number of other scared, frightened passengers. And with some Haitians barely scraping by on a paltry one hundred dollars a year, many had to rely on the grace of relatives already in the States to send the required price of passage to the smuggler captains who ran the surreptitious trips. Over the years, many had fled, trying to escape the economic and political miasma that was Haiti under Papa Doc, and continued under his son, Baby Doc. The notorious brutality of the *ton ton macoutes* had been bad enough, but after the devastating earthquake, many from the Haitian diaspora sought a better life. And so, the smugglers stayed in business.

It was ill-advised to aim directly for the shores of Key West en route from Haiti. No one sought to leap from the frying pan into the fire. To do so would court the possibility of washing ashore in Cuba. Add to that the watchful eye of the United States Coast Guard, and the Keys was simply not a viable option. Haitians were viewed by the U.S. as economic refugees, not political ones. As such, no asylum was offered and Haitians who managed to make it to American soil were frequently deported.

Yes, to head north was a more likely course. The run through the archipelago of the scattered Bahamian islands not only was safer but often the islands served as a stopover point. With favorable weather and winds, the voyage lasted a little less than a week. If the odds fell less in the passengers' favor and the weather ran afoul, the huddled refugees could count on close to ten days of rocking seas, no facilities, and no water. Many did not survive the voyage. Some succumbed to insanity. Some simply died, victim to starvation, dehydration, or sickness. These unfortunates often met with the cold murkiness of Davy Jones' locker. If they survived the entire length of the passage, they were subjected to shipwreck, vessels frequently being wrecked with intent, or purposely driven ashore. Passengers dragged themselves into hiding in the hopes of contacting other Haitian refugees already ensconced in the area to help them complete their journey to the States. As Mateo's boat listed heavily to port once again, he began to wonder if he would have been better off staying in Haiti.

Suddenly, there was a loud, crunching snap. There was a rapid flurry of activity. A ripple of panic began an insidious surge through the crowded hold. The ripple turned into a tidal wave as water began to flood through the open hatch lapping at the feet, then quickly the knees of the frightened refugees. White eyes widened in a sea of dark faces. Then the screaming erupted as the crush began for the tiny open hatch. Mateo heard voices over the screams. He tried to decipher what was being shouted.

"*Le bateau coule! Abandonner le naivre! Abandonner le naivre!*"

The meaning was all too clear. The boat was sinking. Abandon ship.

CHAPTER THIRTY-ONE

Los Angeles, California

"Jake! Jake! Jake!" Digger's voice drilled through Jake's consciousness like a pileated woodpecker on pine. The furrow creasing Jake's forehead belied his aversion to Digger's insistent reveille. He swatted at his soon-to-be-ex best friend and yanked the down comforter over his own head.

"Go away, Digger! I had a long night."

"Yeah. I figured as much. P.S. Your 'long night' jacked your shirt. Kiss that deposit goodbye."

Jake emerged from beneath the covers long enough to confirm Melina's absence.

"She's gone," he stated matter-of-factly, then returned to his goose down cave.

Digger huffed. "Come on, man! I'm not jerking around. This is important! I have something you need to see."

"Unless it's a double-pull cappuccino, I'm not interested," came Jake's sharp retort.

"Cool your jets. I ordered more room service. Your go juice is *en route.*"

"Call me when it gets here."

Digger gripped the top edge of Jake's blanket and jerked the linen clean off the bed. "Rise and shine, buttercup!"

The abrupt motion instigated the desired effect. Jake shot to attention, buck-ass naked.

Digger stood a safe distance away from the bed, a cheesy grin plastered ear to ear.

"Don't worry. I brought you a towel." He held up a scant washcloth. He didn't budge as a down-filled projectile smacked into his face with retaliatory intent.

Hector Alonso liked his job. It afforded the young Latino from the barrio an opportunity to sit behind the wheels of a wide menu of luxury vehicles that, under realistic circumstances, would be hopelessly out of reach. At least legally. Lotuses. Ferraris. A Bentley Continental GTC. Once he had even piloted an Aston Martin DB5. He had entertained the fancy he was Bond. James Bond. So what if he only drove them five hundred feet. Give or take. For five minutes at a time, the Four Seasons valet could imagine he was a spy.

The line between fantasy and reality suddenly blurred as a jet black Suburban squealed into the valet lane, rousting Hector from his perch. He tugged the hem of his red jacket and extended a hand toward the passenger door handle.

Before he could get a grip, the front and rear passenger doors flew open. A team of crisply-suited men deployed. They strode purposefully toward the hotel lobby. Hector's sharp eyes caught sight of a Glock-9 as the lapel of one man's suit waved open with the intensity of his stride. Hector's instinct urged him to alert hotel security. He scurried to the valet stand extension. As he ground his index finger into the "O", a very official-looking military I.D. flashed in front of his startled brown eyes.

"I wouldn't make that call," Lowell Mason warned with icy authority.

"Four seasons Beverly Hills. How may I direct your call?" A feminine voice filtered through the receiver. Hector lowered the phone and disconnected the call.

"She's not answering," Jake muttered. He tossed the phone into the cushions of the couch. He rested his elbows on his knees, then dropped his face into his hands.

"Don't take it so personally, *compadre*. Maybe she's just on the plane and had to power down," Digger suggested. Jake had told him about Melina's ticket to Paris.

When he conceded defeat to the errant crumbs of sleep lodged in the corners of his eyes, Jake lifted his head and inhaled a deep breath. "I shouldn't have let her go alone."

"Aw, come on man! She's a big girl. She can take care of herself. She rearranged your ugly face well enough." Digger gestured to the rainbow of colors radiating across the bridge of Jake's nose.

"Is it bad?" Jake asked. Digger pursed his lips.

"Naw," he drawled. "Purple's a good color for you."

Jake sneered. "Speaking of colors, have you figured out the mumbo jumbo on that napkin?"

"If by 'you', you mean 'we', then yes, 'we' have," came Digger's quick riposte. The shorter man took up roost in the nest of cushions opposite

Jake. "While you were busy studying human anatomy, I was busy with some good old fashioned geography."

Jake failed to take the bait. Slightly disappointed, Digger continued. "These numbers, the ones scratched out next to the colors?" Jake nodded as Digger pointed. "Coordinates. Plain and simple. And they are all over the map. See +69° 35' 10.94", +19° 13' 20.89"? Tromsø, Norway. 34° 51' 15.66" N, 136° 6'24.49" E? Uji City, Kyoto Prefecture, Japan. -2° 35' 40.47, -44° 12' 35.90" is Cruzeiro Santa Bárbara. Sao Luis-MA, Brazil. 11° 57' 08.25" S, 76° 52' 30.67" W? That one's Peru. Lima to be precise. This one's Arecibo, Puerto Rico. And care to venture a guess what this one is?"

Digger pointed to the last GPS coordinates listed. 62° 23' 32.36" N, 145° 8'31.81" W.

"Gakona, Alaska." Jake muttered. He picked up the notepad.

Digger rolled into a slow clap. "Give that man a prize."

Jake narrowed his eyes as he reviewed the list. "Laurent's company has holdings in all of these places. That can't be a coincidence."

"It's not." Digger reached for a world map. He smoothed it out in front of Jake. He sketched a series of angled lines between the locations indicated by the coordinates. The resulting shape was a close approximation to the seemingly haphazard design Davenport has sketched out on his cocktail napkin.

"That looks a lot like a constellation," Jake offered.

Digger raised an eyebrow. "That's exactly what your girlfriend said. Care to guess which one?"

"Not a clue. And she's not my girlfriend."

Digger sat back in his seat, lacing his thick fingers behind his head. "The Phoenix."

CHAPTER THIRTY-TWO

Boston, Massachusetts

The Phoenix. A brilliant crimson bird taking wing. The image blurred in and out of focus along with Melina's consciousness. Her head felt like an overripe melon. Heavy. Fuzzy. Her stomach voiced a nauseated discontent. She tried desperately to focus through the pain.

All she could see was black. Something covered her eyes, submersing her in complete darkness.

"Help! Someone help!" The plea came through muffled, sticky lips. Duct tape sealed her mouth. It wouldn't have mattered anyway, she thought. The sound came dry. Cracked. Hildago could have raced across the desert in her mouth. She'd been drugged. But, when? A faint image of a drink at the airport bar. A talkative businessman with olive skin. Stupid, stupid mistake, she berated herself.

Her training sorted through a pharmacy of possible options. Gamma hydroxybuyrate? Ketamine? No. It was flunitrazepam, if she had to hazard a guess.

The synapses in her brain tried to piece together the random images in her head. After a few misfires and several dry heaves, a sequence of events began to fall into place. She remembered trying to leave the hotel to catch the Paris flight. The concierge had stopped her. He had handed her a message. The envelope sported an embossed Phoenix – the Phoenix Research logo – a handwritten note from Laurent folded inside.

"The Storm is coming home. I have arranged a meeting. Boston Harbor. Slip 40. Tomorrow night. Remy."

She had immediately changed her flight.

Boston. It all kept coming back to Boston.

She was supposed to have started a new chapter of her life here, with Paul. Now, if she could not figure a way out of her predicament, it looked like the final chapter might close here. She doubted seriously she had been brought here for brunch with bloodies. No. Her cover had been blown. She shuddered when she considered what fate Laurent had in store for her. Boston's motto came to mind: *Sicut patribus, sit nobis Deus.* God be with us as he was with our fathers.

Maybe, she thought. But God also helped those that helped themselves. She'd better get cracking.

She tried to move, but her limbs refused to coordinate with the signals coming from her brain. Maybe if she just laid here for a moment, she thought. But where was 'here'? She heard a bass-pitched creak. Not the type of creak you hear when someone steps on a loose floorboard. No, this was deeper. Bigger. Like old wooden beams settling against age.

There was a smell, too. Dank. Musty. She tried to take a deep breath and a wave of nausea passed through her. She gave it a precious moment to pass, but she had to focus. Through the fogginess, Melina thought she could hear a wave of another kind. Yes, there was a definite, repetitive slosh – the sound of water lapping against wood. The sudden echoing ding of a buoy bell sounded through the stuffy air. That was it. She was on a boat. She had to be in the harbor.

Her arms were pinned behind her. She struggled against the bonds. Hard plastic bit into her wrists.

Damn it, she thought. Zip ties. She forced another queasy, but deep, focusing breath into her lungs. Don't panic. The cutting plastic restraints weren't easy to escape, but they certainly weren't impossible. Two things were needed to escape her current predicament – opportunity and time. She just wasn't certain how much of either she was going to be afforded. She'd better get to work.

Understanding the basic physics of any restraint was key. Zip ties were nothing more than a strip of toothed nylon and a ridged ratchet at one end. Designed to give under downward pressure as the ridge of each tooth passed through its open housing, the ratchet also responded with a reciprocal upward motion as it experienced each negative divot – the clicking "lock" that made the ties effective as a restraining tool. At that point, there were three options – sever, shim or saw. Between the blindfold and the awkward positioning of her arms, Melina immediately scratched shim and saw from the list. Well, that left sever.

She wiggled like an overstuffed monarch caterpillar, trying to calculate how much room she had to maneuver. Her brain formed a mental blueprint, calculating from the rough dimensions. She prepped for the next step.

The weakest point on a zip tie was the locking mechanism. Simple physics dictated she needed to position the lock and its open housing between her wrists so it would receive the most substantial impetus of pressure. She waggled her fingers, feeling for the bulk of the rectangular

housing. Once located, she began to twist and contort her wrists.
Centimeter by centimeter, the housing migrated to the desired position.
The effort beaded droplets of sweat along Melina hairline, plastering some
of the errant hairs against her forehead. The inability to brush them away
maddened her.

Focus, damn it! Melinda reproofed herself. The clock was ticking and
there was no telling when it was set to alarm. She rolled until her back hit a
beam. She used to the solid wood to leverage the weight of her slight frame
into a standing position. Her equilibrium lurched. She couldn't be certain
which was to blame – the residual effects of the drugs or the ebb and flow
of the tide. The feeling passed. She shimmied her arms downward, past
the curve of her buttocks, until her bound hands rested on the tops of her
quads. She began a slow squat, letting her hands drop till they met the
backs of her knees, until she was seated, knees bent, feet flat on the floor in
front of her. From there it was a simple matter of stepping her feet, one by
one, through the restrained loop of her hands. She leaned forward and
used her teeth to tighten the restraints even further. The tighter they were,
the easier it would be to accomplish what she trying to do. She stood up
once again, wincing from the pain. But, if she had any inclination to cry
out, the sudden voices from above silenced the complaint in her throat.

Two voices. Male. The voices were deep. Footsteps heavy. The men
were likely large. She caught a few words in gruff, guttural Italian.

In mare. Out at sea.

Mollarla. Dump her.

Her clock had run out. Alarm bells railed in her aching head.

She rapidly prodded herself with her elbows, searching for the
curvature of her hipbones to use as leverage. She raised her hands above
her head and yanked her arms downward with speed and intent. Her

elbows splayed out to the side like awkward chicken wings. The thick nylon sliced into her wrist, executing an unkind, stinging cut, but refused to break. Melina gritted her teeth against the hurt. The heavy, trod of footsteps plodded across the deck above. They were coming!

With controlled haste, Melina raised her arms above her head once more and slammed her forearms against her narrow hipbones. The binding plastic snapped as the footsteps sounded closer. Melina's hands flew to the tape around her eyes. Nimble fingers worked the adhesive strip free just in time to see the meaty fist of the olive-skinned businessman connect with the bridge of her nose. Everything went black.

CHAPTER THIRTY-THREE

Paris-Vincennes, France

Covering nearly forty-two hectares, or one hundred three acres in the middle of the Vincennes forest in France, lay the Hippodrome, the racing mecca for harness racing in Europe. In harness racing, horses raced at a specific gait. Sometimes it was a trot. At other times, it was a pace. The animals usually pulled a two-wheeled cart called a sulky, although sometimes in Europe, *trot monté,* racing under saddle, was not entirely unheard of. The sulky, informally known as a "bike", was a light, two-wheeled cart equipped with bicycle wheels. For exercising or training, the drivers use what is known as a "jog cart," a sulky that is heavier and bulkier than a racing unit. The driver would sometimes employ a light whip. With strict rules in place on how much and how hard the whip could be used, the whip was a tool used mainly to signal the horse by tapping the sulky shaft. Cyprien Renaud did not care much for rules. He pulled up to the motorized starting gate as Remy Laurent watched silently from the stands.

Racing was a religion to Renaud, and Laurent knew better than to interrupt a man when he was at prayer.

As he waited for his audience with Renaud, Laurent thought on the grand history of the track around him. The Hippodrome played host to one of the top races in the trotting community, Grand Prix d'Amérique. Indeed, Laurent suspected the horse Renaud was currently putting through paces was due to participate in that selfsame race.

Founded in 1920 as a tribute to America's involvement in WWI, the Grand Prix d'Amérique was the biggest harness racing event in the world. The pinnacle of the sport sees the top eighteen world cracks compete for the title over the classic distance of 2700 metres. The Grand Prix d'Amérique was now a popular and prestigious international meeting. Media outlets for multiple continents covered the Grand Prix. Millions of viewers in more than thirty countries would be glued to their television sets, urging favourites on to victory and a purse of one million Euros. Avid viewers placed ridiculous bets to try and get a piece of that action and share in the surging adrenaline.

The track itself was created in 1879. It was composed of two separate racetracks, the Grande Piste, an outdoor racetrack with a larger, more demanding two-thousand meter circuit than the standard half mile or full mile imposed by the international standard. Its downhill section provided a unique challenge for competitors. While the home straight, which passed in front of the stands, runs into a long descent, it was immediately followed by a long one-thousand meter stretch to the ultimate finish line.

Another feature of the track which established the character of the Hippodrome as unique was its cinder-paved surface. The cinders offered the unique characteristic of speed and flexibility not often seen at other tracks on the circuit. The Hippodrome offered a second, smaller track as well, known as the Petite Piste. It offered a more level racing surface with no uphill or downhill section and was fitted with specific lighting which catered to night-time events.

It was on the Petite Piste that Cyprien Renaud prepared to test his mount. Renaud was a champion trotter driver. He ran his horses through a gait in which the horse moved its legs forward in diagonal pairs, right front and left hind, then left front and right hind striking the ground simultaneously. Renaud lined his horse up behind the slow-moving, hinged gate. The wing moved up and away. The horse took off like a shot.

When the horse had completed a punishing mile under Renaud's whip, Renaud turned the animal over to its trainer and dismounted from the sulky. The cinders on the track crunched under his feet as he strode purposefully toward Laurent, removing his driving gloves in the process.

Laurent gave a polite clap. "1:52.6. Impressive time."

"But not acceptable. It is two-tenths behind Un Mec d'Heripre. We must be faster if we intend to win. And it is nothing without the win. Do you not agree, Remy?" Renaud tilted his head ever so slightly in Laurent's direction.

"*Absolutement*," Laurent agreed. "*Comment allez-vous, Cyprien?*"

"Very well, thank you," Renaud responded. Renaud took a seat at a small white table that had been set with a cheese plate and two glasses next to a stunning vintage of Chateau Margeaux.

"Please. Join me," Renaud suggested. He gestured to the available seat. Laurent pushed a small package, roughly six inches by six inches, across the table toward Renaud.

"For you," Laurent intimated.

Renaud slowly opened the package. He was a man, it appeared, for which nothing was a rush. Once the paper had been cleared, it revealed a near postage-stamp sized portrait, the diminutive self-study done by Rembrandt, and one of the missing pieces from the Gardner collection. A slow smile crept across Cyprien's face.

"Wampum for the savages, eh, Remy? Tell me. What is it you want?"

Laurent inhaled. "You know the men I was telling you about? The ones poking around the operations at H.A.A.R.P.? I'm afraid they will shortly be on their way to Paris."

"I thought your man was going to take care of them stateside."

"Well, we encountered a problem."

Renaud picked up the sharp knife next to his plate and began to polish it. "And now, the problem is mine."

"There is a benefit to you lending your assistance, Cyprien. Let us not forget that."

"Hm," Renaud scoffed. "A benefit I have yet truly to see. What proof can you offer to warrant my continued involvement in your little 'science experiment', hm, Remy? What verification can you give me that your 'Frankenstorm' will be the monster you promise?"

At that moment, the huge, hairy Russian that had been keeping watch over the storm system at NOAA lumbered toward the two men.

Now it was Laurent's turn to smile. He gestured to the large man. "I give you Dr. Frankenstein himself, of course. Alexander Akimenkov."

CHAPTER THIRTY-FOUR

Beverly Hills, California

"The Phoenix?" Jake repeated, incredulity sharpening the edge of his voice.

"Scout's honor," Digger promised.

"And the colors?" Jake reminded.

Digger sat forward on the edge of his seat. His knee bounced in a staccato rhythm.

"Now we're in my wheelhouse!" He tapped his finger on the map. "All these locations? They have something in common besides Phoenix Research Unlimited."

"I'll give. What?"

"They all play host to H.A.A.R.P. type facilities. Remember how I always said something hinky was going down at H.A.A.R.P. Gakona? Well, I was wrong. Nothing was going down. It was going up."

CHAPTER THIRTY-FIVE

Paris-Vincennes, France

As the plane had climbed steadily up at the onset of the eighteen hour flight to Paris, Alexander Akimenkov had watched the flight attendant rattle through the practiced safety spiel. Her practiced fingers had nimbly manipulated the sample safety belt as she moved down the aisle from business class to the sardined sections of economy. Her petulant little mouth demonstrated how to orally inflate the life vest under his seat. And she had made absolutely certain he had no qualms about being located in an emergency exit row.

He had flashed her a wide, nicotine-stained smile. If only she had known his experience with plane doors. She may have had second thoughts about entrusting him with the safety of two hundred fifty passengers at thirty-three thousand feet.

For Akimenkov, there had never been a well-rehearsed safety speech. There had been precious little in the way of life-saving equipment. And the door?

Akimenkov liked his plane doors open – wide open. The buffeting winds threatening to suck him into a blue oblivion. The plummeting gap between his altitude and the vast expanse of the Motherland below. The heady sensation of soaring through the clouds, needing only to reach out to touch the heavens.

In a former life, Alexander Akimenkov had been a Russian military pilot. It had been his job to stand next to that open hatch, mission after mission. That simple task alone was fractious. But, when you complicated matters by shoveling scads of silver iodide and dry ice into insubstantial puffs of cirrus to ensure clear skies over the May Day parade or other important state function, it was downright death-defying. Each trip up was a flaunt in the face of his own mortality. He'd survived so many missions, he had entertained the concept he might just be immortal.

So, it really came as no surprise when Laurent referred to him as "Dr. Frankenstein". Akimenkov welcomed the analogy. After all, Shelly's mad genius had defied the coils of mortality with his monstrous creation. Akimenkov was doing no less by harnessing Mother Nature and forcing her to bend to his will.

"So, you claim to control the weather?" Cyprien Renaud asked as casually as if he'd asked Akimenkov to pass the sugar.

"No," Akimenkov barked in retort. "I do not claim. I do."

Renaud smiled over the rim of his wine glass. He set the crystal goblet on the table before him.

"A man of action. *Tres bon*. Tell me then, Comrade Akimenkov." Renaud leaned forward, his brow knit in keen sobriety. "How?"

CHAPTER THIRTY-SIX

Beverly Hills, California

"They're boiling the mother-freakin' sky," Digger announced.

"What?" Jake shook his head trying to wrap his gray cells around Digger's proclamation. He considered that Digger had finally gone around the bend on this one. Digger read the doubt on Jake's perplexed face. He shuffled through the pile of papers strewn across the coffee table. He found the data he was searching for and waved it authoritatively in front of Jake's face.

"The antenna array. It's a friggin' space heater for the ionosphere."

"And that's bad." The response was fifty-fifty query and statement.

"When some whack job is using it to steer a hurricane? Yeah. It's bad."

Jake simply stared. Oh, yeah. Definitely around the bend. Around, over and through.

"Steer a hurricane?" Jake's left eyebrow arched dubiously. He groaned and dropped his head back into his hands.

"I really need that coffee." His muffled groan filtered between his fingers. "How?"

Digger grinned maniacally. He hopped on the cushion next to Jake. "Water moves through the atmosphere. Typically, it follows the jet stream which, in turn, bumps and grinds its way through high pressure systems. You with me so far?"

Jake nodded. Digger pressed onward.

"When the ionosphere is heated, it rises. Like a hot air balloon. The stratosphere follows suit. A little mad-scientist created high pressure system here and there and you could ping-pong a storm wherever you want it to go."

Jake thought the scenario through. He began to see the order in Digger's chaos. He picked up the narrative baton. "And devastate major cities, cripple ports, and potentially crash markets."

"All you would need is access to a few strategically placed IR arrays."

"Like in every country Phoenix Research owns holdings," Jake continued.

"And you could play God. As long as nobody figured it out," Digger countered. He pointed to the list of seemingly random colors. "Kat knew, man. She was watching the borealis. Not just in Alaska. All over the world. The Northern Lights? They pop at different colors depending on the altitude of the ionosphere. Kat was tracking a pattern. I'll bet a year's worth of MREs that she linked some of the recent weird weather shit to manipulations of the atmosphere."

A sharp rap sounded at the door. Instinct shot Jake to his feet.

"Cool your jets. I'm supposed to be the paranoid one," Digger reminded. He strode to the room door. "I ordered more coffee, remember?"

His fingers were inches from wrapping around the handle when the paneled door swung inward with sufficient force to knock Digger on his backside.

"What the hell?" Digger blurted.

Mason's men swarmed into the space, weapons drawn. A surge of adrenaline replaced Jake's need for caffeinated spurning. His eyes furtively searched for a weapon of his own.

Digger scrambled to put himself to rights. "This is so not what I ordered!"

Jake snatched up the Gideon's bible from the end table and introduced religion to the underside of the man's chin barreling toward him. The man flipped backward in a graceless arc.

"Friends of yours?" Jake asked Digger.

"Don't think so," Digger replied. He ducked a left from the second intruder. "I haven't pissed anyone off lately."

He landed a solid right hook squarely into the nose of his opponent. Crimson spurted. The wide-shouldered man crumpled to the ground. Digger paused, lips pursed. "Then again, there was that letter to the Energy Commission."

"Then who are these guys?" Jake readied himself as his attacker slowly rose from the ground, wobbling.

"They work for me," came the authoritative answer. Lowell Mason strode into the room. Jake and Digger's attentions flew to the doorway. The momentary distraction allowed Mason's men to overpower Jake and Digger, pinning their arms behind them.

Jake struggled against the oppressive custody. His eyes narrowed at Mason. "I know you. You were at the museum. You're cronies with Remy Laurent."

Mason ensconced himself comfortably in the furry Campana sofa. He raised an eyebrow at Jake's suggestion.

"Cronies?" He let out a throaty chuckle. "Hardly. I'm not inclined to be congenial with people who withhold information from me. Mr. Laurent was not forthcoming in divulging his plans for the H.A.A.R.P. facility in Gakona. You, on the other hand, Lieutenant Commander Riesen, were quite chummy with Mr. Laurent. So, as I see it, the current question on the table is…are we 'cronies'?"

Mason leaned forward, helping himself to an apple from the fruit bowl on the coffee table. "Or shall I cross you off my Christmas card list right now?"

Digger raised his hand. "If anybody's interested, I'm agnostic, so, I don't really do the whole Christmas thing. And, really, I don't even know you, so."

"Master-at-Arms Second Class Grover Kelley. Recipient of the Navy Cross and the Silver Star. Quite a résumé. And quite pleased to make your acquaintance."

The familiarity made Digger squirm. He could count his number of friendly acquaintances on one hand – the one missing a digit. So, when any entity numbering beyond four could identify him by name, rank and serial number, it felt like the sudden onset of a vicious case of scabies. It made him want to crawl out of his skin.

"You obviously know who we are, so it's really only fair. Who the hell are you?" Jake demanded.

Mason stood. "Where are my manners? Colonel Lowell Mason, Commander Phillips Research Site and Materiel Wing Director, Space Vehicles Directorate, Air Force Research Laboratory, Kirtland Air Force Base."

Digger started at the mention of the New Mexico facility. Mason nodded to his men, signaling them to release Digger and Jake. Digger vigorously rubbed some feeling back into his arms. "You're eggheads from Area 51."

Mason's features set stonily in his craggy face. "Gentlemen, your country requires your service."

"We've done our tours, Colonel. No more missions," Jake replied.

"Really?" Mason's interrogative was laced with doubt. He picked up the card from the floral arrangement. "Is that why you have such a keen interest in Remy Laurent and his – affairs?"

Jake's eyes narrowed. "Cut to the chase, Colonel."

Mason lowered the card. "Katarina Sørensen."

"What about her?" Jake countered warily.

"Ms. Sørensen had tried making contact with my offices. She had indicated it was a matter of national security. She died before she was able to pass that information on."

"The official report says she was mauled by a grizzly," Digger interjected.

"And we both know we could fertilize Iowa with what the official report is full of." The muscle in Jake's jaw flexed under his morning stubble.

Mason conceded with a tip of his head. "We found her atop the antenna array. She didn't climb up there by herself."

"Really?" Jake mocked.

Mason ignored the jab. "My men discovered a discrepancy in the flight logs for one of Laurent's company helos. And her computer's hard drive was erased. It's circumstantial at best, but our working theory is whatever Ms. Sørensen discovered, it was serious enough to get her killed.

We believe there is a credible threat."

"You could say that!" Digger snorted.

"And you believe Laurent is behind it all?" Jake asked.

Mason nodded. "We know Ms. Sørensen contacted you. I need to know if she divulged any information that can identify the threat."

"You're not gonna believe us," Digger offered. Jake held up a warning hand.

"What if we do know something?" Jake asked. "Why come to us?"

Mason sighed. "H.A.A.R.P. is no longer under military control. If I go through official channels, I'll be drowned in a sea of red tape. I need to go off the reservation on this one and I need a couple of Indians crazy enough to go with me."

Digger sniggered. "Yeah. Too bad I'm a Red Sox fan."

"Look, I've read both your files. I would not have approached either of you if I did not feel I could trust you. You have a vested interest in nailing Laurent. And you already have an established in."

"Melina."

"Yes. But, I believe Ms. Garcia may just be in over her head." Jake's gut roiled.

"So? What do you say? You ready to pow-wow?"

Digger raised his hand. "Just have one question."

"Yes?" Mason replied.

Digger leaned forward, brows knit in serious preponderance. "Just how many aliens do you have in Area 51?"

CHAPTER THIRTY-SEVEN

Mid-Atlantic

The shade of green on Digger's face suggested they may have had a smoother ride to Paris if they had taken a bucking bronco. Currently, it vacillated between the popular avocado shade of the seventies and a more canary chartreuse. He'd been on smoother flights loaded in the back of a C-17 Globemaster III, he thought as he grabbed for the sick bag wedged in the seat-back in front of him. The in-flight magazine tumbled out. Digger snagged it just as the pilot's voice filtered through the cabin speakers.

"Once again, folks, we do apologize for the rough flight. We are skirting a pretty nasty weather system. With any amount of luck, we'll be able to get above this mess pretty soon and steer you through clear skies the rest of the way into Charles deGaulle Airport. In the meantime, I'd ask that you please observe the signs and remain in your seats with your seat belts securely fastened until such time as we can get you into some smoother airspace."

The pilot signed off, not that Jake would have noticed. His attentions were heavily focused on the thick file that Mason had given them back at the hotel in Los Angeles. Digger was more concerned with trying to open the vomit bag. He had already read the Air Force's white paper on weather as a force multiplier. It helped when you owned a personal, dog-eared copy.

Jake, on the other hand, flipped through page after page on cloud-seeding – both glaciogenic and hydroscopic – a crash course in a sort of applied cloud physics. From its less-predictable inception, the more recent use of optical array probes, diodes and lasers could allow scientists to more accurately select clouds ripe for manipulation. Mason only had half the equation, however. When Jake and Digger offered up their theory – that Laurent was using his access to ionospheric antenna arrays to manipulate the ionosphere and, subsequently, the weather – the intent became clear. Laurent was bent on economic domination and was not above inciting global destruction to effect it. And Melina had managed to get herself right in the middle of it.

A loud crack of thunder boomed. The plane lurched and bobbled before finally setting to rights. Jake looked up from the ream of recent weather reports outlining the spate of unusual weather that stretched from the Nicaraguan coast, across the Caribbean hitting Haiti and Cuba, and now marched diligently up the eastern seaboard toward Boston.

"This will be easy. Like stopping a runaway freight train," Jake scoffed. He slammed the file closed. "Even if we manage to locate Laurent in Paris and get him to shut off the arrays, there's no guarantee we'll be able to stop the storm."

He looked at his friend. Digger was favoring a different shade now. More of a lime-green, like…

"Jell-O," Digger mumbled into the sick bag.

"Dig, you can't even keep down air right now. Why would you want Jell-O?"

Digger shook his head. He lifted his head out of the sick bag. "No, man. To stop the storm."

Jake had heard a fair share of crazy spout from his buddy's mouth, between aliens and government conspiracies, but Digger's latest suggestion was convincing Jake that a trip to Bellevue might be advisable sooner than later. "What are you talking about, Dig?"

"There's a company in Louisiana. Sup-R-Absorb. They've got a patent on this thing called a poly – poly – what's this?" His tongue stumbled.

"Polyacrylamide," Jake replied.

"Yeah. Kinda like that stuff you find in diapers. They're claiming that use on a monolithic scale, like, say, dumping it into a hurricane, could force a reduction in wind speed. It supposed to absorb up to several thousand times its own weight in moisture and dissolves harmlessly on contact with salt water."

Digger raised his eyebrows in an "uh-oh" facial expression, then lurched for the sick bag. After a few retches, he looked back up. "I could use some polyacrylamide myself, right now."

He shook his head at Jake's dubious expression. "Look."

Digger handed the airplane magazine to Jake. Jake took the periodical opened to the technology section. Jake skimmed the contents of the article, his blue eyes widening with each paragraph.

"I may be on the Crazy Train," Digger declared, "but maybe it's going to take a train to stop one."

"I'll call Mason." He picked up the air phone.

CHAPTER THIRTY-EIGHT

New Orleans, Louisiana

Lunch hour. Although, with business running a little on the slow side, it was more like lunch hour-and-a-half to an all-day trough feeding. Robert Hebert, owner of Sup-R-Absorb puzzled at the dearth of clientele. When the graduate of Tulane's Environmental Earth Sciences Program first started his business, he naturally assumed New Orleans would serve as a ready-made market for his breakthrough polyacrylamide product. Who better than a moisture-laden city like New Orleans, a city plagued by the threat of hurricanes and fierce summer thunder showers, not to mention a stifling, oppressive humidity, to reap the benefits of what his fledgling company had to offer? The city was a sopping soup bowl at the mouth of the Mississippi delta, for crying out loud. He had even modified his original formula, which would have required over two billion pounds of product and a fleet of C-5 planes to be effectual on a major storm system. Now, it had an efficacy at a mere two hundred fifty thousand pounds, give or take.

It wouldn't stop the system entirely, but it would weaken it, saving billions in storm-caused damages and property losses. He'd expected the government officials to come beating down his door. Things hadn't quite panned out that way.

Ah, well. There was always his father's car dealership.

He sighed and patted the wide expanse of his belly. The lack of business certainly hadn't created a lack of appetite. Like most New Orleanians, lunch was absolutely his most favorite time of the day. God's honest truth, it was a toss-up between that and jazz brunch at The Court of Two Sisters. Then there was boiled crawfish and spicy red potatoes with sweet corn at Deanie's in Bucktown. His salivary glands went into overdrive when he thought of the over-stuffed muffulettas from Central Grocery, with the layers of choice Italian meats and cheeses – mortadella, salami, mozzarella, and provolone - and the *giardiniera*. The marinated olive salad dropped off the quartered sesame bun for lack of room. But, nothing compared to Mamie's home-cooked red beans. Love in a pot. His family's housekeeper favored the dark red kidney beans over the lighter variety.

"Mo betta flavah," she'd say.

He leaned over the plate and drew in an appreciative breath. He could smell the bay leaf. Maybe a speck of cayenne. A hint of paprika. A pinch of garlic. All the spices mingled together in the simmer process to pack a mighty wallop. Not dissimilar from the recipe for a hurricane – but Mother Nature was a bitch of a cook. Her current concoction was roiling up the Eastern coastline of the United States, hell-bent toward Boston. Robert thought back to Hurricanes Katrina and Rita, the twin inspirations for his foray into the environmental sciences. The levees had failed. The man-made embankments built all around New Orleans and her surrounding areas to stave the overflow of the Mighty Mississippi and Lake

Pontchartrain were useless to prevent the surge of flood waters that left people stranded on rooftops, left thousands homeless, and many dead.

Well, Robert thought, when you lived in a bowl, you'd better have a spoon to bail you out.

A spoon! Robert looked around frantically for his. He was going to have a time of it eating his red beans without one. He spied it near the edge of his desk and wrapped five fat fingers around it. He reached for the hot sauce to give the legumes that little something extra. He dashed in a few spicy drops. He lifted the spoonful of red beans and rice towards his open mouth.

The seasoned load of Cajun goodness never made it past his coffee and chicory-stained incisors. The luan door to his office flew open and sent the stacks of blank purchase orders swirling in a carbon paper dervish. The beans dropped in a dark, ruddy splat on his Perlis tie. Robert lifted his considerable bulk from his office chair.

"What in the hell?" His accent placed emphatic weight on the definite article.

The firearms in the hands of the men at the door placed even more weight on the gravity of his visitors' intent.

CHAPTER THIRTY-NINE

Paris, France

Scylla and Charybdis guarded the street level doors of Cercle Magique. Admittedly, the security goons stood stoically dapper at the entrance, looking more Hermes than Homer. The two massive men could just as well have been the six-headed sea monster and churning, ship-crushing whirlpool that terrorized the Strait of Messina. Like the mythological Grecian monsters, the duo presented an inescapable threat to any one they deemed unworthy to pass through the poker club's door. Jake was willing to place a substantial wager he and Digger were not on the invite list. Especially when he looked down at his squirrely pal's canary yellow t-shirt and baggy cargo pants stained with, well, whatever. He and Digger ducked behind a tree on the banquette opposite the exclusive club.

"And Mason said we're gonna find Laurent in there?" Digger jabbed a thumb toward the entrance.

Jake nodded. "Or, at the very least, we'll pick up his trail. The club's run by Cyprien Renaud. Mason has intel that Renaud is Laurent's Corsican contact and also how Laurent is financing his little science project. Clubs like this? Money-mills for the mob. Oddball and I tripped across these guys a few times when I worked for the Bureau. Renaud was rumored to be one of the worst."

"Oh, joy," Digger groaned.

"I said 'rumored'. The guy's Teflon. Nothing sticks. If anybody was in a position to grease Laurent's wheels, Renaud's the guy. We just need to go in there, ask him a few polite questions, and I'm sure we'll get what we're looking for."

"What? A bullet between the eyes?" Digger suggested. Jake wasn't laughing. Digger continued. "Seriously? That's your plan? A few polite questions?"

Jake nodded. Digger waggled his head in less-than-subtle doubt. "Let's entertain the fleeting notion, and note that I do say 'fleeting' here, that I agree with you, which alone should put me in a padded cell. How are we going to going to get past those monsters?" Digger asked.

A wide, toothy grin broke across Jake's face. "By doing what every poker player worth his salt does. Bluff."

Aleisu Rossi never got through secondary school. Quite literally. By the time he was thirteen years old, he had already achieved a height of six-foot four and weighed nearly two hundred eighty-five pounds and, in point of fact, could not get through the narrow doorways at the school in his village. He was a genetic abnormality. The constant taunts and jeers from his classmates soured the concept of education for him. Well, that and the fist he put into the face of Larenzo Sattori for calling him a stupid ape. The assault on his fellow thirteen-year old drew the attention of the headmaster and a swift expulsion.

It also drew the attention of a certain up-and-coming young mob boss. After meeting with the business end of a broken chianti bottle, courtesy of a drunken father, Aleisu began to hang with an even rougher crowd – Cyprien Renaud's boys. He quickly proved his worth as an enforcer and even occasionally as a personal bodyguard for Renaud. He enjoyed his current post as club bouncer. He was compensated handsomely and often found himself the recipient of amorous attentions from attractive women whose pasty, flabby men would otherwise be denied entry to the very exclusive club. With the recent spate of closures of such gaming clubs like Cercle Haussmann, Cercle Wagram and the famous Aviation Club de France, Cercle Magique was a last chance to sit at a table in Paris and throw down Euros with the aplomb of Fleming's gentleman spy. The women would play the coquette and the men would pay liberally. It usually made for a good day.

Aleisu's lip curled at the approach of the mussed tourist headed his way. The man had a slightly crazy look in his eye. He also had no attractive female at his side. His indisputably tacky tourist t-shirt belied the likely presence of a fat wallet.

It was not shaping up to be a good day.

A green, oval-headed alien with slanted, bulbous eyes stared blankly from the man's canary yellow shirt. The red, block letters on the shirt read: "Not from around here."

A haughty sneer escaped Aleisu's lips. No kidding, he thought. No self-respecting Frenchman or Corsican would be caught in such a rag. American, no doubt.

"Excu-say-muah, see voo plate," Digger began in execrable French and removed all doubt.

If he noticed Aleisu's disdain, Digger either didn't care or wasn't going to be dissuaded.

"The taxi driver from the airport mentioned this here might be a good place to play a little cards." Digger traded in his deplorable French for an over-enunciated Texas drawl.

From his position behind a nearby lamppost, Jake winced.

"Distraction not drama, Dig. You're not trying for an Oscar here," he whispered under his breath.

"*Je suis désolé, monsieur, mais c'est un club reserve aux membres,*" Aleisu clipped.

The second guard began to sidle toward Aleisu, ready to offer his assistance if it became warranted. Digger discreetly threw a glance in Jake's direction. Jake gave a curt nod. Digger puffed up his barreled chest with all the pretentious indignity he could muster and bumped it into Aleisu's even broader one.

"Are you saying my money's no good here, *garçon*? Is it because I'm an American? You French think you're all high and mighty because you gave us the French toast and the French fry. Well, maybe you've heard of the ongoing obesity problem in the United States. That's on you, pal!" Digger began an orchestrated tirade. While the two colossal guards were preoccupied with Digger's sudden rant against all things French, Jake quietly slipped behind them and into the ground entrance of the club.

Once inside, it took Jake's eyes a moment to adjust to the dimmer illumination of the club. A narrow stairway lay directly in front of him with no other means of egress.

"Up, it is," Jake muttered to himself. Once upstairs, he was momentarily flummoxed. There was another set of doors barring the entrance to the main part of the club. This set was guarded by a petite brunette with a neatly manicured finger on an electronic buzzer. Digger could handle the goons outside. If he was lucky, they hadn't quite made pâté of him just yet. Jake would handle this one. Take one for the team. He flashed a brilliant smile at the demure receptionist. She buzzed him right in.

"*Bonjour, monsieur et bienvnue sur le Cercle Magique. Comment puis-je vous aider?*" The receptionist queried politely.

"Yes. You can help me. I am interested in a little play," Jake replied. The receptionist batted her long, velvety black lashes at him.

"*Mais oui,*" she replied. "Aren't we all? Do you have a membership with the club?"

"No, I'm afraid I don't," he responded.

"It is no matter. We can easily sign you up. Foreign visitors frequently join. I only need to see your passport and ask for one-hundred fifty Euros." It was a practiced speech and she began the efficient shuffle of paperwork and photo taking. She reached for Jake's right hand. He drew back instinctively.

"My apologies. One last formality. Members are required to scan their index finger. It is just an additional security measure. You will access the club via biometric reader, scan again when you wish to enter cash games, and once more when you exit the club."

A sharp edge of concern began to cut into Jake's resolve, but he proffered the pad of his right index finger. The receptionist smiled sweetly and expertly rolled his print across the glass of the scanner.

"*Tout fait!*" she bubbled cheerily and handed him a sleek, black membership card emblazoned with the Cercle Magique logo, a lop-eared hare. "Again, welcome to Cercle Magique. Enjoy your stay."

"I will," Jake replied. "*Merci beaucoup.*"

Jake did not notice the expedient fingers of the receptionist type in an email address, attach a file with Jake's fingerprints and photo, and hit send.

Jake moved into the main space of the club. A jazz band played on a small stage in a bar off the main entrance. They weren't bad. Jazz was a genre of music that evoked a mental time machine – transporting you back to a more laid-back, romantic era. Jake thought he recognized the signature tune of French cabaret singer Édith Piaf. An ironic chuckle escaped Jake's throat. "La Vie en Rose" was a song about reclaiming love in a time of war. His thoughts drifted briefly to Melina. Then slowly, the guilt crept in. Insidiously, like a dark shadow. He forced the unbearable weight aside. There simply wasn't time.

Now? Now it was time to locate Renaud. He moved through the club, eyes wary. On the plane, he'd studied the photograph of Cyprien Renaud. Clipped white beard over a determined jaw. Hard mouth. Thin lips. Eyes flat. Black. Like a great white. And equally ready for the next kill.

He continued past a well-appointed dining room. Hard to believe such a rumored ruthless killer could play any part in anything so, well, normal. He thought he spied escargot and was that beef wellington? But, no Renaud. What he did see was a broad-chested security guard across the room. Jake ducked his head and positioned himself behind the feathery frond of a majesty palm. His eyes continued to scan the room.

Another couple had already moved on to the dessert course, a golden crème brulée. Jake's stomach growled involuntarily. He was in Paris and the only thing he'd eaten was the stale peanuts on the plane.

The guard reached a hand to an inconspicuous earpiece. The man scowled in concentration. His dark eyes swept the dining area. His intense gaze lit on the potted palm. He muttered something into a communicator on his wrist and began to move in Jake's direction.

Time to relocate, Jake thought. He wheeled on his heel and started a brisk stride in the opposite direction. When he chanced a glance backward, the guard was gaining ground. Jake definitely had a shadow and it was stuck with more than soap.

Damn it, he cursed silently. He continued down the richly decorated hallway. Gilt accents on frames and candelabras gave off a warm glow, but Jake felt anything but warm and fuzzy as he tried to shake his tail.

He ducked into a nearby alcove and waited for the man to pass. He pressed his back flat against the wall trying to become one with the plaster. His gaze fell on the tapestry hanging on the opposite wall. Threaded through with golden filaments, it depicted a pale, yet beautiful lady and a gallant knight who quite clearly was tethered to her, by heartstrings if not solid bond.

La Belle Dame Sans Merci. Jake called to mind the Keats poem. Keats had been one of Stephanie's favorite poets. A lump lodged in his throat with the thought of his late wife. They had met, in fact, over a Keats poem. He spilled his beer all over it. Stephanie had been sitting in front of him at a Red Sox game, reading.

Who *read* at a Red Sox game, Jake remembered thinking, as the crowd had roared all around them. She stood up, dripping and indignant. Jake braced himself against the expected tongue-lashing. It never came. She had laughed. Just laughed. It was a beautiful laugh, clear and true. Her full, wide lips had been parted in a great, bright smile. The corners of her green eyes crinkled with the joy of laughter.

Jake had merely blinked. When her initial laughter subsided, she showed him the poem, now a bit soggy. It was Keats' *A Song About Myself.*

The first line of each stanza began: *There was a naughty boy. A naughty boy was he.* Then, love spoke.

"Talk about your naughty boys! Or does the naughtiness only extend to dumping beer on poor, unsuspecting women?" She winked seductively. For the next ten years, they stayed together.

Then spilled beer flowed into spilled blood. And the blood was on Jake's hands.

Undercover work required a certain type of individual. You needed intelligence. You needed patience. You needed a finger on the pulse of a less genteel society. The work demanded a chameleon. Someone who could code-switch without batting an eye in order to fit in with whomever the assignment lumped them in with at any given time. Jake had been that guy.

Three months into plotting and throwing back one-hundred fifty-one proof alcohol with the Winter Hill Gang was enough to wear at the resolve of any man. But, it had been a shot at the Gardner collection. At the end of it, Jake had looked like Henry Spencer meets Doc Emmett Brown after a long night with Jack Daniels. He worked as an errand boy for the largely Irish criminal organization. Cars. Drugs. Numbers. Whatever was required to enjoin the trust of the leaders of the group. But it did little for maintaining a stable marriage.

At first, the adrenaline kept Jake going — that surge of arousal undercover agents sometimes felt when considering the threat of discovery by the people they were charged with investigating. It was his coping mechanism. But, undercover work was isolated, with little to no support from colleagues. And when that coping mechanism failed?

Jake broke protocol. He risked a phone call to his estranged wife. But, the watcher was being watched. The people he had been investigating discovered his deception. Stephanie had paid for his mistake with her life. The White Hill bosses had showed no mercy.

La Belle Dame Sans Merci. Jake came back to the Keats tapestry. The lady without mercy. Not unlike the roiling tempest that was bearing down on Boston. Jake shook his head violently to dispel the reverie. No one else was going to die. Not on his watch.

He dared a peek into the hall. The coast was clear. He had to find Laurent. And to find Laurent, he needed Renaud. Now.

He darted out into the hallway. A quick survey of the poker tables yielded no Renaud. He did spy a number of discreet security cameras keeping a watchful eye over the gambling tables. Big brother was definitely cramping his mobility.

A sudden surge of thunderous applause echoed from nearby. Jake followed the sound to a crowded theater. The white-hot column of a follow-spot sliced through the throng of clapping patrons. Dust motes danced in the light. Jake tracked the beam to the stage where a voluptuous showgirl stood in a slight bikini and a clutch of feathers. The rounded moons of her areolas were the only surface of her full breasts that entertained coverage. Graduated arcs of diamond chains connected the nipple covers to the abbreviated triangle of bedazzled satin at the intersection of her thighs. Ah. France.

She held one shapely arm aloft, her hand in the grasp of the master magician at her side. It was Cyprien Renaud. He had just successfully performed the Straightjacket Escape and was now enjoying the adulation of his audience.

"*Merci. Merci.*" Jake's gut went cold as he swore Cyprien's steely gaze suddenly locked with his own. But there was no way Renaud could have seen his through the glare of the spot. Jake remained rooted to his position.

Renaud continued with his performance.

"My next trick is not, I fear, for the faint of heart. The first recorded instance of the illusion was noted in 1631. However, it was here in France, fifty years earlier, that master illusionist Coullew of Lorraine successfully performed the trick, catching a fired bullet in his bare hands."

The audience "oohed" and "ahhed", right on cue. For a split second, Jake entertained the notion that the whole thing was scripted.

Renaud let out a calculated, nervous chuckle. "While the trick is, in fact, immensely deadly, Monsieur Coullew arrived at his unfortunate demise not with a bullet, but when he was beaten to death with his own gun by a disgruntled assistant. Now, while I am certain that the lovely Colette would not enact such a barbarous act – well, why tempt fate, eh?" Renaud bowed and kissed the hand of his assistant. She smiled coquettishly and stepped back next to a small table dressed with a pearl-handled revolver. "So, I find myself in need of a brave volunteer from among our audience. Who is feeling *intrépide?*"

The spotlight broke the jewels on Colette's costume into the spectrum of dazzling colors. A rainbow danced on Jake's cheek and glanced into his eye. Jake held up a shielding hand.

"*Fantastique!*" Renaud declared. He held out a hand in Jake's direction. "We are lucky to have such a brave soul among our numbers!"

Jake's eyes drifted to the ominous-looking revolver on Colette's table. His intended *tête à tête* with Renaud had not included firearms. He turned, ready to beat a hasty retreat from the room. Looming in the doorway was his shadow.

"Come to the stage, *Monsieur!*" Renaud insisted. The audience applauded in encouragement. They did not appear to notice as the showman dropped from Renaud's voice and the Corsican mob boss sharpened the edges of his tone. "I insist."

CHAPTER FORTY

New Orleans, Louisiana

"Can it be done?" Mason demanded.

His brain was still trying to sift through the litany of facts Robert Hebert had spewed in the face of so many drawn weapons. The specter of corporate espionage had left him sniveling like an idiot.

Hebert held the patent on the superabsorbent polymer resin. The original process involved the refinement of one hundred percent organic, water-soluble ethylenically unsaturated monomers. While the polymers themselves were water soluble, cross-linking structures were introduced at the molecular level so as to render the polymer water insoluble. The resulting polymer could be mass produced in a uniform, small size with a peak gel capacity – like a million tiny sponges.

The owner of Sup-R-Absorb wished he had a sponge as he blotted furiously at his tie, trying to eradicate the red bean stain. He'd sat down at his desk expecting to enjoy a nice meal. Not be invaded.

"In theory, yes." Robert Hebert's voice wavered.

"Damn it! I don't have time for theories! There is a freak show of a hurricane barreling up the coast, ready to annihilate a major U.S. city! I need results, and I need them yesterday!" Mason smacked a flat palm on the surface of the desk, upending the plate of beans.

Even Southerners had their limits.

"You give me a plane, a pilot that can handle her, and I'll show you results!" Hebert blustered back. He snatched up a blank purchase order and slammed it into Mason's chest.

"But, it's going to cost you a lot of zeros." He looked back at his decimated lunch. "And a plate of red beans."

Mason tuned to one of his men. "Call the Commander at the Naval Air Station at Belle Chasse. He's an old pal of mine when the 926th Wing flew out of NAS New Orleans. Tell him I need a C-130 gassed up and ready to receive a payload."

"Yes, sir, but what makes you think he'll agree?" the man asked.

"He owes me one. A big one. Just do it," Mason ordered.

"Yes, sir. Do we need a pilot?"

"No," came Mason's dour reply. "This mission's mine."

CHAPTER FORTY-ONE

Paris, France

The City of Lights was an exercise in contradictions. In 1907, the city ruled that it was forbidden for casinos to operate within sixty-two miles of Paris. However, under the umbrella of an antiquated Parisian law, certain non-profit organizations that encouraged certain sporting, social, artistic or literary activity were readily allowed within city limits – gambling included.

Through the years, these clubs, or *cercles*, came to be associated with the French mafia or, more specifically, the Corsican mafia. The hot-blooded Corsicans had gotten a firm root in the poker clubs when the French government made the grateful, if misguided decision, to grant ownership of a number of these clubs to members of the Corsican mafia that had supported the French Resistance during World War II. The quick and easy profit that the clubs provided, their ability to facilitate black market employment and especially money laundering, made club ownership a hot commodity. As a result, vicious blood-feuds erupted between rival families broke out on a regular basis during the decade of disco.

Cyprien Renaud remembered it all.

He grew up in Marseilles, a city whose drug kingpins were immortalized by the 1971 film *The French Connection*. The film wasn't nearly as fictional as it was intended. With the biggest port in the western Mediterranean, Marseilles was a natural selection to process massive amounts of raw heroin coming in from the east and Turkey and then facilitate trafficking into the United States and other locations.

The crime was made worse by the poverty. With a large percentage of the population living below the poverty line and unemployment running rampant, the youth of Marseilles saw little prospect. So they turned to crime as a quick and easy way to ascend the socio-economic ladder. Marseilles was a university of crime, and there was an ample supply of willing students and teachers.

Renaud had been one of those students. Now, he was a teacher. Though sometimes the lessons he had to teach were hard ones. Just last week, four young men were shot dead waiting in their idling car at a traffic signal. Their infraction hadn't been that large – just running a few girls on the side – but, nevertheless, the lesson had to be taught.

The White Rabbit, as he was known, had started off in the Brise de Mer organization as a contract killer. There were about ten families in the organization, with a combined capital of over 150 million euro, divided among investments in Corsica, drug operations out of Marseilles, hostess bars, and even some legal ventures like tourism and construction. Renaud had worked for them all. Watching. Learning. Waiting.

By the early eighties, he had positioned himself to be a key figure, someone to contend with – and, equally, someone to be erased. Rival gang members once tried to take Renaud out in a hail of bullets. He was hit over twenty times, yet, somehow he survived – like magic.

That was when he became known as The White Rabbit, the man who magically could cheat death. He liked the name. He had even taken to signing his name in a semi-abstract swirl of swoops and lines that formed the vague outline of a lop-eared hare. He'd somehow even managed to sidestep any serious convictions over his long and storied career, serving only a minor sentence here and there. He began to think he *was* magic.

He'd carried the mystique of the magic angle even further, calling his club *Cercle Magique*. While gambling certainly went on within the confines of the club, Renaud fancied himself a modern day Houdini, and would often perform the late great magician's master tricks.

Now, Renaud was faced with another trick, dropped on his plate by Laurent. His teeth were bared in a theatrical smile as Jake stepped up on the spot lit stage.

"Where is your colleague? I was to understand you were travelling with a companion," he asked Jake, still beaming beatifically at his audience.

Jake grinned right alongside the mob boss. "Stayed home. Not a big people person, if you know what I mean."

"Hm. Americans. Blunt. To the point. But always with a sense of wit."

Jake let out a muffled chuckle. "Well, we try. Sometimes it's a little tricky."

"*Vraiment?* Well, try to escape this little trick."

Renaud turned to face his eager audience. "*Mesdames et Messieurs*! I assume you are familiar with the great magician Harry Houdini," Renaud announced with the booming projection of a consummate showman. He picked up a threatening-looking pistol.

Jake wondered where Renaud was going with this. He had a fair enough idea. It wasn't settling.

Renaud began extracting bullets from a box on the table and, one by one, inserted them into the gun. He continued to enthrall his audience with the tale of magic's greatest illusionist.

"Houdini performed a great many illusions over the course of his magical career. The Water Torture Cell. The Buried Alive Illusion. Even the Straightjacket Escape. There was one, however, that he never performed. More's the pity. It was truly chilling. Death-defying. It would have been a thrilling complement to his repertoire. Perhaps you have heard of it. The effect has claimed the lives of at least 15 magicians."

Renaud paused for dramatic emphasis. "The Bullet Catch."

The audience gasped on cue.

Jake swallowed audibly. This was not going at all according to his plan. Where in the hell was Digger, he thought. Beads of perspiration began to well across his forehead as Renaud continued to load the gun. The beautiful Colette began to tie Jake's hands behind his back.

"In the effect, a bullet is fired directly at the performer, and he or she catches the bullet in the teeth, hopefully without any ill effects. There are a number of ways to perform this trick, of course. Those who are brave enough to perform it are definitely courting disaster. Sometimes things go wrong. Equipment fails," Renaud paused, waving the muzzle of the gun nonchalantly through the air. "Or worse."

"How about a nice card trick, instead?" Jake suggested. "Cards are safe. And if you hold the deck just right, you can make one of those really cool waterfalls."

The audience bubbled with laughter. Renaud just smiled. He wasn't finished with his history lesson. He was the quintessential showman, and Jake was a captive audience.

"The most famous bullet-catching death was that of Chung Ling Soo, shot on stage in 1918. Rumors persisted that his death was not an accident caused by equipment malfunction, but was, *en effect*, a murder."

A collective gasp escaped the audience. "Tonight, we will perform this illusion. However, it will not be me catching the mortal bullet."

Jake looked just as bewildered as the people in the house. He'd caught this trick in Vegas once. This was not how it went. That cold feeling returned to the pit of his stomach.

"Tonight, our brave volunteer will catch the deadly projectile," Renaud paused. "Or, die trying, just like Chung Ling Soo."

A wave of fervor and concern undulated through the crowd. Renaud resumed loading the weapon. "Many people are unaware that Chung Ling Soo was an impostor. He passed himself off as Chinese when, in fact, the illusionist was an American of Scottish descent. He even stole his stage name after a rival magician, Ching Ling Foo. The bullet-catch performance that resulted in his tragic death was spurned by the same magician."

Renaud held his audience in his thrall, but the subtext was not lost on Jake. His cover had been blown. Renaud continued.

"So shocking was the death of Chung Ling Soo that magician Harry Kellar famously pleaded with Harry Houdini not to perform the Bullet Catch. Houdini listened to his friend, and never attempted to perform the trick."

As Renaud set the pistol back down on the table surface, Jake felt a glimmer of hope. Maybe he could still get out of this mess. Renaud stood close to Jake, leaning in for a more private aside.

"That is why I am better than the great Harry Houdini," the older man growled in Jake's face. Jake could smell the pungent vintage of the red wine that Renaud had been drinking.

"I am not crippled by fear. I can escape any trick." Renaud paused at that last. "Even death. Can you make that claim, Monsieur Riesen?"

With that, Renaud grabbed up the pistol, aimed it directly at Jake's face, and pulled the trigger.

CHAPTER FORTY-TWO

The echo of the shot reverberated through the theater. Colette screamed. Renaud crumpled in a heap to the ground. A pall of shocked silence draped the crowd. For a moment, nothing else moved. Then, suddenly, the spotlight operator swiveled the beam directly over Renaud. The large security guard rushed to Renaud's slumped form on the stage. The circular hole in the middle of Renaud's forehead was garishly apparent even without the spotlight. Jake swiveled his head from the direction of the shot. Without the stage lights in his eyes, he could just make Digger's running form line-backing his way through the bewildered crowd.

Digger clambered onto the stage and used the momentary confusion of the room to quickly free Jake from his bonds.

"Always gotta hog the spotlight, dontcha?" Digger admonished.

"Am I glad to see you, buddy!" Jake wiggled free of the loosened ropes. "I think we've worn out our welcome here."

"Oh?" Digger raised a quizzical eyebrow. "Really? What gave you that idea? The gun aimed at your face?"

"Oh, just come on!" Jake and Digger leapt from the stage, drawing the attention of the security guard who quickly fired off a string of French into the communicator at his wrist.

Digger and Jake tore through the club and headed for the door.

"How did you get past the guys at the door?" Jake asked.

Digger shrugged. "I just made some introductions. Their faces to the wall," Digger replied rather matter-of-factly. Jake managed a smirk. This was why he kept the odd little man around.

"Why are you wearing a delivery jumper?" Jake asked as he noticed the blue jumper his friend was now wearing.

"You know, it's amazing how quickly a woman will buzz open a reinforced security door if she thinks you're there to deliver her flowers. And I know where Renaud is, too. After she slipped me her digits, she might have mentioned he was headed to the Eiffel Tower with some chick."

"I thought you didn't speak French," Jake asked as they continued full-tilt toward the door.

"Turns out love is the universal language," Digger replied breathlessly.

"That's music, you idiot!"

"To-may-to, to-mah-to," Digger huffed.

The two men erupted from the steel door of Cercle Magique like they were shot from a cannon. They scrambled across the street and tore open the doors of their rented Peugot. The distinct echoing ping of a bullet ricocheting off rock followed them out the door and urged the duo to dive headlong into their respective seats.

"Drive, Dig! Drive!" Jake bellowed. Digger wasted no time insisting his foot meet the floor of the tiny car. The R-14s on the Peugeot screeched as the car peeled from the cobblestone alley. Digger snatched a furtive glance from the tiny rear window.

"Are they coming?" he demanded.

Jake twisted his neck for his own quick glance. "No."

Just then, several suits came tumbling out of the red door. Jake was not so much concerned with the men. There was no way they could catch them on foot.

The guns in their hands, however, gave him some cause for concern. Especially when the bullets they rapidly began emptying from them began to bounce off the Peugeot's fender.

"Aw, hell. Yes, yes, yes! Go!" Jake insisted.

The small red car exploded from the first roundabout exit at Place Charles de Gaulle onto Avenue des Champs-Élysées like an extra-large Atomic Fireball on wheels. The Arc de Triomphe loomed in the background, standing proudly, like a stiff, decorated general. Perfectly coiffed, close-cropped trees lined the Avenue like regimented bright green soldiers.

It wasn't long before Jake realized they were being followed. Three jet black motorcycles, Jake thought he recognized them as modified BMW R9Ts, plowed the road between them like so much chaff. The Metzeler ME880 Marathon tires made light work of the boulevard that took its name from the resting place of heroes in Greek mythology. Jake had no intentions on joining those heroes today.

"Come on, Dig." He smacked his buddy's shoulder with repeated insistence. "We need to go faster, Dig!"

"*Au point un kilometers, prendre à droite sur l'Avenue Winston Churchill.*" The clipped feminine French voice commanded from the GPS. Digger smacked the device several times.

"I *can't* go any faster! I don't speak French!" he retorted.

Digger swung the car wildly to the right, careening toward Pont Alexandre III. The pursuing motorcycles leaned a little more gracefully into the turn. As the cycles leaned back to rights, one cyclist sent a hail of bullets shattering through the rear glass.

A shower of tempered diamonds showered across the shoulders of Jake and Digger. Jake instinctively ducked. The immediacy of the bullets helped Digger find his *pied de plomb*. His lead foot nearly kicked through the floorboards to the pavement.

The little car leapt forward, successfully putting some distance between it and their pursuers. The gain was only temporary, however. Quickly, the motorcycles shifted gears, ducking and weaving through the congestion of traffic to again minimize the distance between them and the fleeing men.

Digger yanked the car into a hard right, crossing two lanes of traffic and eliciting some extraordinarily colorful French from several drivers. Digger gave a cursory wave.

"*Pardonnez-moi, s'il vous plait,*" Digger pronounced in halting French.

Digger's abrupt move caused one of the cyclists to lose control of his bike. It went skittering across the entrance to the bridge in a shower of golden sparks as metal scraped the length of pavement. Jake slapped the dash in celebration.

"Hah, hah! One down! Way to go, Dig. Only two more to go."

Digger grimaced. "Wow. Yeah. Like, no pressure there. Okay. Let's see if that trick works twice." With that, Digger jerked the wheel right again, this time onto Rue de Grenelle. The bikes stayed with them this time. L'Hôtel National des Invalides and its golden cupola rose up on the left hand side.

"You know I think that's where Napoleon's buried," Jake added as an aside.

"Oh, really?" Digger replied sarcastically.

"Yeah," Jake replied.

"Thank you, Tour Guide Barbie. But, as you may have noticed, I'm a little busy here…trying not to get DEAD!" Digger barked. The engine of the small car whined in protest as Digger bulleted down Avenue de la Motte-Picquet toward Avenue de Suffren and the tighter congestion of the 7th Arrondissement.

Digger dodged the tiny car through parked vehicles, narrowly missing a young mother shuttling her pram. He executed a quick S-move, avoiding certain tragedy.

Digger turned to Jake. "Next time, I pick the vacation destination, alright?"

Jake nodded. The motorcycles were still gaining, and as passage got narrower, Digger was finding it more and more difficult to navigate.

"You know something, Chief?" he asked Jake.

"What's that, *kemosabe*?"

"I really hate French cars."

"Oh, yeah? Why's that?" Jake kept stealing anxious glances at the encroaching motorcycles.

"They're just so, well, French."

"Oh! You mean stuffy."

"Exactly! Me? I miss my Jeep. Now that? That is a car."

"Is that right?" Jake replied. Digger nodded. Jake put one hand on the door handle. Well, I guess there's really just one thing to do then."

Digger and Jake grinned maniacally as Digger slammed on the brakes, tires squealing on the wet brick. Both men simultaneously threw open their doors as two of the cyclists closed the distance in an instant, unable to avoid Newton's Third Law. They connected with the solid doors with a deafening crack, the back tires of their bikes arcing awkwardly in the air behind them. As the motorcycles clattered to the ground, the assailants quickly regained their wits and reached into their zippered jackets for their weapons.

"Dig! Look out!" Jake warned his friend and connected a well-placed kick into the solar plexus of the cyclist on his side.

Digger quickly grabbed the outstretched arm of the gunman on his left and yanked his entire body forward, crashing his helmet into the solid window of the open car door. Jake leaned over to give his pal a hand, but Digger managed to successfully ram the dazed assailant's arm into the door frame, causing his gun to fall skittering onto the roof of the car.

"Oh, damn. Jake! Twelve o'clock!" Jake quickly looked up to spy that the man he had taken down with the kick had regained his wind and was now clambering atop the Peugot to retrieve his accomplice's firearm.

"Punch it!" Jake ordered, jamming his thumb in a backward direction. Digger gunned the car into reverse, ripping the doors off the poor Peugot. The helmeted man on the roof clung tightly, his body swaying dangerously back and forth as they caromed backward through the narrow street, until Digger once again slammed on the brakes and he went sailing into the plate glass of a nearby *poissonnerie*. The man landed on a cart of mackerel. The sign next to his limp head read *Captures du Jour.*

"Heh," Jake chuckled. "Catch of the day."

Digger and Jake look at each other, chests heaving, then broke out in sudden laughter.

"Well. There you go. We did it. Told ya so," Jake prodded.

"What?" Digger scoffed. "You did not. And what's this 'we'? As I recall, I was the one doing all the driving."

Digger was about to launch into a long, drawn out lecture on the subject when he noticed Jake's long stare out the shattered back window.

"You'd better do some more of that driving then," Jake began. Digger followed Jake's stare out the window to see a pack of seven more cycles bearing down Avenue de Suffren and heading directly for them.

"Cause here comes the cavalry," Jake finished.

"Yeah," Digger replied.

"Yeah," Jake nodded in agreement. Against three guys, they had a shot. Seven on two? Not odds they cared to take. The White Rabbit's men certainly wanted them to disappear.

The doorless, windowless compact tore off like a bat out of hell. The rushing wind buffeted Jake so hard he dug his nails into the dash in the hopes of not falling from the car. When he wasn't hanging on for dear life, he kept sneaking furtive glances out the back window frame.

"What's the sit rep, boss?" Digger hollered over the whistling wind.

"Not good," came Jake's reply. "They're gaining, and they're gaining fast. Does the thing have any more get up and go?"

"If it does, it got up and went," Digger yelled. "Hang on. Looks like we got hard right coming up."

Jake braced himself for the turn. Digger cut the corner at Quai Branly so hard the Peugot went up on two wheels. Digger nearly toppled from the vehicle, saved only by Jake's quick snag. As the car bounced back down to all four wheels, Jake looked back one more time to see how much time they had before the cycles caught them.

He didn't see the parked tow vehicle angled directly in front of them, its bed levered down to the pavement in preparation to receive its charge. The Peugot was traveling too fast for Digger to alter his course and the car sailed up the incline.

"Hey, Jake? How do you say 'oh, shit' in French?" Digger shouted.

"What?" Jake shouted back. He turned just in time to see the concrete wall along the banks of Seine disappear beneath them.

"*Merde!*"

CHAPTER FORTY-THREE

Like the long, aquiline nose of a toffee-nosed Frenchman, the dark spire of the *Tour d'Eiffel* thrust upward into the Parisian sky, indifferent to its surroundings. It was not readily apparent what function the three hundred twenty-four meter tower served and, yet, your gaze felt a certain, inexorable pull toward it.

The brainchild of Gustav Eiffel, an architect from Dijon, the towering behemoth had not always enjoyed the adoration of its Parisian subjects. Writers, artists and other societal figures of note had lobbied against its initial construction in 1888, and, in fact, continued to declare the giant "A" over the Champs de Mars a pitiful eyesore. Guy du Maupassant was among the most vocal of the icon's detractors, though nearly every midday meal found him lunching in the tower's dining facilities. It could not be helped. It was as if the two million plus steel rivets were magnetic, eventually drawing one and all to admire it.

Of course, Maupassant would argue he dined within the tower because it was the only location in Paris where he did not have to endure the sight of the ten thousand ton monstrosity!

"It's freakin' tall," Digger blurted, breaking the momentary spell.

He and Jake stood like insignificant ants at the foot of the barbican, staring upward in a kind of slack-jawed reverence. The architectural adoration was short-lived, however, driven by the pressing motive behind their visit.

They were here to barter for Melina's life and try to stop Laurent's insane plan.

A building disquiet urged Jake's steps forward toward the south pillar of the tower and the crisp black awning with the white, minimalist lettering that heralded the Michelin-starred restaurant, Jules Verne.

As the two men stepped into the exclusive elevator car, indeed, they found themselves plunged into the steampunk-flavored world of *20,000 Leagues Under the Sea*. The elevator traveled diagonally, upward four hundred and ten feet toward the tower's second tier and the restaurant. It was no great surprise the riveted leviathan conjured images of Nemo's *Nautilus*. With its dedication ceremony taking place in 1889, the Eiffel Tower was a contemporary of the restaurant's namesake.

"You really think Melina's going to be here?" Digger asked Jake.

"No. No, I don't," Jake replied curtly. The elevator continued its climb.

"So, you think this is a trap?"

"Yes. Yes, I do."

Digger shifted uncomfortably in his new clothes. "So, I don't get it. If you think Laurent is pulling a fast one, why come?"

The elevator began to slow its two meters-per-second-pace. Jake turned to his friend. "Same reason I'd come for you."

Digger dipped his head in an acknowledging nod, then busied himself worrying at the waistband of his pants. The remaining trip ascended in silence.

A cheery ding announced the car's arrival at its final destination. The elevator doors opened and Jake stepped out.

Digger remained in the car, apparently unaware they had stopped. He clutched futilely at the thighs of his tight pants, searching for a hold on the fabric, but there was not an extra centimeter to be grasped.

"I thought the French loved food," Digger groused. "You'd have to live on rabbit rations for these pants to fit right! Stupid river. I mean, really! Who puts a river in the middle of the street?"

"Wasn't a river, Dig. It was a canal."

"River. Canal. Whatever! It was wet!" Digger barked. The elevator doors began to close. He executed a nifty little hop to clear the closing panels. As he looked up, his apparent irritation with all things French melted away.

The two men looked out over the sprawling vista that was Paris. The entire city was framed in the window of the neo-futuristic dining room, like the bottom of the sea from the viewing window of the *Nautilus*. The Arc de Triomphe was represented in one corner, the Champs-Élysées in another. Vigilant eyes could pick out the Basilique du Sacré-Cœur in the distant Montmartre district.

But the visual candy was not reserved to the exterior view. To enter into the dining room of the Jules Verne was a rare moment. It was a calorie-laden step into rich chocolates and toasted beige. One hundred and twenty leather and carbon fiber seats anticipated ravening guests eager to sample *une degustation*, a brilliant pairing of French culinary heritage with *nouvelle cuisine*. Foie gras ravioli with black truffles served in a delicate broth. Or, perhaps the *belle langoustine refraîchie* in cauliflower cream and topped with gold caviar.

Of course, these brilliant epicurean marriages were not simply reserved to the plated fare. The Jules Verne boasted a wine list four hundred thirty selections strong. *Incontournable* choices from wine regions across France, vintages not to be missed. There were even a few incursions into more far-flung provinces – the deep color and pure fruit of New Zealand wines, the noticeable sweetness of Argentina's vigorous grapes, vintages from Spain, Greece and even Switzerland.

Remy Laurent sat like an unflappable Dionysian monarch ruling over his culinary kingdom. A semi-eaten meal occupied the plate in front of him. A swirl of wine twirled in the bowl of his glass, so deeply red it was nearly black. Jake caught the hint of disgust crinkled across the bridge of his nose. He wasn't certain if it was the escargot or the presence of the two Americans that was causing him the apparent intestinal upset. As Laurent spoke, all doubt dissolved.

"I don't believe you gentleman have a reservation." A disingenuous smile pulled the corners of Laurent's mouth up with some effort.

"It's okay. We're bad tippers anyway," Digger parried back. Laurent stood.

"I fail to comprehend you Americans. All I'm trying to do is take advantage of a bear market. Granted, it's a market of my own design, but I would have thought people of your capitalist society would understand that."

"By playing God?" Jake countered.

"*Vraiment?*" Laurent cocked an eyebrow. "Where, then, is the, how do you say, 'smoking gun'? Do you have any proof?" A light chuckle escaped Laurent. "Proof that anyone who doesn't have a tin foil hat for every day of the week would believe."

Digger started. "Hey! I resemble that remark!"

Jake dug an elbow into Digger's side. The shorter man fell obediently silent.

Laurent's smile became a little more real. "Gentlemen. Face facts. The scenario you are purporting is nothing more than colorful science fiction. If there were any validity to what you are claiming, the legitimate scientific community would have come forward instead of you – a washed up FBI agent and a lunatic conspiracy nut."

Jake's eyes narrowed. His voice dropped an octave as he took a step closer to Laurent. "The legitimate scientific community *did*. Her name was Katarina Sørensen and *you* had her killed."

Laurent took his own step in, putting himself nearly nose to nose with Jake. His voice growled out in a guttural whisper. "Call it 'natural selection'."

Jake leaned back and threw a solid right cross. The punch whiffed through empty air. Laurent had deftly dodged the blow. One of his henchmen quickly neutralized Jake, pinning his arms behind his back. Digger started, but checked himself as another man aimed the muzzle of a gun at his face.

Laurent tugged the cuffs of his sleeves straight. "Herbert Spencer explained it best. It is survival of the fittest and I simply did not see Miss Sørensen fit to survive."

Jake thrashed in the vise-like grip of his captor. "You sonovabitch! And Melina? Where is she? What did you do with her?"

"What? The indomitable Miss Flores? I do believe she finally found what she's been searching for." Laurent glanced at his Rolex. "And right about now I'd say she's enjoying a vigorous swim."

Jake and Digger exchanged glances.

"The storm," they replied in unison.

Laurent tugged the cuffs of his sleeves straight. "Oh, I do hope she wore a good wetsuit. I hear the water is quite chilly this time of year."

Laurent nodded toward Digger. The second henchman grabbed his muscled arms from behind.

"I wouldn't do that if I were you," Jake cautioned.

Laurent laughed. "I do not believe you are in any position to direct orders."

"It's not so much a direct order. More like a public service announcement."

"Dispose of them," Laurent barked. "I have a boat to catch."

The next few moments exploded in a blur of motion. Digger snapped his head back. It became readily apparent where some of the crisscrossing scars webbed across his shaved head originated. His skull made crushing contact with the septum of the man holding him. A decided pop cracked through the air, decibels louder than the man's yowls. Everything froze.

A look of stunned surprise altered Laurent's facial features. The Frenchman looked down where his hands covered a crimson stain blossoming across his abdomen. He fell to his knees.

"*C'est quoi ça?*" He muttered with incredulity.

Digger stood in a solid shooting stance across the room. Gun at the ready, smoke still wisping from the barrel. "Survival of the fittest, dumbass."

Laurent fell face forward. The man holding Jake rushed to his side. Jake seized the opportunity. He tucked his head down and charged the man. He body-checked him into the bar with the force of a Pamplona bull. Newton's third law of motion whipped the man's head at a decidedly unnatural angle as his body collided with the curved edge of the bar. His temple cracked against the unforgiving, polished wooden surface. It bounced back, significantly dented, but the man used the momentum and his own body weight to shove Jake to the floor.

Jake felt the rush of wind crush from his lungs. He sucked in against the pain and drew his knees in toward his chest. As the massive Corsican barreled toward him, intent on completing the job, Jake leveraged his legs in an upward thrust, straight into the man's abdomen. Jake drew in his legs once again and catapulted himself to a standing position, right arm extended into a fist-ended battering ram that crunched into the Corsican's nose. Garnet spurted from the man's face. He blindly swung in Jake's general direction. The punch whispered through empty space.

Jake had ducked low. He wrapped his arms around the man's thick waist and gave a mighty heave to the right. The Corsican sailed, arms splayed, and crashed through a wall of frosted glass. Jake leapt over the jagged teeth. Boots crunched across the glass. He descended upon the man and drove his knees into his chest, pinning him to the ground.

Three solid jabs connected with the man's face. As Jake raised his right arm readying to pile drive his fist once more, the man on the ground brought a well-placed knee up into Jake's groin. Galaxies exploded in Jake's vision and the sudden compelling urge to vomit surged through him. He rolled sideways, curled into the fetal position, trying to stave the unspeakable pain. The bloodied Corsican dragged himself to his feet, his face resembling a pound of freshly ground beef. He gave an angry swipe across his face to clear the blood from his vision. He reached down and grabbed a hunk of Jake's hair and yanked him to his feet. Jake wobbled where he stood. The Corsican reached back and swung a mighty sidearm toward the left side of Jake's head. Jake retained just enough wherewithal to duck backward, but the Corsican was helpless to halt the follow-through of his own punch. As he spun round to the left, he left his back vulnerable to attack. Jake seized the opportunity and drove a well-placed kick to the back of the Corsican's knee. The man crumpled, knees crunching into the broken shards of glass. He bellowed like a stuck boar. Jake slapped one hand against the man's thick neck. He quickly slid the other hand under the armpit of his opponent, locking the free arm around his other wrist and squeezed. He held on, even as the big man stumbled to his feet and drove his body weight backward, slamming Jake into the solid wall. He repeated the drive, over and over, but Jake held fast, tightening his grip till the man turned an unsightly shade of violet. The blows grew progressively weaker as his body slowly converted the available oxygen into carbon dioxide waste. Eventually, the man simply collapsed, his brain starved of life-sustaining oxygen. The Corsican fell forward, dragging Jake with him. Jake landed on top of the man's back, near breathless himself and remained there, motionless.

Across the room, Digger was enjoying his own *tête à tête* with the bar. In Digger's case, he was thrown backward, arms flailing, and his neck snapped back, skull connecting hard with the bar surface. The force knocked the gun from his hand. It skittered across the floor, just out of reach.

Digger shook his noggin a bit and gave a curt nod of approval to his opponent, a leaner man with heavily-hooded eyes in a weasely angular face. The angle of his nose was now slightly askance, courtesy of Digger's earlier head smack. It lent his features a slightly Picasso flavor.

"Not bad. Your sister teach you that?" Digger proffered a cocky smile.

Digger may not have spoken much French, or even Corsican for that matter, but apparently trash talk was universally understood. His adversary took three rapid swings in succession – right, left, right – but none of them connected. Digger dodged each one in swift order. As another taunt, he playfully smacked the back of his opponent's head. He took a quick jog forward and spun round to face the man again.

Digger succeeded in swatting away the man's next few blows and managed to get in a few stinging back-handed slaps against The Weasel's face with his knuckles. On his fourth try, he wasn't quite quick enough. The man shoved him across the room into the wall near Jake.

Digger stole a brief glance at his prone pal. "Hey, there, Jakester. How's it going?"

The panting query elicited a low groan from Jake.

"Really? That good? Okay. So when you're done napping, feel free to jump in at any time." Digger paused. "Alright. Good talk."

Digger dove back into the fray. He readied his fists in a traditional boxing stance, ready to jab. Unfortunately, his opponent subscribed to a more unconventional style, Edmund Prys' treatise be damned. With a powerful hook reminiscent of Rocky Graziano, The Weasel cracked into Digger's jaw. Digger spun one hundred eighty degrees and crashed prostrate over one of the dining tables. China shattered. Crystal exploded. Digger groaned audibly.

A satisfied smirk spread across The Weasel's face. He spat a fat glob of blood and phlegm to the floor and began a slow strut toward Digger to finish the job.

"Now who fights like my sister, huh?" The Weasel taunted in heavily-accented English.

Suddenly, Digger shot up, catching the slighter man by surprise. He hooked his fingers beneath the table and flipped it, end over end, toward him. Tableware and linens went flying, obscuring The Weasel's field of vision for just a moment. The man shot his fist out in a blind jab. Digger saw it coming a mile away and neatly blocked it. He countered with a swift left cross to The Weasel's jaw. The punch connected, throwing him off balance. Digger widened his arms out to the sides and clapped his cupped palms quickly and solidly over The Weasel's ears. The blow induced the intended vertigo and loss of balance as twin columns of air forced their way through the skinny man's alimentary canals. The resultant disorientation urged a wild, forceful swing. Digger side-stepped the angry blow easily enough. He drove the heel of his right hand into the man's side. Digger was almost certain he heard a rib crack. A second wild punch swung in from the right. Digger swept his right arm down on a sweeping arc and blocked the blow. He turned into it and threw up his left elbow. It crashed into the man's mandible. The Weasel's head snapped to his left. Digger finished what he started with a well-aimed left cross to the heavy jaw bone and shattered it. He directed another serious blow to the solar plexus. As the man doubled over, Digger felt certain the ribs cracked clean through this time. He leaned back to give himself a counterweight and delivered a crushing, winding kick to the man's diaphragm. The Weasel bent in half at the waist and sailed backward, landing in a motionless heap.

Digger collapsed, adrenaline spent. He crawled slowly, picking his way through the broken glass, and sat braced against the wall next to Jake.

"Next time," he managed through heaving breaths. "Next time can we just go to the place with the mouse? Did you know they have Walt Disney's head cryogenically frozen? Him and Einstein. I'm thinking of having that done, actually."

Jake dragged himself to a sitting position. "You know what we have to do, right?"

"Go back to the hotel and order room service?" Digger opined hopefully. Jake shook his head.

"Aw, man! Come on! Can't you call Ethan Hunt or something?" Digger sighed heavily. "Fine. Rescue the girl. Stop the storm. Save the world. Did I leave anything out?"

Jake smiled as Digger rose to his feet.

"But, just so you know, when we get home, I'm moving my bunker and I'm *not* leaving a forwarding address!"

CHAPTER FORTY-FOUR

The Atlantic

As Melina came to, she felt the undulating motion of water beneath her. This wasn't the gentle bobbing of the harbor, though. No. This time Poseidon was dry-heaving after an all-nighter at the sand bar. The outer bands of Hurricane Hera must have reached Boston already.

She planted her palms flat on the deck, half in an effort to steady herself and half to push herself to a sitting position.

"What?" She drew her hands back in surprise when they splashed into an inch of water that was rising fast. She was no merchant marine, but she was pretty certain that wasn't normal. She fought the violent pitch and sway of the ship and put herself to rights. Her captors must have assumed she would still be out cold from the blow she took to the face for they hadn't bothered re-securing her bonds. No doubt they had figured on dumping her limp, lifeless body into the murky depths of the Atlantic long before she regained consciousness.

"Sorry to be a disappointment, fellas, but Daddy always said it was a bad idea to assume," she muttered to herself and started looking for an escape route. A sudden thought brought her up short. Why *hadn't* she been schlepped overboard yet? She stole a glance at her watch. Liquid had beaded under the crystal. She tapped the face. Probably from the water accumulating in the hold. It didn't really matter. There was no way she could be certain of the elapsed time, but it certainly didn't take that long to sail out past the Harbor Islands and out into the Atlantic. If what she had heard the men say was true, she should have been shark bait by now.

She spied a door across the way. Melina stumbled towards it, bracing herself clumsily against the bulkheads as the ship tossed. She had almost made it when the ship began a sudden, heavy list. Everything, including Melina, slid to the right, piling against the starboard bulkhead of the compartment.

Every item that hadn't been battened down was on top of Melina – an assorted mismatch of crates, cylindrical tubes, and heaving line. Blood trickled from a wound on her forehead where one of the crates had gouged her. She shoved the offending wooden box off her.

"Damn it!" She probed the cut to gauge its severity. "That's gonna leave a mark."

She muttered a few more colorful epithets before her eyes fell on the crate's labeling. A large, red bird had been spray-painted on the side along with the letters P.R.U.

Melina started. "Phoenix Research Unlimited!"

That's when she began to register the shapes of all the detritus that had clobbered her as it slid across the deck. The crate was just about large enough to hold a missing Chinese *ku*. She did the mental math and quickly added up the number of containers. Twelve. Nearly the number of

missing pieces from the Gardner collection. She scrabbled through the pile
and grabbed the cylinder nearest to her. Her fingers felt like uncoordinated
sausages as she tried to work off the threaded end of the cylinder. She
wasn't sure if her heart was hammering because of what she might discover
in the tube or because the inside or the boat was beginning to resemble an
Escher drawing as it continued to list. Down was becoming up and vice
versa. Melina was running out of time.

The cylinder popped as the end finally came free. Melina quickly
looked inside. A rolled canvas! She stuck her long fingers into the empty
space, pinched the canvas and drew it from the container. She unrolled the
old canvas with controlled reverence. Her eyes immediately flicked to the
dark, lower right hand corner of the painting. She knew what she was
looking for. There, inscribed on a rudder, was the prize – a signature with
an artistic, calligraphic flow.

Rembrant f/ 1633

Experts often contended over the missing letter in Rembrandt's
signature, omitted in many of his earlier works. Some suggested that it was
omitted for practical reasons   the artist had merely run out of room. It
mysteriously reappeared sometime after 1635.

A shaky laugh bubbled up inside Melina. Like the missing letter, the
painting had resurfaced.   And she had found it. She quickly opened the
remaining containers. Napoleon's finial. Vermeer's *The Concert*. The Flinck.
Chez Tortoni by Manet. Degas. She had found them all!

The ship groaned a warning. Melina shook herself from her reverie.
Unless she wanted to disappear into history like the Gardner artwork had,

she had to get to a radio.

Six inches of water now lapped at her calf. She needed to get to one fast.

She rapidly replaced the canvases in the waterproof cylinders. She closed the crates with the *ku* and the finial as best she could. Her eyes darted for a secure spot to safeguard the precious cargo while she searched for a radio. Water seeped in faster by the minute. She lodged the canvases up high in a wooden support beam. Though, at the rate the ship was heeling over, up would not be up much longer. As she began to wedge the last cylinder in the beam, she hesitated. What if she couldn't get all the paintings out to safety? It was impossible to put more worth on any one of the particular pieces. But, *The Storm?* It was Rembrandt's only seascape. It was the main reason she had ventured on this crazy search to begin with.

The Storm on the Sea at Galilee. A piece on faith. In the turbulent scene depicted by the painting, the disciples had lost faith. Melina thought of the tumultuous storm that was her life. She, like the disciples, had lost faith. Then she met Jake. A beam of hope had begun to cut through the chinks in the dark clouds.

On impulse, she slung the cylinder holding *The Storm* over her shoulder and started to scrabble for the door, fighting for purchase with every step.

"Save a little faith," she mumbled to herself.

She hadn't heard a peep from her captors, but she erred on the side of caution and opened the door carefully. A quick recon confirmed the coast was clear. Melina pulled the door wide. The bottom edge sloshed through the continued rise of salty water.

As she opened the path to the ship's engine room, a wall of suffocating heat crushed Melina in the chest. It had to be over one hundred degrees in the machine-filled room. Two diesel engines on either side moaned in futility against the power of the storm. Her hands searched for a surface to brace against the vicious rock of the ship, but everything was scalding to the touch.

There were two generators to run complementary power to the diesels – one port, one starboard. Only the starboard generator appeared to have any life left in it. An ironic chuckle escaped Melina's throat. If she didn't find a radio soon, she wasn't going to have much life left in her either.

She squeezed past the large fuel bays, sweat and saltwater plastering her clothes to her lithe body. She reached a ladder and started to climb. She made her way to the bridge, unaccosted. Her captors were nowhere to be found. She gulped audibly.

Neither were the vessel's life rafts.

She rushed into the radio room. Without hesitation, she fired up the radio. What was the damned marine emergency channel? She dredged up the life-saving numbers from the recesses of her memory banks. Quickly, she dialed in frequency 161.400. She pushed the DSC button. Even if the Coast Guard couldn't hear her mayday call, at least her GPS coordinates had a chance of getting through. She grabbed the handset and hit the PPT button.

"Mayday. Mayday. Mayday. This is Melina Flores aboard *The Fortune's Tide. The Fortune's Tide. The Fortune's Tide.*" She repeated the vessel name several times per maritime distress protocol.

Melina lost her footing as the ship lurched. The handset flew from her hand. She scrambled to pick herself up and retrieve it. She continued her distress call.

"I repeat. Mayday. The vessel *The Fortune's Tide* is currently located," her eyes darted over the instrument panel and quickly gathered necessary information. "Position 54 25 North 016 33 West, drifting at one knot with a bearing of 228 degrees. We are taking on water quickly and are in need of immediate assistance. This is *The Fortune's Tide*. Over."

Then, suddenly, Melina came to the world's end. A twelve foot wave crashed over the tilted deck and snapped off part of one of the two hundred foot masts. She ducked just in the nick of time as some of the splintering wood shattered the glass above the computer console. Briny water washed over the electronics. Sparks erupted and all the lights on the panel died.

"No, no, no!" Melina swore. She pounded an ineffective fist on the console. It was no use. The radio was not coming back to life. She looked at the angry sea roiling in tempestuous black waves under a morbid sky then looked at the tubular container strapped to her back. She had to have faith that her message got through. Faith that someone had heard her cries for help. She clutched *The Storm* tightly to her chest.

CHAPTER FORTY-FIVE

Raleigh-Durham, North Carolina

"And you're sure she's on board?" Mason asked Jake as they crossed the tarmac at North Carolina's Raleigh-Durham airport. After loading the polyacrylamide in New Orleans, Mason had relocated the C-130 and its crew to the new position. It was the closest airstrip near the hurricane that hadn't been closed due to gale force winds. If they were going to launch this insane plan to quell the storm, this was ground zero. Now, it looked as though they were going to have to launch a rescue mission as well.

Jake nodded as the wind whipped his hair back from his forehead. "A Finnish oil tanker was the only vessel within hailing distance. The captain picked up the call and her coordinates before communications went dark. That was the best he could do with conditions the way they are out there. Wind speeds up to seventy knots in places and the driving rain is killing the radar. You couldn't see the QEII if it was on top of the Titanic through that mess. If it weren't for the distress call, we wouldn't have even know she was out here. Coast Guard can't get its cutters out there. The Jayhawks wouldn't stand a chance. You've got to fly the Hercules out there. Get close enough to establish communication and assess what the hell the situation is. Then drop your cargo and pray to god it's enough to stop this thing in its tracks and we can get rescue choppers out there.

Mason pulled up short. "Rescuing a single individual was not part of this arrangement. It's too risky. The mission is too important."

Jake looked Mason dead in the eye. "You do this, you'll be rescuing two."

For a man who did not play well with others, Mason understood. He gave a curt nod which Jake returned in kind.

"Hey, are we gonna get this show on the road, or what?" Digger called from the hinged loading ramp at the rear of the plane's fuselage. "She's all gassed up and ready to roll."

"I'll stand by with the MH-60s. When you give the go ahead, we'll move out," Jake called over the echoes of Mason's footfalls on the metal ramp. The ramp motor hummed as the jaws of the giant beast clamped shut.

The interior of the C-130 hummed with activity. Special meteorological instrumentation had been loaded onto the aircraft to monitor the storm: several computers; radars; data collection hardware; and a laundry list of scientific and navigation instruments. Aboard the plane, it was a motley crew. Besides Mason and his cockpit crew, a group of electronic engineers were on hand. They busied themselves with powering up computers and monitoring the fragile circuit boards. Maintenance crew members went about pre-flight inspections. Extra care was given to every detail – nothing left to chance. Mason made his way past the flight director's station, set back just behind the cockpit. Stacks of aviation charts covered the flat surfaces along with a copy of the flight plan which would take them directly into the eye wall of the storm.   Cam Jensen, the mission's flight director, stood with a larger, bearded man in a bowling shirt, poring over instrument calibration tables.   Both men turned upon Mason's approach. Jensen held out a hand in greeting.   The bearded man stood slightly back.

"Colonel Mason.   It's an honor, sir.   We've finished our pre-flights checks.   Personnel are geared up. All systems are fully operational."

Mason nodded. "And my crew?"

"Already in the cockpit, sir."

"Good," Mason replied.   "This is Master-at-Arms Second Class Grover Kelley. This whole nutty professor experiment was his crazy idea."

"Well, if it works, I'll be the first man to buy you a drink, Kelley." The bearded man spoke.   "Hugh Peterson.   Head of the science team from NOAA.   It's no exaggeration to say this storm is a downright killer.   My team's been going over the data.   If what we've calculated is accurate, that little dust-up Hera had in Cuba and Haiti will look like camel spit compared to what she's bringing to the northeast U.S.   There will be catastrophic casualties."

Peterson extended a hand to Mason and Digger.   Peterson continued as the men shook.

"And there's something else."   Peterson and Jensen exchanged worried glances.   "One of our scientists is missing.   An ex-pat Russian. Once this system really started cooking, we called for all hands on deck. He never reported in. When we couldn't raise him on the horn, we sent people to his house. Didn't find him. But, what they did find was disturbing."

Peterson paused.

"Well?" Mason barked.

"Our man, Akimenkov? He had worked up hurricane models. Granted, that's part of what we do at NOAA, but Akimenkov? He had worked these models up before Hera was even a tropical depression. What's more, he plotted the exact course that Hera is taking. Almost down to the exact latitudes and longitudes and times it would hit each target. Now, how could he have possibly known which way a monster storm like that was going to go?"

"Unless he was steering it," came Mason's somber reply. "Where does he have it headed next?"

"Right into Boston." Peterson glanced at his watch. "In less than three hours.

Digger cleared his throat. "So, being the resident crazy person in the room, can I make a crazy suggestion? Let's get this bird in the air. Like, yesterday."

"Wheels up. Now," Mason ordered and turned for the cockpit.

CHAPTER FORTY-SIX

Digger followed Mason into the cockpit. Two other men were already strapped in. Mason gestured to the man nearest to him.

"Master Sergeant, I want you to meet Dante Rodrigue, our co-pilot. Flew P-3s for Uncle Sam for twenty years. Damned good at his job, too. Even if he is Navy."

Rodrigue shook Digger's hand. "Good to meet you. I hear we have you to thank for the on-board snack choice."

"The super-size Jell-O cup down in the cargo bay?" Rodrigue prompted.

"Oh, yeah. That. Guess I am," Digger replied with a half-laugh.

Rodrigue returned to his seat. "Man. Would I have loved to see the requisition order come through for that one. Some government bureaucrat probably choked on his five-hundred dollar latte. Classic."

"Hey, I'm Steve McKean. Flight engineer." The wiry young man near Digger shook hands. "It's my job to monitor engine performance, fuel consumption, and other critical aircraft function."

"In other words, if the plane goes down, it's his fault," Rodrigue joked. The two crew members laughed.

Digger chuckled nervously, remembering his last flight and love affair with the sick bag. He looked around the cockpit. "Great. Just point me in the direction of the parachutes."

The men laughed even harder. Digger looked blankly at them. "What?"

"We don't carry parachutes on this aircraft," Mason replied from his pilot's chair. "Wouldn't do you a damned bit of good where we're headed."

"That's it," Digger muttered. "I'm trapped in *Final Destination*."

"Aw, come on. It's not that bad. We haven't lost a bird yet," McKean joked.

Jensen poked in his head. "Twelve bodies present and accounted for, Colonel."

"Did he have to say 'bodies'?" Digger groaned.

"Good," Mason replied. "Better strap in, Kelley. This ride's gonna get a little bumpy."

Digger moaned, but dutifully shuffled back to the flight director's station and strapped himself into his lap buckle and shoulder harness.

"Prepare to start engines," Mason warned his crew. He donned his headset and prepared for takeoff.

The C-130's engines gave the familiar whump as they fired up and roared to life. The g-forces pressed Digger against his seat as the monster plane chewed up the runway then lumbered into the air.

Mason set the big plane on a northeasterly path. The altimeter marked their altitude at ten thousand feet once they leveled out.

"What track are we taking?" Mason called from the cockpit.

Jensen punched in a few numbers and his console and hollered back.

"Take us to oh-six-oh. If we need to adjust once we start hitting funk, I'll let you know!"

"Roger that. Turning to heading oh-six-oh." The massive airplane took a gentle bank to meet the new heading then leveled out.

Digger stole a glance at the swirl of reds and oranges that suddenly dominated Jensen's radar screen. He pointed. "Is that the hurricane?"

Jensen followed Digger's gaze. "What, that? That, my friend, is Mother Nature getting ready to whip our ass. And we're about to tell her she's ugly and her momma dresses her funny."

"Great. Just great," Digger mumbled.

"That's not the worst of it," Jensen responded.

"There's more?"

"Oh, yeah," Jensen began. He tapped a well-defined circular area on the screen, ringed with bright orange and red. "See this tight little space here? This little circle is the eye of the storm. And it's only thirteen miles wide. Hurricanes with eyes this tight and defined? Let's just say I'd rather get a root canal."

"That good, huh?" Digger managed a half-grin.

Jensen nodded. "Without anesthetic. So if we get into trouble, that doesn't leave us much room to maneuver."

"Standby." Mason's voice popped over the loudspeaker. "We're almost at our descent point. Hold on to your stomachs. The drop's going to be fun."

He nosed the big bird into a thousand foot per minute descent. Digger got that roller coaster sensation as his stomach took up momentary residence in his throat.

"Wow! Take a gander at those feeder bands!" Rodrigue exclaimed. Mounds upon mounds of puffy cumulus congestus, looking like so much giant cauliflower, towered in organized lines that corkscrewed toward the eye of the storm. Below, the wind whipped the flat, steel blue of the ocean's surface into a capped froth.

"And there she is," Peterson pointed. The bearded man didn't need to point. It was impossible to miss the colossal flat wall of cumulonimbus before them, obscuring their view.

"Set Condition One!" Mason called into his handset. His voice bellowed loud and authoritatively throughout the whole of the aircraft.

Jensen and Peterson scrambled to stow the charts, documents, bags and other loose gear around their station.

"Condition One?"

"Stash everything that's not bolted to the floor, 'cause things are about to get bumpy," Jensen replied.

Suddenly, heavy, somber clouds consumed them. Day segued into night. The plane began to jostle and rock as winds gusted into the eighties. Joining the symphony of creaks, groans, and steady thrum of the engines, an abrupt, continuous rat-a-tat drummed a syncopated rhythm on the steel exterior. It was over almost as quickly as it had begun.

"That's not bad. The way you guys were talking, I thought this thing was really going to rattle my fillings," Digger chuckled, easing his white-knuckle grip on the seat arms.

Jensen and Peterson exchanged knowing looks. Behind the two men, the intense glow of the bright orange-red eye of Hurricane Hera watched from the radar screen, waiting. Digger blinked first.

They hit the eyewall. Intense gloom blanketed the plane in one fell swoop of darkness. The aircraft lurched back and forth as Mason and Rodrigue fought to keep her steady. Potent knuckles of wind thrashed the plane as Digger watched the right wing contort.

"Is the wing supposed to bend like that?" he hollered over the noise.

"Would you rather it broke?" Jensen yelled back.

McKean's face twisted in concern. "I don't like this, boss."

"What's going on?" Mason countered.

"The pressure's falling crazy fast and the winds are picking up too quickly!" the flight engineer shouted. "Winds at one hundred ninety miles per hour and a surface pressure of 930 millibars. We shouldn't be this low unless you feel like taking a dip!"

A brutal updraft jerked the aircraft upward, sucking the crew into their seats. An equally powerful downdraft left them momentarily weightless as the wind shoved them in the sudden and opposite direction. As the plane lurched, an abrupt crashing noise joined the cacophony.

"What in the hell was that!" Mason demanded.

"Some of the gear worked loose!" Jensen called hoarsely.

"Secure it, damn it! We're getting beaten up enough on the outside. We don't need to take hits inside, too!" Mason ordered as he and Rodrigue fought to maintain control.

Visibility rapidly reduced to zero-zero. None of the crew could make anything out through the cockpit window, and it wasn't long before blinding squalls began pelting the glass. The plane continued to buck and bump as it met the brunt of the storm. Digger was missing the convenience of the commercial airline's sick bag. Cloud layers were as thick as pea soup. Mason began to curse.

"Hand me those night vision goggles," Mason ordered. "If I'm going to pick out anything in this mess, I'm going to need them." Rodrigue complied. Mason worked them onto his head.

"Jesus, Mary, and Joseph!" Mason exclaimed.

The other men looked out the window. You didn't need night vision goggles to see what had made Mason gasp. A massive, towering wall of angry clouds, electric with lightning – and they were flying directly into it.

"Drop altitude to one thousand feet," Mason ordered.

"Dropping to one thousand feet," Rodrigue responded, looking askance at Mason. The turbulence continued to rock the plane. A loud screech reverberated, followed by a metallic pop.

Digger dug his nails into the arms of his seat. "Is that normal?"

"Define normal." McKean twisted up his face. He tapped a few of the instruments. "Come on, girl. Hold it together."

The flight engineer had every justification to worry. The gale force winds of hurricanes had been known to shred the tough metal exteriors of planes brazen enough to fly through them. If the hurricane turned their plane into scrap, the mission would be scrapped as well. Then there was that whole missing parachute thing, too, Digger thought. The strap of the harness cut cruelly into his shoulders as the tumult of the air stream they were traveling in met a pocket of slower moving air.

"Drop to five hundred feet," Mason directed. Once again, Rodrigue complied. There was a sudden chink in the clouds, then vision opened onto stormy seas.

"What do you see? Anything? Anything at all?" Digger asked. He sat as near to the edge of his seat as his harness would allow. Rodrigue has the best view.

"Call Bruckheimer. Ask if he's missing a boat," Rodrigue replied.

"What?" Mason asked, confused.

"I see a freaking pirate ship."

Mason banked the Hercules tightly for a second pass. Rodrigue wasn't wrong. It was as if the storm was a wormhole into the 18th century as the twin masts of *The Fortune's Tide* clawed at the sky. The *Tide* was in serious trouble. The brigantine was heeled over, her entire starboard side practically under water. Twenty foot waves pommeled her hull relentlessly.

"Jesus!" Rodrigue exclaimed out of the blue as Mason sent the C-130 into a steep bank to narrowly avoid a joust with the ship's tall rigging. The enraged ocean bobbled *The Fortune's Tide* like a cork – a cork with two hundred foot lances.

"There!" Digger called. "I see something in the water! Can you see it? It's red!"

There was, indeed, something floating in the water near the overturned ship. Whatever it was had a strobe light attached.

"That's not normal," Rodrigue stated.

"You tell me what's normal about any of this!" Digger suggested, gesticulating wildly to the demonstration of nature's fury surrounding them. The light continued to blink, but the men kept losing sight of it in the undulating waves.

"Could be a raft, or possibly a life jacket. I can't tell and I can't get any closer," Mason said. Sudden thundering booms echoed throughout the plane's cabin and it pitched into a steep left bank.

"Fire! We've got fire in the number two engine! And I've lost the number one!" McKean yelled.

In the midst of chaos, came calm. It was a momentary reprieve as the massive aircraft broke into the relative peace of the storm's central eye. Then, suddenly, the boiling froth of the water below grew closer at a dizzying pace. The interior of the plane exploded into activity.

McKean hit the kill-switch on the number two engine. The massive flames jetting like forty-foot flares ceased almost immediately with no fuel to feed them.

Mason yanked the plane out of its perilous left-rolling dive, mere hundreds of feet from the unforgiving surface of the ocean. Rodrigue noted a bank of dark, low-lying clouds coming up fast.

"Is that just scud, or are we headed back into hell?" Rodrigue's query immediately quashed any relief afforded by the crew's quick response to peril.

Mason's eye's narrowed. "No time to debate. If it's not scud and we slam into that eyewall this low, we're in more trouble than that ship."

"Clear to the left!" McKean shouted. Mason snapped the plane into a hard left roll.

Jensen snatched a glance at the radar on the screen. "No! No! No! You're wrong! You're taking right back to the eyewall!"

McKean watched the wind speed indicator spin like a top. A fortification of foaming black clouds rotated past the window.

"Bank it!" Mason bellowed.

"If you push the angle past thirty-five degrees, we won't be able to sustain it without the number two engine!" McKean cautioned.

"Then I won't hit thirty-six!" Mason agreed with a wry grin. He began the bank, the right wingtip practically grazing the angry eyewall.

A jutting clump of clouds leapt into their path. Too late to turn, Mason gritted his teeth as they were sucked into the eyewall. Mason rolled the plane even harder to the left, the sharper angle climbing well-past thirty-six degrees, and one which threated to stall the massive plane.

An eternity passed in ten seconds. Then light broke through the darkness.

"Booyah!" Rodrigue whooped. The plane was back in the eye!

"Time to get the hell out of Dodge." With that Mason lipped the nose of the plane up and began a steady, spiraling climb.

A low groan emanated from Digger whose head was now between his knees.

"You okay there?" Jensen asked.

"Next time, I'm taking the train," Digger moaned.

"Boss, there's a problem," McKean informed.

"Another one?" Mason gruffed.

"The G-meter shows six G's up and three and a quarter G's down through all that mess," McKean reported, a look of serious concern on his angular face.

"What? What's that mean?" Digger asked rapidly.

"This baby's not rated to take that degree of gravity. We're torn up. We don't drop some weight soon, it's going to be a water landing," Rodrigue reported.

"Dump the fuel," Mason ordered.

"If we dump the fuel, will there be enough left to get us to where we need to spread the polyacrylamide?" Digger asked.

"It'll have to be," Mason declared.

Digger watched as a steady stream of jet fuel sailed out into the atmosphere to lighten the plane by fifty thousand pounds. Mason continued to spiral the plane upward, taking them to the necessary altitude to drop the absorbent polymer. The altimeter kept climbing. The storm kept raging. Finally, they had reached the requisite height.

"Drop it," Mason ordered. The two hundred and sixty thousand pound payload was released, and the C-130 added its own cloud to the swirling soup below. Mason continued to circle the monster until every last bit of the polyacrylamide had been dumped. He only hoped it would turn out to be the miracle they all hoped it would be.

"That's that, then," he said. He tuned to Digger. "Call your pal. Tell him to watch the screens. If this works, he'll need to get out there as soon as possible, or his girlfriend's not going to make it. Those waves will crush her. If they haven't already."

Digger nodded, unstrapped from his harness, and headed for the radio.

Mason turned to Rodrigue. "Take us home."

CHAPTER FORTY-SEVEN

The Fortune's Tide had decided for her. When her communications were cut, Melina realized that she had to make the decision to bail or bounce. At first, she had rushed bank down to the engine room and tried to revive the ship's bilge pump. Initially, the plan seemed to be working. Then, the second generator failed. The water was coming in too fast and rising too high. She was going into the water one way or another. Melina determined it was going to be on her terms.

She located and donned an emergency suit, the kind with a strobe light attached for location, and made her way back topside. Waves the size of New York skyscrapers towered over the heeling ship threatening to devour her and the ship whole at any moment.

"Come on in," she muttered. "The water's fine."

She adjusted the tube on her back and tightened the vest belt. "Yeah. Right."

With that, she hit the water surface. Almost immediately the power of the waves sucked her under. The pressure of the water crushed the breath from her lungs. Instinctively, she breathed in and was rewarded with nostrils full of salty diesel and debris. It was a substantial effort to get back to the surface and expel the vile mix and replace it with life-sustaining oxygen. The wind howled like an impassioned reaper searching for its prey. Melina couldn't help but float low in the water. The effort of trying to combat the constant crush of the waves drained her energy at a rapid pace. She weakened by the minute. Her tired brain began to imagine each wave as another vessel coming to rescue her. There had to be another ship out here somewhere. She wasn't going to die like this. She couldn't be alone.

She gripped the canvas, safe inside its cylinder. Have faith. Just have faith. She repeated the mantra, over and over. Consciousness began to slip away as her brain registered a steady whump-whump over the crash of the ocean. Just moments before she blacked out completely, she could have sworn the rains seemed to lessen, but then, maybe that was just her addled brain playing tricks on her. Then darkness enveloped her.

Jake had worn a track in the floor at the Coast Guard station. Mason and his crew had left over two hours ago with no word. Suddenly, the radio crackled to life.

"Payload away. Some close calls, but mission accomplished." The sound of Digger's voice stopped Jake in his tracks. He grabbed the handset.

"Dig! Man, oh man, am I glad to hear the sound of your voice. You dumped the polyacrylamide. That's great!"

"I don't know, Jake. This storm is an unbelievable bitch." Digger's voice took on an uncertain edge.

"No. No, no, no, Dig. You believe in some of the craziest crap on the planet. It's got to work!"

"I'm with you, man, but this storm is bigger than any of us imagined."

"Damn it!" Jake pounded a furied fist into the desk's melamine surface. A million scenarios played out in his head. "Hold on, Dig. Put the guy from NOAA on the horn."

"Hugh Peterson." The big voice of the bearded atmospheric scientist crackled over the handset.

"Dr. Petersen, can we use IR arrays to redirect the hurricane? Keep it out over open water and steer it towards colder water where she'll die out?"

"No," came Peterson's disappointing reply. Jake's face fell. "There are no IR arrays where we would need them in order to manipulate the ionosphere."

"What if we could put one where we needed it?" Jake suggested wildly.

"You just happen to have an IR array hanging around?" Peterson joked.

"No. But the Navy does," Jake replied.

"The SBX-1," Peterson replied. The line went static as Peterson conferred with Jensen. Jake waited with bated breath. Peterson's voice cracked live over the line. "We'll make the call. Let's hope we're not too late."

Digger came back on the line. "Look, Jake, I hate to be a party pooper, but, you know how I am with crowds. And we're, uh, running a little low on fuel, so I'm afraid we're gonna have to bow out of the rescue mission."

"You found her?" Jake's heart leapt into his throat. Melina was alive!

"We found something. *The Fortune's Tide* is definitely out there, but we spotted something else in the water. We can't be sure, but it could have been Melina."

Jake whooped. "Dig, I owe you one!"

"I sure hope you're keeping score, 'cause this makes it, like, a million. One day, I'm gonna collect. Over and out."

The MH-60 pilot strode briskly into the room. "Sir, a break's opened up in the weather. It's not ideal, but if we're going to attempt a rescue, there's a narrow window. Wheels up in five minutes."

A chink had broken in the clouds, Jake thought. In more ways than one.

CHAPTER FORTY-EIGHT

The rescue helicopter had covered miles over dark, foam-capped water. They were losing daylight fast. If they had any hopes of finding Melina, time was running out. The pilot had them on a course for the coordinates Mason and C-130 had last seen the strobing light. They had been crisscrossing over the same patch of turbulent water for an hour. The brute force of the storm had lessened, enough to allow the chopper to fly, but conditions were still less than ideal.

"I don't know how much longer we can stay out here, sir," the pilot cautioned.

"As long as it takes," came Jake's quick retort. He didn't want to admit it, but the pilot might be right. His eyes had grown weak from the draining to pick out a tiny red bauble on the broad chest of the water.

The pilot nodded. "I understand, sir. But, it's like looking for a needle in a very big haystack. Wait! Hold on here a moment, sir. I've got a call coming in."

While the pilot responded to the call coming in over his headset, Jake continued to comb the water for a sign. Any sign.

"Sir, I've got orders to abort. We've got a distress call in from a fishing trawler nearby. Crew of seven in the water. I've got their coordinates. We've got to go."

"Five more minutes!" Jake pleaded.

"I'm under orders, sir."

"Five minutes!" Jake barked. He blinked hard. He argued to himself it was against the strain. The welling moisture in the corner of his eye told another story.

He suddenly squeezed his eyes very tightly. He reopened them and squeezed again. This time when he reopened them he stared intensely over the shoulder of the pilot. He nearly threw his shoulder out with the sudden and abrupt point over the water.

"There! I see something!" Jake started. The pilot rotated to catch sight of what Jake pointed to.

"It might be a life jacket. I can't make it out from this distance. Turn this bird around. Do a fly-by!" Jake snapped

"Roger." The pilot nudged the helo into a slight bank.

"I see it!" he exclaimed. "We have a body in the water. I'm going in."

The waves were still thrashing below, grasping at least twenty-five feet into the still gray sky. The pilot was hard pressed to keep the bird out of any trouble. But, he kept it as even as possible. Still, the altitude bobbed between thirty and forty feet above the angry water.

A lone red object dipped through the waves. It was Melina.

Jake leapt from the cockpit to the back of the helicopter where the flight mechanic readied the rescue gear. It had been decided that Jake was going in as the swimmer. His SEAL training more than qualified him.

They were using the sling. If there was a God, Jake thought, they would be able to hoist Melina up from the cruel water and to safety.

Into his arms, Jake thought.

"Swimmer to the door," the flight mechanic called. "Ready for deployment!"

Jake nodded, and slipped, feet first, into the open air above the ocean. The flight mechanic momentarily lost him in the height of the waves.

"Swimmer's away!" he called when he picked up sight of him again.

Jake swam with everything he had. He fought against the potent heave and swell of the water. The waves were cruel, bringing him within inches of touching Melina, then sweeping her in a watery embrace only to carry her further away. He replayed the same cat-and-mouse scenario, his fingers brushing Melina several times, as nature toyed cruelly with him. Melina appeared unconscious, unable to give any effort to the endeavor.

"Melina!" Jake shouted hoarsely over the crash of the waves. "Melina!"

It was maddening! She was right there! Jake took one final breath, then dug in, his powerful arms pulling through the water. He reached out and finally succeeded in wrapping a hand around her slender arm. Her head rose weakly at his touch, eyes barely opening.

Jake lifted up his mask as he drew Melina weak arms around him. "Hey. I heard you needed a ride."

She managed a weak smile.

The flight mechanic whooped. "He's got her! Hold! Preparing to take load!"

Jake noticed the odd cylinder. He started to pull it off Melina's shoulder to fix her into the hoist. Melina found a sudden burst of strength and energy. She clutched for the cylinder.

"No!" she cried. In her weakened condition, it was little more than a squeak, but she was clearly not letting go of the container. She tried to explain to Jake, but the sound would not come.

"Okay. Okay. I understand. Let's just get you to safety. You can tell me about it later."

Jake fixed a sling around Melina. The flight mechanic readied the hoist. As soon as Jake gave the thumbs up, the winch began to wind and then they were both hoisted back up into the aircraft together.

The flight mechanic immediately wrapped her in a dry blanket. Jake stripped off the top half of his wetsuit. He leaned over Melina.

"It's okay. You're okay. You're safe now. Everything's going to be alright."

She smiled and reached up to touch his face.

"I know," she whispered. She rattled the container. "I had a little faith."

Jake gave a puzzled look, then gently pushed a plastered lock of wet hair from her forehead. "What do say after all this, we take a little vacation?"

She nodded weakly.

"Deal. Only," she began. Her voice cracked hoarsely.

"Only what?" Jake leaned in closer.

"Only, can we go someplace away from the water?"

Jake chuckled. "What did you have in mind?"

"I'm thinking." she paused for a considerable moment. "I'm thinking the Sahara."

EPILOGUE

Willamette, Oregon

"And Bostonians breathed a little bit easier today when the National Hurricane Center downgraded Hurricane Hera, the surprise super storm of this year's hurricane season, to a tropical depression after she took yet another surprising turn against predicted models and lumbered into the colder waters of the North Atlantic. Residents of the Massachusetts capitol narrowly avoided the devastating flooding and major damages caused in Manhattan by Hurricane Sandy, a storm remarkably similar in its erratic development and path. There has been some speculation, since both storms were so unnatural in their behaviors, that there was human involvement both in their creation and control. However, scientists at the National Oceanic and Atmospheric Administration assure that there is no basis in fact for this wildly speculative claim."

"Sounds like Digger wrote another letter," Jake muttered as he nuzzled Melina's neck. A half-eaten large pizza lay forgotten on the coffee table as the couple curled on the couch in Jake's cabin watching the national news wrap-up of their adventure.

Mason and the scientists at NOAA had worked together with the United States Navy to maneuver the portable SBX-1 antenna array into a position to manipulate the ionosphere just enough to turn the hurricane out of Boston's path. Now Mason was in Washington, D.C. to answer for his misappropriation of a government plane for an unsanctioned mission, not to mention the damage said plane incurred in the process. To his credit, the Air Force Colonel had kept Jake, Digger and Melina's involvement out of it. In fact, somehow, the whole incident had remained strangely amorphous — names, dates and facts lost somewhere in the mounds of dust swept under Washington's innumerable rugs — the fodder of conspiracy theorists' dreams.

"The near miss with a hurricane was not the only news on the lips of Boston citizens this morning. Curators at the Isabella Gardner Museum were stunned yesterday when the opening of an anonymous package revealed one of the long lost paintings from 1990's Gardner heist. Rembrandt's *The Storm on the Sea of Galilee* has returned home and museum officials are planning to hold a grand unveiling of the oil canvas when it goes back on display in the Dutch Room in its original frame."

The wide-screen went dark as Jake pushed the power button on the remote. "I wonder how long it will take them to realize it's a forgery," he murmured as he leaned his lips to Melina's.

"I'm sure Connor will have the authentic painting back in place before they even realize it," Melina mumbled through Jake's kiss.

Jake managed a chuckle. "I'll bet it's the first time he will have ever broken into a museum to put a painting back. It's got to be killing him!"

"You're probably right," Melina replied throatily. The shoulder of her satin nightgown slid seductively from her shoulder. "He's more about liberating art. He just thought, after all we'd been through, that we should be able to spend a little one-on-one time with the art that brought us together."

"I am totally on board for one-on-one time. Speaking of 'liberating', how's about I 'liberate' you from this nightgown, huh?" Jake taunted.

"Really! Mr. Riesen!" Melina laughed. "I'm not that kind of girl."

"Oh, yeah? What kind of girl are you then?" Jake countered.

A split second passed before Melina had Jake pinned, flat on his back.

"The kind that's going to keep you out of trouble," she whispered, then kissed him full on the mouth.

"By the way, it works," Jake voiced whisper soft.

"What works?"

"The St. Anthony medal," Jake replied, slowly tugging the halter tie of her nightgown.

"Yeah?"

"Yeah." The gown slid a few inches south of proper.

"So? What did it help you find?" Melina whispered as she nibbled on his ear.

"Trouble. Nothing but trouble."

Jake's cell phone warbled, vibrating off the top of the pizza box and onto the floor. Jake absentmindedly picked it up and answered. "This is Jake. Leave a message. I'll get back to you."

He blindly fumbled to put the phone back on top of the pizza box, but he was more interested on putting the moves on the sultry Melina.

"Maybe," he mumbled to empty space. The phone dropped, still engaged, to the floor.

"Jake? Jake? It's Mason. Things did not go as expected in

Washington. Well, in truth, they went exactly as expected. I was relieved of my position at Kirtland. They weren't too happy with my, er, unorthodox methods. Good news is, someone thought unorthodox is exactly what the doctor ordered. I've been offered my own team, a special unit. Asset Recovery Investigation Specialists – A.R.I.E.S. they're calling it. The team will be tasked with tracking down some of the world's most priceless stolen art and secrets. I want you, Kelley, and Miss Garcia to be on the team. You all have unique qualifications for the job. Each of you would be an incredible asset. Jake? Jake? Did you hear me?"

Jake and Melina were oblivious, lost in each other. Cody, Jake's dog, was completely interested in what Mason had to say. Or, it quite possibly was simply the pizza sauce on the receiver. The Husky snuffled into the mouthpiece.

"Damn it, Riesen! What's your answer? I know you're there! I can hear you breathing! Riesen? Riesen!" Mason's voice echoed in a tinny bellow through the small speaker.

Jake came up for air for just a moment.

"What do you think?" he asked Melina.

She put her long fingers aside his cheek and kissed him again.

"Sounds like trouble," she muttered. Jake cracked a wide smile. Melina returned it in kind. They went back to kissing, leaving Mason's voice barking angrily from the phone.

"Riesen!"

Rembrandt's *Storm* hung serenely over the fireplace.

ABOUT THE AUTHOR

M.T. Falgoust is a veteran of the United States Navy and an international award-winning author and illustrator. Her work has appeared in *Reader's Digest* and *Writers' Journal*. She currently resides in New Orleans, Louisiana where she continues to writes adult fiction and children's literature. Visit at her website www.melindatfalgoust.doodlekit.com for more information.